Whisked Away

As they bowled along Brook Street, Deborah admired Fairfax's competent handling of his horses. The pair seemed a bit skittish, the off leader shying a bit when the wind gusted, which it seemed to be doing with increasing frequency, but he kept them up to their bits seemingly without effort. In truth, she admired everything about the duke, from the perfect fit of his dark blue morning coat and buff pantaloons to the understated elegance of his nubby silk waistcoat, neatly tied cravat, and gleaming Hessians, and she could not help but wonder what he thought of her.

She did not want to distract him, but neither did she want him to think she was a ninny with no conversation. "I was not sure you would return," she ventured after they crossed New Bond Street.

"What?" His eyes slewed to hers. "Did you think I would sit tamely in White's or the House when there was a chance, however slight, that you would drive with me?"

With me or with one of the Woodhurst twins? She shrugged off the thought. "I didn't know."

"After my disappointment yesterday, nothing short of a downpour would have kept me away this afternoon."

Oh my, that does sound promising—if it is my company specifically that he sought. "Were you disappointed yesterday?" she asked, greatly daring, then blushed at the boldness of her question.

"Exceedingly disappointed."

Such honesty deserved an equally candid response. "So was I."

Twin Peril

Susannah Carleton

A SIGNET BOOK

SIGNET
Published by New American Library, a division of
Penguin Group (USA) Inc., 375 Hudson Street,
New York, New York 10014, USA
Penguin Group (Canada), 90 Eglinton Avenue East, Suite 700, Toronto,
Ontario M4P 2Y3, Canada (a division of Pearson Penguin Canada Inc.)
Penguin Books Ltd., 80 Strand, London WC2R 0RL, England
Penguin Ireland, 25 St. Stephen's Green, Dublin 2,
Ireland (a division of Penguin Books Ltd.)
Penguin Group (Australia), 250 Camberwell Road, Camberwell, Victoria 3124,
Australia (a division of Pearson Australia Group Pty. Ltd.)
Penguin Books India Pvt. Ltd., 11 Community Centre, Panchsheel Park,
New Delhi - 110 017, India
Penguin Group (NZ), cnr Airborne and Rosedale Roads, Albany,
Auckland 1310, New Zealand (a division of Pearson New Zealand Ltd.)
Penguin Books (South Africa) (Pty.) Ltd., 24 Sturdee Avenue,
Rosebank, Johannesburg 2196, South Africa

Penguin Books Ltd., Registered Offices:
80 Strand, London WC2R 0RL, England

First published by Signet, an imprint of New American Library,
a division of Penguin Group (USA) Inc.

First Printing, August 2005
10 9 8 7 6 5 4 3 2 1

To Linda Brandon and Laura Littrell,
the best, most wonderful sisters in the world,
and to our second cousin, Jenny Presnell,
whose twin-like resemblance to Laura
inspired this story.

And to Nonnie Saad and Sandra Heath,
with my heartfelt thanks for
their friendship, advice, and encouragement.

Chapter One

Fairfax Castle, Kent, 1 November 1813

"*F*airfax, it is time and past for you to do your duty as duke."

Irritation stiffened the spine—and frosted the voice—of Michael Winslow, the Twenty-fourth Duke of Fairfax. "I have been doing my duty to the dukedom since I was four years old." A fact his grandmother knew very well, since it was she who had instructed him in his role and its obligations.

The diminutive dowager duchess, garbed in purple satin, her posture regally erect, waved one thin, beringed hand dismissively. "I do not refer to your responsibilities to your estates and dependents or to your country, but to your duty to the dukedom itself. If, God forbid, you should die in a carriage accident like your father did, what would happen to the title, then?"

It, along with all the entailed properties, would pass to a distant—very distant—cousin. Michael refused to state the obvious, since his grandmother undoubtedly knew the exact degree of the relationship, down to the number of removes, but the validity of her argument could not be denied.

Conceding her point, he nodded. "Siring my successor is the one obligation I have not yet fulfilled. When I go up to Town for the next session of Parliament, I will look over the young ladies on the Marriage Mart. But London is generally thin of company this time of year, so I may not find a suitable bride until spring, during the Season." His word given, he hoped his grandmother would not pursue the subject.

The dowager duchess was not quite five feet tall and had nearly seventy years in her dish, but she was as tenacious as a terrier. She pulled several crested sheets of ivory vellum from her reticule. "I have been considering the matter for some time now, and have drawn up a list of potential brides."

Michael managed, barely, to stifle a groan. To gird himself for the coming confrontation—and there was no doubt in his mind that he and his grandmother would clash over the definition of a "suitable" bride—he glanced around the room. The Winter Parlor, despite its blood red velvet hangings and upholstery, was not a battleground. Elegantly furnished but comfortable, it was the smallest of the castle's three drawing rooms, and one of his favorite rooms in the castle.

"What do you think of Greenwich's daughter?"

The Duke of Greenwich had only one daughter. A hoyden as a child, Lady Christina Fairchild had made her come-out last spring, and she was still given to mad starts. "Lady Tina is only seventeen. A bit young, don't you think, Grand-mère?"

"Nonsense! If you marry a young girl, you can mold her into the kind of bride you want."

Michael had no wish to add the responsibility of molding his bride's character to his already lengthy list of duties. Nor could he imagine taking to wife a girl a dozen years younger than he. He wanted a partner and helpmeet, not another obligation. "I don't believe Lady Tina and I would suit."

"It would be a good alliance, Fairfax."

An alliance was all it would be. Good for the dukedom certainly, but not for the duke. And since all of his predecessors—twenty-three dukes and nineteen earls before that—had made dynastic alliances that increased the dukedom's holdings and filled its coffers—more than seven hundred years of noble sacrifices for the title by the men who held it—Michael thought it was time for a Duke of Fairfax to marry for love.

It would not be easy to find a woman who loved him more than, or even as much as, she loved his title and fortune, but Michael was determined to try.

He knew that the matchmaking mamas of the *ton* considered him a matrimonial prize of the highest order. Their daughters, however, did not. Not unless they had their eyes on his coronet instead of on him.

His assets were plentiful, but his looks were not one of them. He was not handsome and dashing, like his friend, Viscount Dunnley. Nor did he possess his friend's height or famed address. Neither handsome nor ugly, Michael was an ordinary man of average height with medium brown hair and unremarkable blue-green eyes. The only extraordinary thing about him was his title.

He dressed well—neither his valet nor Weston would countenance aught else—but he wasn't a fop or a dandy. He rode and drove well, and he was an excellent fencer, but he was not a Corinthian. Michael did not dislike sporting activities, he simply preferred more intellectual pursuits.

"Surely you must agree, Fairfax!"

The slightly strident note in his grandmother's voice refocused Michael's wandering attention. *What had she been talking about? Oh yes, Lady Tina as a prospective bride.* "I cannot deny that allying Fairfax with Greenwich would be advantageous for the dukedom. Particularly if the patent for Greenwich's title allows it to pass through a daughter to her first-born son. But an alliance between Lady Tina and me is quite another matter. Instead of being beneficial to either of us, it would likely be disastrous for both."

"But—"

"Grandmère, do you wish to see a flibbertigibbet in your place?" Given his grandmother's penchant for formality and her many strictures on manners, Michael knew it was a compelling argument. He devoutly hoped it would be a silencing one.

"No chit of a girl will ever take *my* place."

"Of course not." His tone soothing, he tried to smooth her ruffled feathers. "You will always and forever be revered as the twenty-second duchess. What I meant was, do you wish to see a hoyden as your successor? Lady Tina is the most impetuous, outspoken girl to make her come-out in the past decade."

His statement took her aback, but only for a moment. The dowager's retort was predictable—and predictably crusty. "I am shocked that Greenwich and his duchess did not raise their daughter more strictly."

"Perhaps it is difficult to be strict when one has only one child on whom to lavish one's affection."

"You are my only grandchild, and I didn't indulge you excessively."

"You did, you know." Michael smiled fondly at his irascible grandmother. "You doted on me shamelessly, and taught me everything I needed to know to become the man I am today."

Flustered by the apparent compliment, although there was blame as well as praise attached to it, the dowager harrumphed and glanced down at her hands, folded atop the sheaf of papers on her lap. Ignoring his last statement, she picked them up, rattling them to ensure that she had his attention. "Perhaps Greenwich's girl is not the best choice, but I am sure we can find you a suitable duchess."

Well aware that his grandmother's ideas of suitability were far different than his own, Michael knew it was time to take a stand. "There is no 'we' about it, Grandmère. I told you that I would look for a bride. I did *not* say that you could choose one for me."

"But I, having held the position, know what qualities and abilities your duchess must possess."

"Undoubtedly so, but I—and I alone—will choose my bride." Softening his tone, he added, "I am perfectly capable of doing so, thanks to your instruction." It was both a sop and a reminder, and Michael hoped that it would mollify the dowager.

She thrust the sheaf of papers at him, clearly annoyed by his intransigence. "Here, then, is a selection of young ladies with which to start your search."

With a polite but perfunctory "Thank you," he accepted it and flipped through the sheets. *Seventeen pages*!

Stabbing the finely patterned burgundy and gold Savonnerie carpet with her cane, the dowager rose and reached for his arm.

Michael stifled a sigh and set the papers on a Sheraton side table, then escorted his grandmother, still in high dudgeon, up the stairs. At the door of her suite, he bent and kissed her cheek. "Good night, Grandmère. Sleep well."

Returning to the Winter Parlor, he poured himself a brandy. Then, knowing that he had not heard the last from his grandmother on the subject of his future wife, he sprawled in a wing chair near the fireplace, his feet stretched toward the blaze, and donned his spectacles.

As he perused the sheets of her list, he shook his head in amazement. Not only had she listed most of the unwed daughters of nearly every duke, marquess, and earl in the realm, she also had summarized each family's connections, described the young ladies, and catalogued their dowries. How she had obtained the latter information, he could only guess, but he did not doubt that it was accurate. Or, rather, as exact as the dowagers' grapevine could determine. And usually the gossip-loving old dears were demmed accurate about such matters.

It amused him that there was not a single viscount's or baron's daughter on the list. And, he realized, flipping through the pages again, quite a few earls' daughters had not merited a mention. Michael was acquainted with most of the young ladies listed. While all of them undoubtedly had the necessary training to become a duchess, only two were worthy of consideration as his wife: Lady Deborah Woodhurst, the elder daughter of the Marquess of Kesteven, and Lady Sarah Mallory, the Earl of Tregaron's daughter. Not because of their families' connections, nor because of the size of their dowries, but because he liked them. And also because he believed that their hearts, not their heads, would dictate their choice of husband.

Both girls were beautiful, intelligent, and talented musicians. They were also well-mannered, kind-hearted, and could—and frequently did—converse about subjects other than the weather, fashions, and the latest *on dits*. But Lady

Deborah was Michael's first choice. For some inexplicable reason, he had felt an urge to protect and care for her since the day he'd met her. Lady Sarah's reserve, coupled with Michael's own reticence, might prove a formidable obstacle. Not an insurmountable one, but conversing with her was not as easy as talking to Lady Deborah.

He would please his grandmother—and himself—by considering Lady Deborah first. Provided the ability to distinguish her from her identical twin sister, Diana, had not deserted him over the winter. Lady Diana's tongue and nature were not as sweet as her sister's, and he had no wish to end up married to the wrong twin if he could no longer tell them apart.

Finding a duchess would be easy. Finding a suitable wife was a much more difficult task. To do that, he would have to reveal the man behind the ducal mask. Michael wondered, rather bleakly, if he remembered how.

Chapter Two

Woodhurst Castle, Lincolnshire, New Year's Eve, 1813

"*T*raditions are stupid."

Lady Deborah Woodhurst glanced at the mutinous expression on her twin sister, Diana's, face and stifled a sigh. Maintaining her smile with an effort, Deborah mustered a light tone as she replied, "Christmastide is rich in traditions. Are you railing against one or two in particular, or all of them?"

"I am *railing*," Diana said, "against the stupid Woodhurst end of the year 'evaluate what you accomplished this past year and what you want to achieve in the coming year' tradition."

Deborah had, indeed, known the answer before she'd asked the question, but she'd felt compelled to ask it anyway. And to do so in a way that emphasized the fallacy of her sister's opinion. "If it was a stupid custom, it wouldn't have become a tradition, would it? Traditions only become so because people believe in them. Like"—she gestured at the evergreen boughs and holly decorating the Great Hall and the riband-bedecked garland entwined around the banister—"Yule logs and kissing boughs."

Diana rolled her eyes and started up the stairs. "That is different."

"Why?"

"Because *everyone* decorates their home for the holidays. But no one else in the world has the stupid yearly evaluation tradition."

Deborah arched one delicate blond eyebrow. "Is that so? No one else in the *whole world?* And you know that to be a fact because . . . ?"

Her sister's blue eyes drilled her with an annoyed glare. "Well, I suppose it is possible that some other family does it, but . . ." She huffed out a breath. "Who started this stupid tradition anyway?"

Deborah knew that Diana's question was rhetorical. No one knew how or when the ritual had begun, nor who had begun the custom, but it was firmly established. It had been part of the Woodhurst family's Yuletide celebrations for generations. No member of the family ever had been—nor probably ever would be—exempt from the practice, but human nature being what it was, some took the matter seriously, while others only paid lip service to it.

On the last day of every year, the members of the Woodhurst family, individually and collectively, reviewed their accomplishments during the past twelvemonth and set objectives for the coming one. Deborah knew that their parents, the Marquess and Marchioness of Kesteven, established goals not only as individuals, but also as a couple and for the family. When she was young, Deborah thought the custom was rather silly, but her opinion had changed as she'd grown older. Now, at one-and-twenty, she participated wholeheartedly, as did her eldest brother, Jonathan, Earl of Oldham. Her older brother, Henry, and Diana, however, still viewed the ritual as a whimsical caprice.

"What," Deborah asked with real curiosity as they reached the top of the stairs and turned toward their rooms, "do you hope to accomplish this year, Di?"

"I *intend* to catch a husband. A rich, titled husband."

"You make it sound as if any wealthy peer will do."

Diana shrugged. "I suppose just about any one will, if he's rich enough."

Shock halted Deborah in her tracks. "You can't mean that!" Her sister occasionally behaved quite shockingly, and she'd had some outrageous ideas in the past, but nothing like this!

"Indeed I do." Twin sets of blue eyes met in challenge, but Diana's were not the first to fall.

Dear God, she isn't bluffing! "But . . . but what about love?"

Diana shrugged again. "What about it? It isn't necessary to love one's husband. If it were, the married women of the *ton* wouldn't have affairs."

Stunned, Deborah walked past the door of her bedroom, where she'd intended to evaluate the past year and consider the coming one, and followed her sister into the sitting room that adjoined their chambers.

"You wouldn't take a lover, would you?" Dread and curiosity compelled the question, but Deborah was not at all certain she wanted to hear the reply.

"I daresay that will depend upon whom I marry."

Sinking into a chair, Deborah said with some acerbity, "Just imagine how Mama and Papa are going to react to such an ambition! Especially one so baldly stated. They will probably lock you in the dungeon for the next twelvemonth."

Diana laughed, then with a sly look said, "I have no intention of mentioning that particular objective. Instead I will vow to improve my performance on the pianoforte."

"That's what you said last year."

"And the year before, too."

"Did you even touch a pianoforte in those two years?"

"Touch one?" Diana pondered the question for a moment or two—which was answer enough. "Possibly. Did I practice? No."

"Why set a goal if you don't intend to work toward it?"

"Because I have to say something when Papa asks, and that objective, absurd as it is, suits the stupid tradition."

If Diana said "stupid" one more time, Deborah was likely to scream. Not willing to test her patience—or her sister's vocabulary—she rose and left the room.

Feeling—and hating—the silent reproach of Deborah's abrupt exit, Diana glared at her sister's back. But several moments after Deborah closed the door of her bedchamber with rather more force than necessary, Diana's expression shifted from a glower to a sneer. *Deb is such a fool! And such a prim and proper miss.* There was nothing wrong with marrying for convenience. Nor, if the patronesses of Almack's were an example, with a married woman taking a lover. After she had given her husband an heir, of course. To do so before she'd fulfilled that particular obligation would cause a scandal.

Contemplating her plan for the coming year—and despite what she'd told her sister, Diana did, indeed, have one—she smiled. She was tired of being second best, of being the twin who did not measure up to the family's standards. This year she intended to show their parents, as well as the *ton,* which twin was the smarter. And, judging from what Deb had—and had not—said, it appeared that she was, for once, going to make it easy for her twin. If Deb intended to make a love match, no doubt to an impoverished baronet or younger son, then Diana's marriage to one of the wealthiest, highest-titled peers in the realm would, in comparison, glitter like the finest diamond. Diana had set her sights on a rich, powerful duke, and four were currently unwed: St. Ives, a grieving widower twice her age; Aylesbury, a tall, gangly young man only a year older than she; Devonshire, who seemed older than his three-and-twenty years and had vowed never to marry; and Fairfax. The latter was her target. And since she did not share her twin's fine sense of right and wrong, Diana was quite certain that she would succeed.

Even if she had to compromise the Duke of Fairfax to wrench a proposal from him.

And even if she had to impersonate her sister to accomplish the feat.

Scruples were for namby-pamby misses like her sister. Diana knew what she wanted, and she was determined to get it.

Deborah closed the door connecting the sitting room to her bedroom, then leaned against the portal, hoping the barricade was sufficiently strong to keep the shocking senti-

ments her twin had just voiced from invading the chamber.
For good measure, she turned the key in the lock—something she had never done before.

Knowing she would not be able to settle to her task until
her mind had cleared, Deborah allowed her astonished
thoughts free rein. *How is it possible for two sisters to have
such opposing goals and opinions?* They had the same parents, had been taught by the same governesses, listened to
the same sermons in church every Sunday, yet Diana's beliefs could not be further from Deborah's own.

*Diana is a fool to believe that a fortune and title might
recompense for a life of misery.* Deborah was certain that
marriage to a man one did not love could bring naught but
misery. A woman might, with equanimity, share a meal or
two with a man she did not like, but a lifetime? Never!

She shuddered at the thought of years of living in the
same house—and sharing a bed—with a man she did not
love. There was no fortune large enough to compensate for
that!

Much as she might like to think that she could change
Diana's mind, Deborah knew her twin too well. Diana could
give a mule lessons in stubbornness, and once she formed an
opinion, right or wrong, nothing could alter it. In twenty-one
years, she had never, ever been dissuaded.

Sighing at her sister's folly, Deborah shook her head. Although she could not banish the troublesome thoughts from
her mind, she hoped to relegate them to a far corner, at least
for a while. It was time to evaluate the past year and choose
goals for the coming one.

Crossing the rose and green floral-patterned Aubusson
carpet, she sat in the window seat, her favorite perch. Outside, the fog continued unabated, as thick as at its onset four
days ago. Her back against the linenfold paneling of the embrasure, she drew her feet up onto the seat, wrapped her
arms around her legs, rested her head on her knees, and
began her review of the past twelvemonth. After several
years' delay due to mourning and illness, she—and Diana,
of course—had made her bows to Society in the spring, and
her Season could only be considered a success. She'd made

a number of new friends, including five very special friendships that would likely endure forever, and she'd received—
or, rather, her father had—a flattering number of offers for
her hand. She had refused to consider any of them—either
wisely or foolishly, depending upon whom one asked—because it was impossible to believe vows of undying love and
devotion from a man who could not distinguish her from her
twin. And none of the men who offered for her could. In
fact, none of them had made an effort to do so. How, she
wondered, had they decided which sister would be the re-
cipient of their proposals?

*Am I foolish to expect a man who loves me to be able to
tell us apart?* From the curly blond hair on their heads to the
tips of their toes, she and Diana were identical in appearance,
but even so, Deborah did not think it was an unreasonable
expectation. After all, her parents and brothers could tell
them apart, and two members of the *ton* had unerringly done
so since first meeting them.

Thinking of the pair brought to mind one of the disap-
pointments of the past year. Early in the Season, the Marquess of Elston had courted her—or had seemed to court
her—but he had fallen in love with Miss Karolina Lane and
married her last June. His defection had not broken Deborah's heart, nor wounded aught but her pride, but she'd been
disappointed all the same. Despite—or, perhaps, because
of—her friendship with Karla, in whose newfound and
richly deserved happiness Deborah delighted.

But if Elston, who loved neither Diana nor her, could distinguish between them, surely a man whose affection was
engaged would be able to do so. While it seemed unlikely
that other gentlemen of whom she was unaware could tell
them apart, it was not impossible.

Or perhaps you are building castles in the air?

Her thoughts a tangle, she welcomed the interruption
provided by the knock on her door. Hoping it was not her
sister come to plague her, Deborah was pleased to find her
mother instead.

"Am I interrupting, dearling?"

"No, Mama, not at all." Deborah smiled and ushered the marchioness to a slipper chair in front of the fire.

"Did you and your sister cross swords? She was wearing a face like a thundercloud when I passed her in the hallway."

"Really?" Deborah could not hide her surprise; her opinions rarely carried weight with her sister, and it was difficult to credit that today would be any different. "We didn't have an argument. I was astounded by something Di said, but even though I offered no dispute, she undoubtedly realized that my feelings on the subject did not match hers."

Her mother gave her a searching look. "Would you like to discuss whatever she said that so astonished you?"

Although Deborah would have liked to do so, it smacked of talebearing. "No. At least not today," she temporized. "Instead I would like your opinion on another subject."

"Of course, dear."

She opened her mouth and closed it. Twice. *How can I ask without sounding like the veriest goosecap?* Finally, haltingly, she explained, "I have always had the notion that a man who loved me would be able to distinguish me from Diana. Yet of all the gentlemen we met during the Season, only Elston could tell us apart. That is," she amended, recalling her earlier musings, "he is the only man I know of who can. Is it foolish to think that a man who loves me will be able to identify me?"

"'Tisn't foolish at all, my dear. But it is unrealistic to expect a man to be able to do so instantly. I had to dress the two of you differently for several months before I could tell you apart. Your father and Jonathan were not able to do so until you were almost a year old. And Henry couldn't, not reliably, until you were almost two."

"Really? I didn't know that!"

"I daresay we don't often tell that tale, since it doesn't redound to our credit."

Deborah reached for her mother's hand and squeezed it gently. "I am very glad that you told it today, Mama."

"Is there a gentleman you wish could tell you and Diana apart?"

The delicate probe was so typical of the marchioness that

Deborah smiled. "Are you asking me if any gentleman has captured my heart? Or my fancy?" She shook her head. "No, Mama. But I hope that, someday, one will."

"You can be sure of that, dearling."

"No one can be sure. Not even you, O Wise and Knowing One," she teased.

Her mother's smile seemed a bit mysterious, but Deborah did not press the subject. Instead she stood and said, "I shall leave you to . . . whatever I interrupted."

"I was just reviewing the past year. I haven't yet thought about goals for the coming one."

"I don't know what you hoped to achieve this past twelvemonth, Deb, but from my perspective, you had a successful year."

"Thank you, Mama."

After escorting her mother to the door, Deborah sat at her writing table and opened the drawer, searching for the sheet of paper on which, a year ago, she had written her goals for 1813. She knew that one had been to have a moderately successful Season, and she had not only accomplished it, she had surpassed her expectations. Another was to not allow her inherent modesty and reticence to prevent her from meeting like-minded people and forming new friendships. She'd succeeded in that as well; she was one of "The Six," a group of musical young ladies who had become fast and firm friends.

Finally finding the elusive paper, she reviewed the third objective. Of the six harpsichord and pianoforte sonatas listed, she'd learnt five, although she had not yet completely mastered the fifth one. Even though she had not attained this goal, Deborah was not displeased with her progress. When setting it, she had not known how little time she would have to practice during the Season.

Taking a new sheet of vellum from the drawer, she sharpened her quill as she considered goals for 1814. What she wanted most was a husband and family of her own. But not just any husband would do. Deborah wanted a love match— to love and be loved by a man who recognized her as an individual, not just one of the Woodhurst twins. Making a love match was an impossible goal, though; a lady could only receive marriage proposals, not make them. She could, however, set herself the task of finding a man she loved who could differentiate between her and her twin.

If such a man existed.

Her second goal required a bit more thought, as well as a trip to the music room, but she soon settled on four pianoforte sonatas to learn, one each by Beethoven, Mozart, Hayden, and Scarlatti. Her third and final objective, however, was more difficult to decide. She considered possibilities for the rest of the day, including a variation on this year's friendship goal, with the aim of furthering her acquaintance with the most personable gentlemen she had met last Season, but she eventually discarded them all. Either the goals did not hold great appeal—which, she knew from past experience, doomed them to failure—or their success depended on things beyond her control. It wasn't until after dinner, when her father asked each member of the family to state one of their aims for the new year, that Deborah realized what she wanted to achieve.

Surprisingly, it was recalling her twin's true purpose that focused Deborah's mind and enabled her to formulate her final goal. It was unlike any other she had ever attempted. And she was not at all certain that she would succeed. But she was determined to try.

Chapter Three

"*F*airfax, you have not made the least push to engage the affections of any young ladies—"

"I told you I would look for a bride this Season. I did not undertake to choose one before the Season begins." Michael lifted his coffee cup and sipped the fragrant brew, hoping the action would help to keep his temper in check. He ought to have known that his grandmother's appearance outside her rooms well before her usual hour presaged trouble, but he had not expected her to carp at him over the breakfast table. A man ought to be able to eat his eggs and bacon, drink his coffee, and read the newspapers without interference, damn it!

"Why not select your duchess now? You will have ample opportunity to get to know her once you are married."

Explanations were futile, given their different perspectives, but he provided one anyway. "Choosing a wife requires more thought than selecting a horse at Tattersall's. Blood, breeding, and appearance are not the only factors."

"What else, aside from the size of the dowry, is there to think about?"

"The size of her dowry does not matter."

"*What?*" The dowager bristled as if he had blasphemed in church. "Of course it matters. You have to take into account what money and properties each girl will bring to the dukedom."

"Grandmère, I have more money than I could spend in three lifetimes. I have fifteen estates—"

"More money and more estates will make the dukedom even more powerful."

The dukedom, the dukedom, always the bloody dukedom! She never considers anything else, least of all the poor, beleaguered duke. He pushed his untouched plate away, his appetite gone. "I am not suggesting that I will take a dowerless girl to wife, although I would, if she were the most suitable choice."

"Fairfax! A girl with no dowry would be completely unsuitable. You must—"

"No more, Grandmère."

"But you must—"

"I said no more!" Michael threw his napkin on the table and shoved back his chair, then strode from the breakfast room, muttering imprecations under his breath.

"Your Grace!" The footman on duty was disconcerted by Michael's abrupt appearance in the entry hall. "They . . . they haven't brought your horse around yet."

"I am a bit early, I believe," Michael said with commendable calm, given his roiling emotions. "I will go to the stable." He grabbed his crop and gloves from the demilune table in the sunlit, two-story entry hall, then headed toward the back of the house. Reaching the door to his study well in advance of the startled footman, Michael barreled inside. The *crack* of the door hitting the paneled wall made him wince, but did not break his stride. The French doors opening onto the terrace received gentler treatment, but even so, he took the three steps down to the garden at a trot. Once on level ground, he checked momentarily, inhaling the cool, crisp air deep into his lungs, then set off across the lawn.

His unexpected appearance in the stable sent the grooms scurrying for his mount. "Not Monarch. Saddle Diablo," he ordered.

"But you—"

"Having trouble with your ears, Perkins?" Michael inquired edgily. "I said, saddle Diablo."

When the horse was brought out, he rubbed a hand down

the stallion's nose, then mounted and galloped down the drive as if chased by the hounds of hell.

Less than an hour later, he was in London, pounding on his best friend's door, although it was only nine o'clock. "Is Dunnley home?" Michael demanded of the startled footman who opened the door.

"Yes, Yer Grace. But he is still at breakfast."

He brushed the servant and his protest aside. "I will announce myself."

Michael's precipitous entrance into the dining room startled all three occupants. Captain Stephen Middleford came to his feet, wielding his cane like a saber. Michael Middleford, the Bishop of Lymington, peered at the duke over the top of his spectacles and ordered his great-nephew back to his seat. "Fairfax may look like the wrath of God, but he presents no danger."

Theodore Middleford, the Viscount Dunnley, took a long look at Michael, arched a tawny eyebrow at his brother, who promptly returned to his chair, then asked the butler to bring the duke coffee, eggs, and ham. "Have a seat, Fairfax, and tell us what brings you to Town on a Wednesday, and so early in the morning."

Michael almost laughed. The scene was so ordinary, so normal. *How many times over the years have I sat at this table? A few dozen? A hundred?* Dunnley was his closest friend, and had been since their early days at Eton. When they'd first met, Michael had been rather awed, as well as a bit intimidated, by Theo, who could chatter like a magpie in several languages and was a dab hand at all sports. But within a few weeks, despite their differences—or, perhaps, because of them—they'd become fast friends. Michael had helped Theo hone his fine mind and appreciate scholarly pursuits; Theo had taught the young duke that there was more to life than duty and responsibility. They'd run tame in each other's homes during the holidays, and Dunnley's family had always welcomed Michael with open arms. Although initially taken aback by the Middlefords' camaraderie and easily expressed affection, Michael had come to revel in it.

He and Theo could talk to each other about anything and

everything, and over the past nineteen years, they probably had. But even though he'd opened his budget in front of Stephen and the bishop many times, Michael did not feel comfortable doing so on this subject. At least, not completely. And not until the servants were dismissed.

Leaning back in his chair, he sipped his coffee. "My grandmother is pushing me to marry. And she is meddling."

Theo looked at him with sympathy. The bishop muttered, "Oh, Lord."

"But if the Season does not start soon, I am going to lose all chance of finding a wife. Because if the Season doesn't begin soon, I am likely to do violence. And a man, even a wealthy duke, who murders his grandmother will not be considered an eligible *parti*." He mustered a wry smile. "Even if the old harridan is the most vexing creature on the face of the earth."

"Wealth and a title atone for any number of sins," Theo said dryly, "but not for the murder of one's nearest and dearest."

Stephen snickered. "The dowager may be Fairfax's nearest relative, but I bet she ain't his dearest one right now."

"I love her," Michael said simply. "I always will. But she seems less lovable now than she was a few months ago." He rubbed his hands over his face, then raked one through his hair. "I love her as much as before, but it seems harder to love her now that she is bent on destroying my life."

"Now just a minute." The bishop pushed his plate away, then leaned forward and planted forearms on the table, elbows akimbo. "Marriage is a sacrament. It won't destroy your life."

"Marriage to the wrong woman could," Michael shot back.

"Marriage to the wrong woman could make a man miserable, but the dowager isn't going to choose an unsuitable bride."

"My grandmother won't be doing the choosing. I will. But she wants me to pick a duchess. I want a wife."

Frowning, Stephen glanced from Michael to the bishop. "Is there a difference?"

"Yes." Michael reached for the coffee pot and refilled his cup. "The dowager wants a dynastic alliance that will increase the dukedom's holdings. I want a wife who will be a partner and helpmeet. I don't care how blue her blood is, I don't care about the size of her dowry—"

"You will choose a woman, while the dowager would select her family." Stephen's summary was, perhaps, oversimple, but it was close to the mark.

"Yes." Michael threw caution to the wind and said what was in his heart. "What I really want is a bride who will love me for myself, not my title, but I don't know if it is possible for a man of my rank to find one."

"It may not be easy, but I believe it is possible." Surprisingly, the optimistic opinion was Dunnley's, not the bishop's. "Since I hope to find just such a lady myself when the time comes for me to choose a bride, why don't we go to my study and discuss the best ways to do so?"

Once they were seated in comfortable wing chairs in front of the fire, Michael was again subjected to his friend's perceptive scrutiny. "You look better than when you arrived, but you still aren't happy. Was it the dowager's meddling that sent you racing neck or nothing across the countryside, or something else?"

The ride to Town had given Michael ample time to ponder just that. "It was her meddling that triggered my temper this morning. She has been badgering me since November to marry, and I gave her my word that I would look for a bride this Season. But apparently that isn't enough for her, although she knows better than anyone that I am a man of my word. Every time I turn around, she is shoving some girl at me. In the three weeks we have been in Town, there hasn't been a single afternoon that the drawing room wasn't chock-full of feather-headed chits and their mamas. Every single day, even Sundays! Grandmère tells me they all dropped by for tea."

Theo roared with laughter. Michael understood his friend's amusement, but he could not share it. Had he lived in Mayfair, such a coincidence, however unlikely, would have been possible. But The Oaks was not a townhouse on one of the fashionable squares. It was neither a townhouse nor in London, but an Elizabethan mansion set in the middle of a parklike estate on the banks of the Thames about a dozen miles southwest of Town. It was *not* a place people just happened to pass by.

His friend gave one last chuckle, and Michael felt an answering smile twitch the corners of his mouth. "I admit, I thought it was funny the first day, but it ceased to be weeks ago. The real problem is the silly widgeons themselves. I can put up with their coy looks and fluttering eyelashes. I have borne all the whacks on the arm from the ladies' fans without complaint—and I sport an array of bruises as proof of my forbearance. But I absolutely could not endure another afternoon of inane conversation about fashions and the weather."

"Then spend the day here, with me."

"Thank you, Theo. I would like that."

"So it is the girls the dowager has selected that you dislike?"

"Yes. They are enough to put any man off the idea of marrying. But since I have promised that I will do my duty, I can only thank God that I am acquainted with other young ladies who aren't so . . . so insipid."

Theo's arched brows invited Michael to confide the names of those ladies, but he was reluctant to do so. Instead he said, "Since my grandmother is as likely to stop matchmaking as pigs are to fly over the dome of St. Paul's, I have been praying that the time until the Season's opening ball will pass quickly. And hoping that, having withstood three weeks of her machinations, I could endure thirteen more days without losing my temper." With a grimace, he added, "Obviously, I did not succeed."

"Perhaps not, but the provocation was great."

"Yes, it was. But you know what is really strange?"

"What?"

"Despite my grandmother's stratagems, I would like to find a wife—a lady I can love who will be my partner and helpmeet. And, even more astonishing, as much as I love The Oaks—its seclusion and . . . pastoral serenity—there have been times, particularly during the past few days, that I wished I lived in Mayfair or St. James's, amid the hustle and bustle that I have always found abhorrent."

Theo's brows rose at the admission, as well they might. In the nine Seasons since they'd come down from Oxford, attained their majority, and taken their seats in the House of Lords, Michael had lived in Town for only two of them—the first one, and three years ago, during the prolonged deliberations of the Regency bill. By the time the bill had been debated and passed, he'd been too weary to even think of changing residences.

"Michael, you own huge tracts of Mayfair. Of St. James's, too, no doubt. I don't know if it is Fairfax House you dislike, or if your objection is to St. James's Square, but it makes no difference. There are other houses on your lands, are there not? Live in one of them if you don't want to live at Fairfax House."

"The others have been rented for the Season."

"Then boot out the tenant of your favorite house."

Theo made it sound so simple. And, Michael conceded, perhaps it was. "If I am going to live in Mayfair, I will live at Fairfax House. I suppose it won't be so bad—not like last time. And it will probably be easier, not to mention less exhausting, to court a lady if I live in Town."

"Undoubtedly so. Paying calls will be easier, too. As will getting to the House, or to Whitehall."

"You live here, so there must be advantages to it," Michael quipped. "I daresay you even know which families have arrived in Town, and those that haven't."

"You know as well as I do who has been in the House, and who has not yet made an appearance."

"But the men often come up before the ladies, don't they?" He knew that the Marquess of Kesteven, Lady Deborah Woodhurst's father, and the Earl of Tregaron, Lady Sarah Mallory's father, had arrived in advance of their families. In response to Michael's rather oblique queries, both gentlemen had said that their wives and children would not arrive until later in the month. Exactly how much later had not been specified.

"Yes, they do."

"The thing is, Theo . . . I don't want it known that I am looking for a wife. The Marriage Mart is hazardous enough for eligible men who aren't known to be on the hunt for a bride. When a man is known to be seeking one, there are more hazards than a golf course designed by Satan himself."

Theo laughed. "Very true. But, much as I hate to say it, my friend, I suspect that the dowager's machinations have put paid to the chance of your search for a bride remaining a secret."

"Isn't it possible that people will think she is looking, but I may not be?"

"Hmmm . . . I suppose it is possible. Unlikely, but not *im*possible. I think you'd best be prepared to find yourself *very* popular with the ladies."

Michael sighed. He only wanted to be popular with one lady. Well, one lady and her parents. "You could help. Why don't you look for a bride this Season, too? That might distract attention from me."

"You are a duke, I am a viscount. I wouldn't provide much of a distraction. Besides, I am only eight-and-twenty—too young to be seeking a bride."

"Cut line, Theo. Your birthday is in two days."

Unabashed, the viscount smiled. "I don't feel quite ready to be fitted for a leg shackle. Not even for you, dear boy."

"You need an heir as much as I do," Michael argued. "Even though you have a brother, his occupation puts him in constant danger."

"I will certainly look over the ladies on the Marriage Mart this Season—I always do—but I have no immediate plans to take a bride."

"The problem is . . ." Michael leant his head against the chair's high back, feeling almost overwhelmed by the enormity of the task he'd set himself. "Ignoring for the moment the problems created by my grandmother having all but trumpeted my intentions to the *ton*—and I shudder to contemplate the havoc that will wreak—there are still two huge obstacles. The first is that I have never tried to win a lady's favor before. Aside from dancing with her at balls, calling on her, and taking her for drives in the park, I have no idea *how* to court a lady."

"You should send her flowers and take her small gifts, too. When the time seems right"—Theo's smile hinted at the rake he was sometimes reputed to be—"when you are comfortable with her and think she is attracted to you, touching her is also good. Touch her hand, her arm, the small of her back if you are standing beside her or walking with her. Eventually, embrace her. Kiss her."

Michael nodded, hoping he would remember all his friend's advice. The touching seemed a good idea—a way to determine if the lady was as attracted to him as to his title. The same was true for embracing and kissing her, although he suspected it would take him a great deal longer to reach that point.

"What is the other obstacle?" Theo prompted. "You said there were two, but you have only mentioned one."

"The other problem is that it would be much easier to do as Grandmère wants and find a duchess, instead of a wife. Because in order to find a wife, I have to reveal the man beneath the ducal trappings. And I . . ." Michael swallowed hard, the words seeming to stick in his throat. "I am not sure that I can. It has been so long since I tried."

Theo wasn't the type to offer false assurances. Instead he asked, in a level yet compassionate tone, "How long has it been?"

"Since Oxford." Michael knew his friend would understand what—and to whom—he referred. He had fallen in love with a young woman who professed to be the daughter of one of the dons, but was, in fact, the man's much younger second wife. Michael had discovered—too late—that she regularly had affairs with her husband's students and had chosen him that year because of his rank. She'd never before had a duke, she'd informed him after the one and only time they'd made love, then laughed as she'd recounted some of the things he'd confided during their "courtship." He'd scrambled into his clothes as quickly as he could, desperate to get away from her and sickened by her perfidy, then returned to his room and was violently ill. He had wooed her as only an earnest young man in the throes of first love could, and she had broken his heart and shattered his confidence in himself as a man. He had not trusted a woman since, nor attempted to court one.

"Not all women are like Mrs. Nichols. Although it is true that some of the *ton*'s matrons play their husbands false, it is generally because their husbands are doing the same to them. And it is often done, if not with the husband's consent, at least with his cognizance."

"That doesn't make it right."

"Of course it doesn't," Theo agreed. "But the *ton*'s morals, or lack thereof, aren't worth discussing. Your situation is."

"Discussing it won't do the least bit of good. What I need is a plan."

"What kind of a plan?"

"A plan for courting a lady, of course. I wonder . . ." Propping his elbows on the chair arms, Michael steepled his fingers and tapped them against his lips. "Perhaps I should make a push to secure a lady's affections before the Season begins."

"The first thing you must do," his friend advised, laughter lurking beneath his tone, "is find a lady you think will suit. Suit *you*—and, if possible, satisfy the dowager, too. Do you have someone in mind?"

"Two ladies, actually, although I have a decided preference for one over the other. Not because the second one is any less suitable, but because . . . well, because I like the first one a bit more." That was as much of his feelings for Lady Deborah as Michael was willing to admit. "And because talking to her is easier."

Theo's brows had risen when Michael admitted having two specific ladies in mind, so his next question did not come as a surprise. "Are you going to tell me who the ladies are?"

"I would rather not. If I make a mull of it, I don't want anyone to know. Not even you, old friend."

"Understandable." Theo nodded, and if he felt slighted,

he hid it well. "But it does make it difficult to offer advice. Have you called on the ladies?"

"I don't even know if they are in Town yet!"

"They haven't been amongst the maidens cluttering the drawing room at The Oaks?"

"No, although both are on Grandmère's list."

"The dowager has a list?" Theo asked, astonished, then answered his own question. "Of course she does. How many ladies are on it?"

"Thirty-four."

"At least she is giving you more choices than Elston's father gave him."

Although Michael was fairly well acquainted with the Marquess of Elston, he had no idea what his friend meant. When he said as much, Theo explained that a codicil to the late marquess's will had given his son one year to marry one of the twenty ladies listed therein, or face unknown consequences. "Like you, Elston wanted a wife, not a marchioness, but he was willing to consider a few of the ladies on his father's list. Miss Lane was one of them, and they fell in love and married, so Elston never learnt what those consequences were."

"I hope I will be as fortunate. Not that Grandmère has threatened anything should I marry a lady who isn't on her list, but if she were displeased, she might well take it out on my wife."

"Getting ahead of yourself, aren't you? First you have to find a bride."

Michael sighed again. He seemed to be doing a great deal of that lately. "I know. And to do that, I have to court her. But I would prefer not to single out the ladies by calling on them. At least, not until after I have encountered them about Town."

"In case no one has mentioned it, old trout, ladies are rarely found in the House or at Whitehall. And never at White's." Although he did not laugh outright, Theo's amusement was obvious.

Conceding the point, Michael smiled. "Very true. So what do you suggest? The best idea I have come up with is to stroll along Bond Street or Oxford Street in the mornings in the hope of encountering the young ladies and their mothers while they are shopping. But it is a haphazard method, at best, and could take days—or even weeks—to yield results. Not to mention the inherent risk of being cornered by ladies with whom I don't wish to speak. Or, even worse, being dragooned into escorting a friend of my grandmother's."

"Bond Street would be the better choice. Many of the premier modistes and milliners have their shops there. But how will meeting the ladies there help your cause?"

"Once I have met them, calling on them will be quite unexceptional."

"Ahhh . . . Not a bad plan. If you hadn't ridden up, we could put it to the test this morning."

"I am not in the mood today." Nor did Michael want Theo, with his dazzling good looks and famed address, beside him if he met the ladies.

He must have sounded as dispirited as he felt, because Theo took another long look at him. "What is wrong?"

"I can't help but wonder if any wife is worth the effort a man must make to claim her as his bride." Michael could only hope so. He knew which lady he wanted as his wife—and duchess—but whether or not Lady Deborah would want him remained to be seen. As did her reasons for making the choice.

If, in fact, she did choose him.

Chapter Four

"*W*hat are our plans for today, Mama?" Deborah posed the question over breakfast in the morning room at Kesteven House.

"This morning we have fittings at Madame Celeste's. This afternoon we will, of course, be making calls."

Diana groaned. "Not more calls! Surely we have paid enough of them? I vow, I cannot stand another afternoon—"

"You need not come with us, Diana."

Ignoring her younger daughter's exclamation of delight, the marchioness continued, "But if you choose not to come, you must also refrain from comment—and from pouting—when your name is not included on invitations."

"That is not likely to happen, Mama," Diana scoffed. "Deb and I were the rage of the Season last year, and we were invited everywhere."

When, Deborah wondered, had her sister become so puffed up with conceit? "No one is disputing that we were popular last year, Di. But there may be another set of twins making their come-outs this Season who will cast us in the shade. It behooves us to pay calls so that we will remain on the best hostesses' guest lists."

"Pooh! No one is going to refuse to send us invitations merely because we don't call on them."

"I will cut from my invitation list any woman who doesn't call on me before the Season begins," the marchioness averred. "Think about it from a hostess's perspective. Parliament opened on March first, but the Season won't begin until the Tuesday after Easter—April twelfth. If a woman can't be bothered to call in those six weeks, what are the chances that she will attend a ball or rout I host?"

"Not very likely, I would think." Deborah had never considered calls in quite that light. "If a lady doesn't respect you enough to call, then she probably won't attend your entertainments. Why bother writing out an invitation?"

"Why indeed?"

"Very well, I will go," Diana conceded with poor grace, "even though I think you are both wrong."

Their mother smiled. "You will be grateful later, when the invitations resulting from these calls arrive."

"I am certain that we will, Mama," Deborah answered for them both. She was hoping for a deluge of invitations. How else was she to find a man who loved her and could tell her apart from her twin?

An hour later, Deborah, her sister, and her mother were in the town chaise the marchioness favored and on their way to Madame Celeste's shop on Bond Street. The elderly Frenchwoman had reigned supreme as London's premier modiste for more than two decades. Every spring she was inundated with customers, both young and old, all vying for her attention—and for the exquisitely fashioned ensembles she created. Her gowns were the *dernier cri*: well cut, sewn with impossibly tiny stitches, and certain to flatter the wearer. Unless, of course, Deborah amended, thinking of Karla Elston and her stepmother, the purchaser deliberately chose unbecoming styles.

Deborah had nothing to fear in that respect. Her mother's eye for flattering styles and colors was almost as fine as Madame Celeste's. But Deborah was a bit concerned how her sister would react when she discovered that their gowns would not all be nearly identical, as they'd been last year. As the coachman drew the carriage to a halt in front of Madame's shop, Deborah gave a mental shrug. She had a very good idea of her twin's reaction to the change and was not at all eager to witness it. Or to bear the brunt of it.

Madame Celeste herself came forward to greet them. "Madame la Marquise, eet ees a pleasure to see you and your lovely daughters. You have come for ze fittings, yes?" Although she still spoke with a marked accent, her English was perfectly understandable.

"Indeed we have, Madame," the marchioness replied.

"Four gowns are ready for ze young ladies, three for you. Who will be fitted first?"

"The girls first, Madame."

After seeing the marchioness seated on a sofa in an alcove, with a pot of tea at her elbow and a stack of new fashion plates to peruse, Madame Celeste turned to the twins. "Lady Diana, my niece, Giselle, will fit your gowns while I do ze same for your sister."

It was clear from Diana's scowl that she was not best pleased to be relegated to Madame's assistant. A reed-thin spinster with forty-odd years in her dish, Mademoiselle Giselle gave the younger girl no chance to protest, ushering her briskly toward one of the fitting rooms and talking volubly about one of the new evening gowns.

Madame nodded and turned to Deborah. "Come with me please, mademoiselle, and we shall try zese new gowns."

Four gowns—all chosen by Deborah, and some of them different from her twin's in color—awaited them in the fitting room. As the modiste helped her remove her morning gown, Deborah ventured a question. "Madame, how did you know that these"—she gestured to the garments—"were mine and not my sister's?"

A frown creased the Frenchwoman's brow. "You are Lady Deborah, are you not?"

"Yes, I am."

Crossing to a small table in the corner, she peered at a piece of paper lying there, then nodded her head. "Just as I thought. Zese are for you. Do you not remember—"

"How could I forget such lovely gowns?" Deborah exclaimed, smiling. "I wondered how you knew that I am Deborah."

"How could I not know?" Madame countered, dropping a pale blue sarsenet evening gown over Deborah's head.

"Your faces and forms are identical, but not your hearts. You are kinder zan your sister."

"But you cannot see our hearts." Then, belatedly, "Thank you, Madame."

"No, but zey are reflected een your eyes and your smiles."

"They are?" Deborah was not sure if she was more astonished by Madame's ability to distinguish her from her twin or by the Frenchwoman's assessment of their characters.

"Indeed." Satisfied with the drape of the gown, the modiste tugged at the neckline and muttered something under her breath, then knelt to pin the hem. "Would you have frowned if I said zat Giselle would fit your gowns?"

"No, of course not."

Nodding, Madame glanced up. "Your sister did."

Deborah started to apologize, but thought better of it. It was her sister's place to offer an apology to Madame and her assistant, although Diana probably would not. Instead Deborah said, "Even though we are twins, sometimes I do not understand my sister's actions." *Or her motivations,* she amended silently, still troubled by her sister's stated intention of marrying a wealthy peer, whether she loved him or not.

"You are not ze first sister to feel zat way, nor will you be ze last."

The modiste's philosophical statement was unexpected, but also vastly comforting. Deborah smiled, her sunny mood restored. "Undoubtedly."

Silence reigned for several minutes, broken only by Madame's soft-spoken requests for Deborah to "turn to ze right, please." When the hem was pinned, the modiste rose and, with a frown puckering her brow, again tugged at the gown's neckline. Tilting her head slightly, she studied it, then picked up her tiny scissors and made a cut in the center.

"Zis will be better." Her nimble fingers began making alterations, deepening the décolletage.

Once it was pinned, Madame gestured to the mirror. "What do you think, Lady Deborah?"

"It is a lovely gown, Madame, and the neckline is perfect. Neither too deep nor too high."

"I agree. Eet ees just right for a young lady." Motioning for Deborah to turn around, the modiste asked, "Which gown do you want to try next?"

"The green silk, please."

Diana knew she was spoiling for a fight, but Mademoiselle Giselle would not oblige her. Fuming, she waited for the Frenchwoman to finish fastening the next gown, a primrose silk ball gown with light green trim. The moment she looked in the mirror, Diana knew she ought not to have insisted that the garment be made exactly as shown on the pattern card. Deborah had argued against the color, suggesting several others, but Diana had held firm. The proof that her sister had been correct spiked Diana's temper.

Madame would just have to fix it. Yanking the hem out of Mademoiselle Giselle's hands, Diana stormed from the room. A plunging décolletage was the only way to draw gentlemen's eyes from the unfortunate color to the wearer, and nothing Madame Celeste said would sway her.

Pushing into the next fitting room, she announced, "Madame, the neckline of this gown is too high."

The modiste fastened the last three buttons of Deborah's pale green gown and tied the sash before sparing Diana a glance. "No, Lady Diana, eet ees not. Eet ees exactly ze same as your sister's, and she ees not complaining."

Deborah turned around slowly, almost as if she were reluctant to do so. Diana could not imagine why . . . until she realized that her sister's gown was not the same as hers.

"What have you done?" Diana barely recognized the shrill shriek as her own voice. It seemed to grow, echoing throughout the shop like the death knell of all her hopes.

"You knew I didn't like that color"—Deborah gestured to Diana's primrose gown—"so I reversed the colors."

"But we always wear the same dresses. Sometimes identical, sometimes with different trims. We agreed to that compromise before we came to Town last year."

"That was last Season. This year, we will have some

identical gowns, some with different trim, and a few, like this one, that are the same style but of different colors."

"But—but—"

"We can't dress alike all our lives, Di. We are two different people. Twins, yes, but also individuals. Once we marry, surely you don't expect to coordinate your outfits with mine every day?"

Diana had not thought beyond this Season. "We aren't married yet! There was no reason for you to change the color of your gown. No reason at all."

"The fact that I didn't like the color was reason enough. The dresses are the same style, just opposite in color."

Deborah's reasonable tone made Diana even angrier. "You have ruined everything!"

"Don't be silly. The *ton* knows we are twins. They aren't going to forget if we wear different colored gowns once or twice a week."

"Did you change the colors of others?" Diana gasped, seeing her plans falling around her like a house of cards.

"Yes, of two—no, three—others. But the variations in hue are more subtle."

Subtle would not do. It would not do at all. "I hate you! You have ruined everything!"

Unable to look at her traitorous sister for another second, Diana spun on her heel and ran from the room. Perhaps outside she would be able to catch her breath and think.

Chapter Five

$\mathcal{D}$ressed in his favorite blue superfine morning coat, a maroon silk waistcoat, dove gray kerseymere pantaloons, and Hessians polished to a mirror shine, Michael walked down Bond Street, his eyes drawn to every blonde present. None was the lady he sought—*who knew there were so many fair-haired women in the beau monde?*—but he'd seen the Kesteven town carriage parked farther down the street, so he hoped that he would eventually achieve his goal. In the past hour and a half, he had traveled the length of the street twice—down one side and up the other. He'd also made six purchases, spoken to a goodly portion of his acquaintance, both male and female, and looked in at Angelo's and Gentlemen Jackson's. And that did not take into account the time he'd spent in Weston's shop, where he'd ordered several new coats and waistcoats.

Given his eagerness, it was difficult to keep his pace to a stroll. But since he wanted his encounter with the Woodhursts—and, at this point, any member of the family would do—to appear casual, not contrived, Michael made a conscious effort to slow his steps.

He would allow himself another half hour, he decided as he started back down the street. Then he had a meeting with his man of business, after which he'd eat at Brooks's or White's before this afternoon's session of Parliament. Gazing ahead, looking for Lady Deborah Woodhurst's sunny blond hair, he was unprepared when a woman's precipitous exit from a dressmaker's shop nearly bowled him over. Instinctively, Michael reached out and grasped his assailant's arm, hoping to keep them both from toppling to the pavement.

Well, hell! As he gasped for breath—she had plowed into his side like one of Stephenson's locomotives—Michael told himself to be more careful what he wished for in the future.

"Let go of me, you clumsy oaf!"

"Clumsy, am I?" he queried, releasing her and stepping back a pace. He swept a gaze from the top of Lady Diana Woodhurst's curly blond hair to her feet. The primrose silk ball gown she wore bore witness to the fact that her exit from the modiste's had been both abrupt and unplanned. While the gown's simple, flowing lines flattered her tall, slender figure, the color, unfortunately, did not. It was fashionable—he'd seen many ladies garbed in similar hues this morning—but it did not become her as well as the pastel blues, pinks, and greens she and her twin sister usually wore.

"It was you who ran into me, my lady." The reminder was ungentlemanly, but her unjust, shrill-voiced accusation had been more suited to a Billingsgate fishwife than a lady of quality.

Her posture radiating insulted indignation, Lady Diana retorted, "You were in my way." No doubt she was glaring at him, but her eyes were hidden behind several locks of hair that had been dislodged from her topknot when they collided. Advancing on him, intent on continuing the argument, she shoved her tresses out of her eyes. But the instant she saw him, her glower changed to a smile, her tone from strident to sweet—and fawning. "Oh, I beg your pardon, Your Grace. I did not realize it was you."

"So I am not an oaf? A clumsy oaf?"

"Of course not, Your Grace—"

But if I were not a duke I would be. Michael kept that opinion to himself, but had no doubt about the truth of it.

"—I was not watching where I was going."

The door behind her opened, and Lady Kesteven stepped outside, her expression harried. "Diana! What was—Oh! Good morning, Fairfax. I see you have rescued my errant daughter."

"Mother!" Lady Diana flounced back into the shop.

The marchioness grimaced at her younger daughter's rudeness, but gamely continued the conversation. "Thank you."

Bowing over Lady Kesteven's hand, Michael returned her greeting. With a start, he realized that he had, indeed, rescued Lady Diana. It was scandalous for a lady to walk unescorted on Bond Street, but quite unexceptional for her to converse there with a gentleman—provided her maid or a chaperone was present, and if the man had been properly introduced. "It is a gentleman's duty to rescue damsels in distress. I am pleased to have been able to perform such a service for you."

"I hope you will allow me to return the favor by inviting you to join us for luncheon."

Exultant at his success, he wanted to dance a jig. But dukes who danced on Bond Street were likely to be carted off to Bedlam, so instead he bowed again and said, "Thank you, my lady. Much to my regret, I have another engagement. May I call this afternoon instead?"

"We aren't At Home today."

"Perhaps on Thursday?"

"Thursday is fine," the marchioness confirmed. "You are welcome to call at any time, Fairfax."

The door opened again, framing one of the twins in the portal. Michael knew immediately that it was Lady Deborah, although, if pressed, he could not have said exactly how he knew. Perhaps because his heart turned a somersault or two before settling back into place, pumping at a faster rate than usual. Or the smile of pure delight blooming on his face.

Lady Deborah smiled. "Good morning, Your Grace."

"A very good morning to you, Lady Deborah." He bowed over her hand and murmured for her ears alone, "Fairfax, please."

Wearing a blue velvet spencer over a white, sprigged muslin morning gown, she was even lovelier than he remembered, and he basked in the warmth of her sunny smile. She nodded, but did not have the chance to either grant or deny his request before her sister, still sulking, flounced out of the modiste's again, this time trailed by a middle-aged maid.

Good manners obliged him to incline his head to acknowledge her. Although her ensemble matched Lady Deborah's and their features were identical, his heart performed no acrobatics.

Turning back to Lady Kesteven, he offered, "Allow me to see you to your carriage, ma'am."

"Thank you, Fairfax. It is kind of you to offer, but unnecessary." She gestured to the curb, where the coachman was drawing rein.

Waving off the footman who had opened the door and let down the steps, Michael handed the marchioness inside, then turned to offer the same service to her daughters. Lady Diana pushed in front of her sister, smiling coyly as she placed her hand in his. When she made no attempt to enter, he dropped her hand and stepped back. "If you prefer to have the footman assist you, you need only say so."

Clearly stung, she clambered inside without aid.

Her expression pained, Lady Deborah stepped forward. "Your Grace, I hope you will overlook my sister's behavior. She—"

Michael interrupted without remorse for his rudeness. "Your sister is quite capable of offering her own apologies, should she choose to do so." They both knew how unlikely that was. With a smile, he asked, "May I assist you, my lady?"

"Yes, of course." She placed her hand in his, and Michael swore the sun shone brighter. Softly, she added, "Thank you, Fairfax."

As he watched the carriage pull away from the curb, he ran his finger around the edge of his shirt collar, hoping a stray breeze would waft down his neck.

The silence was deafening.

Eerie and frightening, too, given the tempest of emotions roiling within the close confines of the carriage.

As the coachman tooled the rig through the streets of Mayfair, Deborah darted glances from her mother's pinched, set face to her sister's stony one, wondering when the storm would break. And how long it would last.

It was like waiting for a volcano to erupt. Fascinating, but dangerous for the victims caught in the explosion.

A tempest of a storm, all *Sturm und Drang* and emotional lightning bolts, was inevitable. Mother would wait until they were at home and in private to take Diana to task for her behavior, but the marchioness's tightly pursed mouth and taut features guaranteed a scold. The critical question was whether Diana would maintain control of her temper until they reached Kesteven House. Her sullen expression and defiant posture gave mute testimony to the fact that not only was she unrepentant, but she had vented only a small portion of her wrath. Deborah still did not know what had triggered her sister's outburst. She was, however, absolutely certain that she had not yet heard the last of it. In fact, Deborah suspected that she might well hear about it for a long time to come.

She darted a glance at Ogden, the lady's maid she shared with her sister, and caught the slight shake of the older woman's head. Perched side by side on the rear-facing seat, Deborah and the maid huddled in their respective corners. There was no doubt about it—when the storm broke, it would be a tempest of epic proportions. Deborah squeezed more tightly into her corner and took refuge in thoughts of the pleasant and delightfully unexpected encounter with the Duke of Fairfax.

Charming, attractive, intelligent, and oh so eligible, he would make some young woman a very fine husband. Since the end of last Season, Deborah had nurtured the hope that she might be the fortunate lady who won his regard.

Michael could not have said why he felt so inclined to dance today, but he did. It was a strange, rather exhilarating feeling. One he had never experienced before. Not that he had anything against dancing; truth be told, he rather enjoyed it—in a ballroom with a partner who did not tread on his toes. But Bond Street was not an appropriate milieu for dancing. Nor was Threadneedle Street.

Grinning from ear to ear, he descended from his carriage in front of his solicitor's premises. Lady Deborah Woodhurst had smiled at him as if he were handsome and dashing. And

Lady Kesteven had invited him to call at any time. If that wasn't reason enough for a man to dance through the streets of London, Michael did not know what was.

The defeat of Napoleon, perhaps. Or the Prince Regent suddenly becoming a penny-pinching miser.

With a leap worthy of the great Armand Vestris, Michael took the first three stairs. Lady Deborah's radiant smile was enough to make a man feel ten feet tall, able to move mountains and perform the most daring deeds. Michael was rather surprised to discover that his jump had not taken him all the way to the second floor. A few more such smiles might well be enough to wrest an eloquent proposal from a reserved, rather diffident duke.

By the time they reached Hanover Square, the tension in the carriage was palpable. Diana knew that she was in for a rare trimming. Her mother wore an expression suitable for an avenging Fury. Or a diminutive Valkyrie, in lilac jaconet instead of armor and a horned helmet, preparing to wreak havoc on the unwary.

Diana, however, was not unwary. Uneager, yes; unhappy, too, but not unwary. Always honest with herself, she admitted that she deserved the scold for her shocking lapse of decorum. But it was difficult to remember one's manners when provoked past bearing. And Deborah had done just that—and more—by arbitrarily changing the colors of several of her new gowns.

The marchioness led the procession from the street to the front door of Kesteven House, her teeth gritted as if to prevent a stray word from escaping. The moment her foot touched the top step, Driscoll opened the door and bowed. Although Diana had spent several weeks last Season trying to discover how the butler managed to perform that feat with such remarkable consistency, she still did not know. Butler's magic, she supposed.

"Thank you, Driscoll," the marchioness said as she sailed through the door. Then, "Don't ask, please."

Deprived of his usual question about the success of their outing, the august, ever proper butler stood, mouth agape and rigid as a statue, for several seconds. Finally he nodded, apparently still unable to muster a response. Odgen, having divested all three ladies of their spencers, bonnets, and gloves, made a beeline for the upper reaches of the house. Halfway up the stairs, she met Pettibone, the marchioness's dresser, who deftly extracted her mistress's garments from the pile in Ogden's arms. After a searching glance at the three ladies in the entry hall, Pettibone, too, beat a hasty retreat.

Turning to the butler, Lady Kesteven issued a series of rapid-fire instructions. "We are not at home to anyone. Not the king. Not St. Peter and the heavenly host. No one." Driscoll carried out all orders to the letter, but suffered agonies of distress—and indecision—if his instructions were not precisely detailed.

"Yes, my lady."

"My daughters and I will be in the drawing room. We are not to be disturbed unless the house is ablaze or the angel Gabriel appears to sound the last trumpet."

"Yes, my lady."

"You and the footmen should eat your midday meal now."

The butler's dismay at having to leave the front door unattended was unmistakable, but he nodded his acquiescence. "Yes, my lady."

Diana knew that her mother was ensuring there would be no bystanders in a position to overhear the imminent confrontation. By the time the marchioness turned back to her daughters, Deborah the Perfect was already halfway to the staircase. Diana hastened to follow.

She would endure the reprimand, no matter how harsh, but she vowed to make Deborah pay in kind before the end of the Season. It was only fair, since this debacle was all her fault.

Diana was a firm believer in fairness and justice. *An eye for an eye and a tooth for a tooth.*

Chapter Six

Thursday, 31 March 1814

*M*ichael awoke with the same feeling of excitement he'd experienced on Christmas morning as a boy. The day beckoned, full of glittering, seemingly limitless possibilities, luring him out of bed several hours earlier than was his wont, much to the disgust of his valet. But not even Meecham's grumbling could dampen Michael's spirits. And grumblings there were, plenty of them, offered with the ease and freedom that only twenty years of loyal service can provide.

He cut off the valet's complaints by saying, in a mild tone free of censure, "You should be thankful it is raining."

Meecham frowned, his grizzled brows forming a *V.* "How so, Your Grace?"

"If not for the storm, I wouldn't have rung. I would have dressed in an old coat and buckskins and gone out for a ride before breakfast."

"Not—"

"Yes, indeed," Michael interrupted cheerfully. "That blue coat you so deplore and my oldest pair of boots."

"Thank God for the rain! That coat is a disgrace."

"That coat is *comfortable.* Besides, I never wear it beyond the gates."

"And I thank God for that, too."

"While I bathe, why don't you choose my garments for the day? *Comfortable* clothes this morning, but after luncheon, Meecham, I want you to rig me out in the first stare.

This afternoon I am paying a morning call on a young lady—and her mother, of course. If the weather clears, I hope to take her for a drive in Hyde Park."

"The mother, Your Grace?"

Michael rolled his eyes at his valet's feeble attempt at humor. "You know I mean the young lady."

Meecham gave a knowing nod. "Her Grace finally found a young lady you like, eh?"

"No." Michael's tone was flat and purposefully repressive. There would be no gossip amongst the servants on the subject of his wife. He unbent enough to add, "*I* found her. I met her last Season."

Accepting the rebuke with a nod, Meecham straightened, his craggy face suddenly solemn. "Your Grace, I have known you since you were in short pants. Known the dowager duchess for more than two decades, too. I haven't always agreed with her, but I respect her. And I know my place. It is indisputably your right to pick your duchess. And it is far more important that she meet your criteria for the role than your grandmother's."

He cleared his throat, shifted from foot to foot. "But you must be aware that your grandmother might not agree. With all due respect, sir, if the dowager doesn't like your choice, she could make your wife's life a living hell."

Indeed she could. Would, too, if she took umbrage at Michael's choice. Well, she could take umbrage all day long, but she demmed well would not do anything to upset his duchess. Michael would see to that.

"She could," he agreed, heartened by the old man's concern, "but she won't. She is not likely to object to this young lady." Doffing his dressing gown, he pointed to the wardrobe and stepped into the tub. "Clothes, Meecham. Then see if Gibbs thinks the rain will stop before noon." Gibbs was the head gardener, and his rheumatic joints predicted the weather with astonishing accuracy.

"One more thing, Meecham," Michael added, a steely edge to his tone. "If my grandmother gets wind of my intentions, or the fact that I have found a young lady I think might suit, I will pension you off to a cottage on my estate in the Scottish highlands." He should not have needed to give the warning, and perhaps it was unnecessary, but he felt compelled to add it. Meecham's tongue had flapped a bit too freely a few years ago while courting the dowager duchess's dresser, and Michael still felt the repercussions from time to time. Not because of the information the valet had let slip, but because the dowager believed that confiding in a servant was a breech of ducal dignity.

Tension still permeated the air at Kesteven House, although it seemed to affect only the ladies. Deborah suspected that defied the laws of physics and chemistry, but even so, it was indisputably true. Equally indisputably, Diana was the source.

Deborah did not understand why her sister was sulking, but a glance down the length of the breakfast table showed that she was. There was no denying that the scold Diana had received on Tuesday after the aborted trip to Madame Celeste's had been a harsh one. It was the first time their mother had ever invoked all four names when rebuking one of her children. Even when the twins were eight and had fallen into the Home Farm pond, then arrived in the entry hall—mud-covered from head to toe, missing one shoe (Deborah) or both (Diana), and trailing brackish water from their brand-new, irretrievably ruined white muslin dresses— at the same time three of the highest sticklers in the realm had appeared for tea, she had only resorted to three names. That had been enough for Deborah, and she hadn't done anything since that required more of a reproach than her given name could support. Whether her sister could say the same was open to debate.

Given the nature of the offense—ladies did not disrupt another's fitting, argue heatedly with their dressmakers, or yell at their sisters for all the world to hear—its public venue, and its possible repercussions, Deborah did not think the four-name reprimand, unprecedented or not, had been unreasonable. Especially since the only punishment the marchioness had decreed was an apology to Madame Celeste and Mademoiselle Giselle when she and the twins returned the next day to have the new gowns fitted—and one to Deborah, which she had yet to receive.

Diana's opinion was obviously quite different, but Deborah did not know why. No doubt she would eventually learn. Probably when she least expected it.

Her most recent attempt to coax her sister out of the sullens having been as unsuccessful, and as firmly rebuffed, as the previous dozen, Deborah resolved to leave her to her pouting. Diana could, and usually did, hold a grudge for days. Sometimes weeks.

Pinning a smile on her face, Deborah turned to her mother. "What are our plans today?"

"You may do as you please this morning, but this afternoon, I will expect both of you in the drawing room to receive callers."

"Whom do you expect to call?"

"A number of the ladies on whom we have called will undoubtedly return the favor. And"—the marchioness's steel-blue eyes twinkled—"I believe the Duke of Fairfax will also call upon us."

"Really?" Diana said. It was the first time this morning she had deigned to join their conversation.

"Yes. The other day"—there was no need for their mother to specify which day, since it was irrevocably stamped in all of their minds—"he asked if he might."

"And you said that he could?" Despite her nonchalant tone, Diana was clearly interested in the answer. Of course she was, Deborah scoffed, surprised by her own foolish blindness. Fairfax was exactly the kind of wealthy, high-ranking husband her sister hoped to snare, but he deserved far better.

"Yes, I did."

Any mother with a marriageable daughter would have done the same. Fairfax was one of the greatest prizes on the Marriage Mart, and had been for several years. Last year he had shown no interested in being caught, nor in pursuing a young lady. Deborah wondered if that would prove to be the case this year as well.

She hoped not. Not that she had any reason to think that

he would want her for a wife. But she hoped that he might. She liked the rather diffident duke. She could not claim to know him well—she suspected that few people did—but she liked him. Quite a lot, in fact.

While her mother and sister discussed other callers they might expect this afternoon, Deborah mentally reviewed her wardrobe and tried to decide what to wear. Should it be the new blue jaconet afternoon dress or the blush pink muslin carriage dress? Both were fashionable and becoming, but the latter might encourage him—or another gentleman—to invite her for a walk or drive in the park. Which would be lovely, of course, if it ever stopped raining.

Unfortunately, the carriage dress might also rouse her sister's ire. Deborah did not understand why her sister was so upset that a few of their new outfits differed in color, but there was no denying the fact that she was. Any mention of gowns or clothing elicited a shrill lecture about Deborah's fickleness, disloyalty, and lack of honor. Although she did not believe that she had violated last year's compromise about their attire, her sister did.

And had said so repeatedly.

Diana plopped into the seat beside her. "What shall we wear this afternoon?" she demanded.

Startled, Deborah stared at her sister. Gone were all traces of the tears and accusations, sulks and pouting of the past two days. Such a quick recovery was not extraordinary—Diana's memory was, at times, rather selective, remembering only the things she wanted to recall and forgetting the rest—but Deborah found the abrupt volte-face a bit suspicious in this instance. Wary, but eager to see the end of her sister's hostility, she suggested, "Perhaps the blue jaconet afternoon dress?"

"An excellent choice," their mother remarked, nodding her approval. "It is very flattering."

"Why not a carriage dress?" Diana countered. "Fair—a gentleman might ask us to go for a drive in the park."

"One of them might, if it isn't raining," Deborah readily agreed. "But if we are asked, we can change clothes. It seems a bit presumptuous to wear a carriage dress when we have not received such an invitation."

"I suppose it might." Diana appeared to be debating the advantages and disadvantages of such overweening behavior. Deborah was much relieved when her sister finally said, "Very well, the blue jaconet it shall be."

"If you are invited for a drive," their mother said, "you could wear that dress with the pale pink velvet spencer and the villager bonnet with matching ribands, or with the cream merino spencer and the Gypsy bonnet with the blue ribands."

Both ensembles would be lovely. "Yes, we could," Deborah agreed.

"But, Mama, don't you think the new peach muslin carriage dress is vastly becoming?"

"Indeed it is. But I thought you did not want to make this hypothetical gentleman wait while you changed?" the marchioness quizzed.

"I daresay that will depend on who invites me." Diana's outrageous comment was accompanied by a flirtatious toss of her head.

"That kind of attitude will lose you admirers faster than anything, young lady." The marchioness's tone was not harsh, but her frown made the statement more than an admonishment, but not quite a reprimand.

Deborah held her breath, fearing the criticism, mild as it was, would spark her sister's volatile temper. Diana merely tossed her head again and said, "Some of them would be better lost."

Recognizing Diana's mood, their mother forbore from further comment. Deborah expelled her breath on a sigh of relief.

Peace, however tenuous, reigned for the rest of the morning.

The fastest means of travel from The Oaks to London was by boat. Michael usually made the trip that way if Parliament was his sole destination, since there were stairs and a wharf conveniently located at Westminster. If, however, he had other engagements and needed to use one of the horses or carriages he kept in Town, the advance planning and complex logistics required would do a field marshal proud. Particularly if he wanted to use a rig other than his curricle. In that case, his coachman had to go up with him, and the master of the ribbons hated traveling on the water. Making the trip by carriage often took considerably longer, especially if it had rained recently, but making the journey by river in the rain was not always comfortable, either.

Michael had no control over the weather or the state of the roads, but he did over his boats and the eight boatmen in his employ. All were young and strong, and three of the crew had won the Doggett Coat and Badge Race the year after they had completed their apprenticeship as watermen. They could ferry him the ten miles up to Westminster in an hour, regardless of the weather.

Today, however, one thing after another had gone wrong, and by the time he reached Hanover Square, shortly before two o'clock, Michael was not feeling very sociable. His greatcoat was decidedly damp, his Hessians only slightly less so, and the beginnings of a headache throbbed at his temples. The rain was to blame for the soggy state of his attire, and his coachman's grumblings for the state of his head—although the fact that his carriage hadn't been waiting at the Parliament stairs had not helped either condition. A duke of the realm shouldn't have to trudge through the streets in the rain, especially not one who had sent a messenger to his stables in Town two hours in advance of his own departure.

At least the rain was beginning to taper off, so Michael could look forward to the possibility of taking Lady Deborah for a drive in the park later. If she hadn't already accepted a similar invitation from another man, and if she was willing to favor him with her company. Philosophically, he shrugged, knowing he would ask again if she had a prior engagement today.

As he climbed the steps of Kesteven House, the door swung open, and the butler bowed him inside.

Michael pulled out his card case. "The Duke of Fairfax to

see Lady Kesteven, Lady Deborah, and Lady Diana." He did not particularly wish to see Lady Diana—not unless her temperament had sweetened over the winter, which, judging from their encounter outside the dressmaker's shop, did not appear to be the case—but courtesy demanded that he ask to see all three ladies.

"Yes, Your Grace." Instead of taking his card up to the marchioness, the butler took Michael's walking stick, hat, and gloves, then his greatcoat. "If you will follow me, please."

Michael nodded, striving to conceal his delight that Lady Kesteven had accorded him such preferential treatment and idly wondering if anyone had ever refused to follow the august butler. Escorted upstairs to the drawing room and duly announced, Michael greeted the marchioness and her daughters, pleased to see that no other callers were present.

As she asked the butler to bring a tea tray, Lady Kesteven gestured Michael to a seat, the chair she indicated next to hers—and next to the sofa on which the twins sat, as identical in appearance as two peas in a pod, their pretty blue dresses the same in every detail. Not certain which twin was seated closest to him, Michael nodded impartially to them both and, flipping up the tails of his dark blue superfine coat, sat down as he'd been bidden.

But before his cream kerseymere pantaloons made contact with the seat, his heart began leaping about in his chest, giving him the answer: Lady Deborah was sitting next to him. Catching her gaze, he smiled, and was rewarded when she returned the private greeting.

It was her sister, however, who spoke first. "Did you call to see if I was well after our collision on the pavement the other day?"

The urge to give the audacious chit a set-down was strong, but Michael restrained himself, lest he lose credit with Lady Deborah. "No, I didn't. Since I prevented you from toppling to the pavement after you careened into me, it never crossed my mind that you might have been injured." While not the most polite response, it was an honest one, and Michael prized honesty above all else. He refused to utter the polite, social falsehoods that tripped so readily off the tongues of most of the *ton*. Not only did he abhor such deceit, but the false phrases tied his tongue into knots.

A startled gasp to his left made Michael wonder if he had gone too far with his rather ungentlemanly reminder of who was at fault and discredited himself in Lady Deborah's eyes. "Were you injured, Lady Diana? Do I need to beg your pardon that I happened to be passing by when you burst out of the dressmaker's?" Maintaining a pleasant, even tone was an effort, but Michael managed to keep any hint of frost or hauteur from his voice.

"I wasn't injured." The rag-mannered twin flounced back in her seat—something he would have thought impossible in that position had he not seen it with his own eyes. Lady Deborah shot him a surprised glance, but he did not know if it was because of what he'd said or because she had not known of the incident. Even the marchioness looked at him askance. It was *not* an auspicious beginning, and Michael feared it boded ill for his plans.

Determined to make amends, he plunged into the social pleasantries. "Are you ladies looking forward to the Season's entertainments after the long winter?" He glanced from the marchioness to Lady Deborah, allowing his gaze to linger on her for a moment, then to her sister, then back to their mother.

Lady Deborah smiled. "I am. At times I thought the snow would keep us in Lincolnshire until summer."

"Of course we are," her sister declared almost scornfully, as if she thought him obtuse for asking a question to which the answer must be evident.

"I am, also, although I do enjoy the less frantic pace in the summer and winter," the marchioness said.

Turning to Lady Deborah, Michael returned her smile. "I wondered the same thing at times. My grandmother claims it was the worst winter since 1760, and the snow must have been much deeper in the Midlands and farther north than it was in Kent."

"Is your seat in Kent? Or did you spend the winter at a fa-

vorite estate?" Lady Deborah's questions were hesitant, as if
she feared he might think her too forward.

"I am more fortunate than some peers. Fairfax Castle is
one of my favorite estates."

"Is it old, like Woodhurst Castle, or a newer structure
given the same name as the old one?"

Never having been to Woodhurst Castle, Michael had no
idea how old it was. "Old enough that most people consider
it ancient. Fairfax Castle was built in the late thirteenth century, but it is the second structure to have the name. The first
was more keep than castle, built mostly of wood, but burnt
to the ground in 1287." He was proud of his ancient title,
which dated back to the late eleventh century, but feared he
would sound pompous or arrogant if he did more than recite
the bare facts.

"Is it dreary and drafty?" Diana asked—and received a
reproving "mind your manners" glare from her mother.

"Neither dreary nor particularly drafty, although some of
the larger rooms are difficult to heat in very cold weather."

Lady Kesteven deftly turned the conversation. "Did the
dowager come to Town with you this year?"

"Indeed she did." Michael heartily wished his grandmother would return to Kent, but that was as unlikely as
snow in August. He had been fortunate enough to escape the
house without her inquiring into his plans for the afternoon,
but she had not ceased her matchmaking efforts on his behalf. Or, more accurately, her meddling. "Like you, she is
looking forward to the Season."

The butler entered with the tea tray, and Michael used the
interlude to glance around the large, high-ceilinged room. It
was elegantly furnished, with blue damask hangings and
blue and cream upholstery on the chairs and sofas, which
were arranged in groups for ease of conversation instead of
against the walls. The tables and chairs were from the work-
rooms of Sheraton and Chippendale, and a beautiful harpsichord stood in front of a window at one end of the room. At
the opposite end, a pair of wing chairs sat in front of the fireplace. Despite its size, the room felt cozy and comfortable,
with embroidery hoops and books scattered on side tables

near the ladies' chairs, and a chess board on a game table between the center pair of windows.

After inquiring whether he wanted milk or sugar, Lady
Kesteven prepared a cup of tea for him. Lady Deborah rose
to help her mother, passing plates and forks, cups and
saucers, then offering a mouthwatering array of tarts, cakes,
and biscuits. "The raspberry tarts are Cook's specialty, but
the Queen cakes are also very good."

Michael selected a raspberry tart and won a smile from
Lady Deborah. He looked longingly at the Queen cakes and
lemon biscuits, but limited himself to the one tart. He had a
fondness for sweets, but an even greater aversion to being
fat. And he did not want to become a figure of fun like the
Prince Regent or Baron Whately, whose creaking corsets
and splitting seams were the stuff of legend amongst the *ton*.

Lady Diana made no move to assist, seeming quite content to leave the hostess duties to her mother and sister.
When everyone had been served, the marchioness inquired,
"Fairfax, did you attend the concert of ancient and modern
music last Wednesday at Drury Lane? I understand they performed works by Handel and Mozart, including Mozart's
Requiem."

"We were looking forward to attending," Lady Deborah
added, "but we didn't arrive in London until the end of the
week."

"Yes—"

"*You* may have been looking forward to it," her sister
muttered, just loudly enough to be heard, "but some of us
prefer to spend our evenings at balls and routs and other,
more lively entertainments."

"There are no balls and 'lively entertainments' during
Lent, Lady Diana." Michael's repressive tone was more for
the slight to her sister than because she had interrupted him.
He allowed himself a quick glance at Lady Deborah, catching her eye and the smile he'd earned by championing her,
then turned to the marchioness and answered her question in
his normal accents. "I did attend the concert, and it was
splendid. They also played some of Haydn's work."

"What makes you think I am Diana, Your Grace?" that young lady asked. "I might as easily be Deborah."

A number of replies sprang to mind, not all of them polite. He chose the simplest. "Lady Deborah is known to be fond of music, and it was your sister, not you, who expressed a wish to attend the concert."

"Are there upcoming musical entertainments we should be certain to attend?" Lady Kesteven inquired.

"I am not aware of any events of particular note." He vowed to have his secretary make a list of all likely occasions in the morning. "But the Italian Opera will open a week from Tuesday with Madame Grassini singing the role of Sabina in Cimarosa's *Gli Orazi e i Curiazi*."

"I believe we are promised elsewhere that evening." The marchioness replied before either of her daughters could comment.

"Lady Oglethorpe's ball, perhaps?" Michael suggested. "I am promised there myself, but plan to attend the Opera on Saturday. I could make up a small party, if you and your daughters would like to attend with me. The Opera always seems more enjoyable with congenial companions than when one attends alone." He looked from Lady Kesteven to the twins, trying to gauge their reactions to his invitation. Deborah was smiling in delight; her sister's expression was as blank as a freshly washed slate.

"Does Her Grace not go with you?" Lady Kesteven's smile was rueful and a bit chagrined. "As many performances as I have attended over the years, I shouldn't need to ask, but I cannot recall if I have seen her there or not."

"I daresay that my grandmother's erratic habits are to blame, not your memory, my lady. She does attended occasionally, but usually only once or twice a Season. It isn't that she dislikes the Opera, rather that she doesn't like the long trip home afterward. Although that never deters her from attending a ball or rout," he added wryly. "Or a card party given by one of her friends."

"From Haymarket to St. James's Square is a long trip?" This from Lady Diana, in an incredulous, slightly scornful tone. "'Tis a good thing your seat is in southern Kent, not Scotland or Cornwall."

How, he wondered, did she know the location of both his townhouse and his seat? Neither was a secret—there were few secrets in the *beau monde*—but he doubted that many women knew the latter, since there had not been a house party there, save for his grandmother's elderly cronies, for more than two decades. "Not St. James's Square, my estate near Kew."

"Kew?" she echoed in stark disbelief. "Why would—"

A glare from her mother silenced the chit—and promised a lesson in manners. A much-needed one. With a smile of apology, Lady Kesteven turned back to him. "We would be pleased to have your escort to the Opera, or to join your party, if Kesteven is unable to attend." She colored charmingly, then with a moue confessed, "But rack my brain as I might, I cannot remember his plans. I fear I am growing forgetful as I get old."

"Old, my lady? You don't look much older than your daughters."

Delighted, she laughed, which enhanced the resemblance. Half a head shorter than her daughters and not quite as slender, wearing a pale green gown that seemed to brighten her tawny hair, she was, in truth, every bit as lovely as they were. She looked as if she had not yet seen forty summers, but her eldest son was about Michael's age, so she had to be nearer fifty than forty.

"As for my invitation, I would be happy to call tomorrow so you can give me your answer. Or, if you will not be at home then, you can send a note to Fairfax House, and I will stop there on my way to Whitehall and Westminster."

"You may call at any time, Fairfax. And we should be at home tomorrow, if you don't mind coming again. I dislike taking you out of your way, but . . ."

"It would be my pleasure to call on the three of you again tomorrow." He shot a quick look at the twins, both of whom wore pleased smiles, although Lady Diana's seemed to have an underlying smugness that her sister's lacked.

Lord Henry, the marchioness's younger son, and several

of his friends burst into the drawing room like a litter of boisterous puppies. Two or three years older than the twins, Lord Henry was a bit of a fribble. He was also an aspiring dandy, prone to waistcoats in eye-popping colors and patterns, elaborate cravats, and rather high shirt points. But, to his credit, he did not indulge in the other sartorial excesses of that set. No fault could be found in the dress of his companions—Lord Howe and Viscount Llanfyllin, Lady Sarah Mallory's brother—nor with their manners. Lord Henry remembered his soon enough and, at his mother's behest, crossed to the bellpull to ring for another pot of tea and more cups, then ruined the effect by sprawling in his chair.

Michael used the interruption to proffer another invitation, this one in a quiet voice he hoped would be heard but not overheard. "Lady Deborah, if the rain stops, will you drive with me in the park this afternoon?"

Her blue eyes widened in surprise, and Michael feared she would refuse . . . until her sunny smile blossomed, brightening the room and his heart. "Thank you, Fairfax. I would enjoy that."

"Shall we say five o'clock?"

"Five o'clock is fine. But if it is still raining then, please don't feel you must return." She blushed, looking adorably confused, then amended, "I would be happy to see you again, of course, but there is no need to risk your health just to tell me something the weather will have already made obvious."

When he took his leave a few minutes later, he carried the memory of her smile with him, to sustain him until he saw her again.

Throughout the afternoon and an ever-changing but significantly smaller than usual parade of callers, Deborah monitored both the time and the weather. The latter changed not at all, and there were times she would have sworn that the ormolu clock on the mantle suffered from the same affliction. Enough callers, all male, braved the elements that the ladies of the house were never reduced to talking amongst themselves, and Deborah blessed them all because without their presence, Diana would surely have pouted. Or, even worse, indulged in a fit of the megrims.

As she chatted with their visitors and passed cups, saucers, and cakes, Deborah hugged two secrets close to her heart. Fairfax had invited her, by name, to drive in the park with him. And he had apparently not given her sister leave to call him by his title. Some people might not consider those indications of his favor—and perhaps they were not as remarkable as she believed—but she could only hope they were. She was delighted that he had remembered which twin she was, although given that a proper morning call only lasted for twenty minutes—and the duke was always all that was proper—it was not a prodigious feat of memory. Still, he had made the effort, and that was more than could be said for the rest of their visitors.

Shortly after the last of the callers departed, the clock's silvery chimes sounded five times. Deborah wandered to the window and gazed out at the square, watching the rain fall and waiting for Fairfax. The pang of disappointment that jolted through her several minutes later, when she realized he was not coming, was sharp enough to steal her breath. Even though she had told him that he should not return if it was still raining, she had been hoping that he would come anyway, if only for a few minutes of conversation.

"What *are* you looking at, Deb?"

She started, her heart leaping to her throat when her sister suddenly appeared at her side. Affecting nonchalance, Deborah shrugged and dropped the drapery, then turned her back on the empty square. "Just the rain."

Diana waved a hand at the window. "Aren't you glad we decided not to wear carriage dresses this afternoon? We would have looked quite foolish, since it rained all day."

"Yes, indeed," their mother said without reproach. "Presumptuous, as well. And that, my dears, is a fatal combination, guaranteed to put off any—all—discerning gentlemen."

And that was the last thing they wanted to do. One of the main purposes of a Season—and the sole purpose of a second or subsequent Season—was to find a husband. Preferably a wealthy, titled, attractive one who would consider his wife more than just a broodmare with whom to beget his heir. And probably a spare or two, as well.

Linking their arms, Diana tugged Deborah back to the sofa on which they'd sat that afternoon. Her sister always insisted that they sit side by side, on display like a matching pair of bookends. Deborah thought it completely unnecessary, since there was not a member of the *beau monde* who did not know they were identical twins, but Diana could not be swayed. She had reveled in the attention they'd received last year when they had first made their bows to Society. And she still did. Which, no doubt, was part—perhaps a large part—of the reason she wanted them to dress identically.

Deborah had not understood her sister's insistence on emphasizing their sameness last year, and still didn't. It was only on the surface, after all; their characters and interests were vastly different. And while a gentleman might buy a matched set of blooded horses to pull his curricle, or a pair of identical vases to grace the mantel in his drawing room, he could only take one woman to wife. Better by far, then, to emphasize their individuality, not their similarities, so that a man could choose which sister he wanted to marry.

Unfortunately, Diana seemed unable to understand that. Nor was she willing to try. Thus, Deborah had felt compelled to take a stand, having grown increasingly uncomfortable with being displayed as one half of a matched pair.

Diana settled into the corner of the sofa, one foot tucked beneath her. "The Duke of Fairfax would be an ideal husband if only he weren't so unattractive."

"Unattractive?" Deborah was certain her sister had misspoken.

Their mother's reaction was even more pointed. "You must be attics to let, child! There is nothing unattractive about the duke. He may not be the most handsome gentleman in the *ton,* but in no wise can he be considered unappealing."

"Perhaps he isn't unattractive," Diana conceded, huffing out a sigh, "but he is . . . plain."

"Some featherheaded misses might consider him so," the marchioness conceded. "But any woman who chooses a husband because of his looks is doomed to misery. Her marriage will be as shallow as she is."

Knowing that her sister's goal was to marry a man of wealth and high rank, regardless of her feelings for him, Deborah ought not to have been surprised by this further evidence of shallowness, but she was.

Fairfax, unattractive? Or even plain? Deborah shook her head in disbelief. She thought the duke was one of the nicest—and nicest-looking—men of the *ton*. He was no Adonis, but his smiles, though rare, could charm the birds out of the trees.

And turn the bones in her legs to jelly.

Chapter Seven

Friday, 1 April 1814

*M*ichael was again able to leave The Oaks without an interrogation by his grandmother. Nor had she cut up stiff about his early departure yesterday, though he'd been informed by Sanders, his butler, that the drawing room had been full to overflowing with young ladies and their mothers yesterday afternoon. The fact that he had not seen the dowager accounted for Michael's good fortune, but he was not about to question a benevolent fate. His grandmother's reproaches would keep until later. His call on the Woodhurst ladies was not something he was willing to put off. Seeing Lady Deborah suddenly seemed essential to his happiness.

Arriving at Kesteven House—without, thank heaven, the problems that had plagued him yesterday—Michael was immediately escorted up to the drawing room. The marchioness and her daughters greeted him with smiles, looking as lovely as ever. Lady Kesteven's gown was light purple today, while the twins wore identical pale pink dresses, one with a white sash, the other with a sash of darker pink.

It wasn't until he took a seat, in the same chair he'd occupied yesterday, that Michael realized that the twins had changed places today. Resigned but wary, he turned his attention to Lady Kesteven.

And prayed that he would have the opportunity for a moment or two of private conversation with Lady Deborah.

After the usual social pleasantries and comments on the weather, which was still deucedly damp, the marchioness brought up the reason for his call. Well, one of the reasons. There were, in fact, three, although Lady Kesteven knew only one of them. "If you are still willing to escort us to the Opera, we would be delighted to join your party."

Michael allowed himself a pleased smile, but stifled the urge to shout with joy. "It would be my pleasure to escort you. And to have you join my party." He made mental note to invite two gentlemen—one to escort Lady Diana, the other for Lady Kesteven. Perhaps one to gallant his grandmother, too, if she decided to attend, so that he would not have to dance attendance on her.

"Will your box be large enough for all of us?" The question was Lady Deborah's, although Michael did not understand why she seemed slightly hesitant about asking it.

Hoping to reassure her, he caught her eye and smiled. "Yes. Although I cannot say for certain yet who will attend, I believe there will be seven or eight, and my box can easily accommodate ten people."

"Who are the others?" The sharp tone bordered on rudeness and was, predictably, Lady Diana's.

"Woolgathering, Di?" Lady Deborah asked in a mildly teasing tone before the marchioness could voice the stronger reproach that accompanied the frown she directed at the younger twin. "The duke just said that he was not certain who would attend."

The butler's entry with the tea tray forestalled Lady Diana's reply—something for which they could all be thankful, given her propensity for verbal barbs. Michael darted a glance at the window—and the weather. Although the skies had not cleared, the rain was now only a drizzle or mizzle. If Lady Deborah passed 'round the cakes, as she had yesterday, he would have a chance to invite her to drive in the park.

Lady Kesteven, however, asked her younger daughter to help. Judging by the scowl that soon appeared on Miss Rag-Manners's face, her mother also used the opportunity to deliver a soft-voiced but pithy lecture on proper behavior. As the tea was poured and served, Michael debated the wisdom of openly asking Lady Deborah to drive in the park with him. There was no question of keeping such an invitation a secret—her mother would have to approve the excursion, and her sister was certain to learn of it—but even so, he would prefer to extend the invitation in private. Doing so not only gave him a better chance to gauge Lady Deborah's reaction, but also gave her the opportunity to refuse. A private invitation had two other advantages: he would not get saddled with her twin if Lady Deborah had another engagement, and it lessened the possibility that her sister would feel slighted. He'd heard tales about Lady Diana's methods of expressing her displeasure, and he did not want Lady Deborah to feel the lash of her sister's anger. And it was always other young ladies who bore the brunt of Lady Diana's ire, never gentlemen. She was too canny not to know that reprisals against a gentleman, no matter how well deserved, might put paid to her chances of making a good match.

Michael suspected that Lady Diana was out to snare a husband with the highest title and largest fortune she could contrive. And he did not doubt that she would resort to contrivance, if she deemed it necessary. In fact, he would be surprised if she did not have a scheme or two in mind.

It was enough to make a wealthy duke tread warily in her presence. And to consider every word before he voiced it.

Unlike yesterday, there were no fortuitous arrivals or interruptions. Michael mentally girded his loins, ran the words of invitation through his mind again, then stepped into the breach. "Lady Deborah, if it stops raining, would you drive in the park with me later this afternoon?"

The object of his affection smiled and looked to her mother for permission. The marchioness glanced out the window, then rose and crossed to look outside. "The rain appears to be letting up, but those dark clouds tell a different story." Returning to her seat, she smiled—at him and her older daughter. "If the weather clears, a drive in the park should be pleasant."

While Lady Kesteven did not disapprove, Lady Diana clearly did. Or, rather, she was not pleased. "Your Grace, just think how envied you'd be if you drove both of us."

"No doubt you are correct, Lady Diana. Unfortunately,

the only vehicles I keep in Town are a curricle and a closed carriage."

"I am sure we can all squeeze into your curricle." Her coy smile did not have the desired effect; it only served to annoy him.

"Perhaps so," he conceded, striving to maintain an even tone—and battling the urge to give the outrageous girl the set-down she deserved. "But I have never driven with more than one passenger, and the change in balance might well cause me to overturn." It wouldn't, of course, but she didn't know that. "For safety's sake, I will take your sister today, and you another time."

She opened her mouth, no doubt to protest further, but after a darkling look from her mother, subsided with a sulky, "I will hold you to that promise."

Michael felt certain that she would. Hound him about it, too, probably. How ironic that the rules of Polite Behavior decreed he must extend such an invitation to a woman whose manners left much to be desired!

Those same rules required him to take his leave in a few minutes, so he turned back to Lady Deborah. "Shall we say five o'clock?"

"Five o'clock is fine." The marchioness and Lady Deborah answered almost in unison.

"But if it is raining," she added, "please do not feel obliged to come merely to postpone the outing. The weather will tell me that, so there is no need for you to court the ague to do so."

"Thank you for your consideration, Lady Deborah. Sitting in Lords in damp clothes would be unpleasant."

"You are, of course, welcome to return if you wish," said Lady Kesteven.

"Thank you, my lady."

With that, and a smile for Lady Deborah, he took his leave. As he made his way downstairs, he prayed that the rain would stop. And wondered once again how twins absolutely identical in appearance could have such different temperaments.

*   *   *

The moment the front door closed, the marchioness rose to her feet. "Diana Eleanor Caroline, I am ashamed of you!"

Diana knew that she had no grounds for argument. Her behavior had, by any standard, crossed the line of what was pleasing. Ducking her head as if ashamed, she uttered the apology her mother expected. "I am sorry, Mama. I guess I did overstep a bit."

"You guess?" It was her mother's "awful" voice, which Diana particularly disliked—mostly because she knew she would have to all but grovel to get back in her mother's good graces. "You *know* you did. Even worse, you were well aware of your rudeness, yet you persisted. No doubt you gave Fairfax a disgust of you."

Diana pretended contrition. "I hope not."

"A faint, and most likely false, hope." Mother was in full flood now. Diana let the words wash over her, disdaining to listen to the all too familiar harangue. The duke's good opinion was not essential to her plan. She would wring an offer from him, one way or the other.

Michael headed for the familiar comfort of White's. With any luck, he would find several of his friends there. And, more importantly, would be able to persuade them to join his party for the Opera.

The main room was, perhaps, a bit more crowded than usual at this hour. Brummell and Alvanley were in their usual spot in front of the bow window, probably gossiping. Or trading barbed comments on the attire of the other men present. Idly, Michael wondered how many of the peers scattered about the room would be occupying seats in Lords at a quarter 'til four. He had been shocked to learn, shortly after reaching his majority and taking his seat, that not all gentlemen were as conscientious as he. While he could understand that the attractions of the Metropolis might distract younger men from doing their duty, older peers could not use the same excuse to explain their lack of attendance.

Not espying his quarry, Michael made his way to the reading room, returning the greetings of several of his acquaintances and nodding to a trio of older men deep in conversation. As always at this hour, several of the room's occupants were napping behind newspapers. But he also found the man he was seeking—his best friend, Viscount Dunnley.

Taking a seat nearby, Michael waited for Dunnley to finish his conversation with his uncle, Andrew Winterbrook, the Marquess of Bellingham. Seeing the older man sent Michael's thoughts scurrying in another direction. A widower for two decades, Bellingham enjoyed the Opera—indeed, it was he who had taught Michael, Theo, and his own sons to appreciate it—and he would be an unexceptional, utterly respectable escort for Lady Kesteven. If he could be persuaded. Michael could not recall ever seeing Bellingham squire any lady other than his widowed sister or his late brother's wife. If he was unwilling or had a previous commitment, Theo's great-uncle, the Bishop of Lymington, was another possibility. The amiable clergyman did not often attend the Opera, but, despite his bachelor status, he was a bastion of propriety.

"Good afternoon, Opposite." Dunnley greeted Michael with a grin. Their schoolmates at Eton, seeing only the contrasts between the talkative, boisterous, good-looking viscount-to-be and the quiet, careful, plain duke, had dubbed the pair "The Opposites." Michael and Theo had derived great amusement from the inaccurate epithet, and still did.

Dunnley patted the chair beside him. "Were you looking for me or Uncle Andrew?"

"You," Michael answered. "But when I saw you, my lord"—he nodded at Bellingham, who had started to rise—"I realized that I need your help, too."

Bellingham settled back in his seat. "What can I—or we—do for you, Fairfax?" More warily, he asked, "Does the duchess need an escort to a social event?"

"I thought you vowed never to undertake that duty again," Michael said with a grin. "This will be far more pleasant. I am hoping you will agree to join my party for the Opera next Saturday."

Dunnley shook his head. "I am sorry, but we cannot. My cousin David and his wife are coming to Town for a week or so, and Stephen and I are having a dinner party for them—

for the entire family, actually—after which we will attend the Opera."

Panic stabbed through Michael, making him aware of just how much he had been counting on his friend's assistance and support. Somehow, he mustered a smile. I hope you have a very enjoyable evening." Turning to Bellingham, he added, "Much as I like your younger son, sir, I can't help but wish he had chosen another time to bring his bride to Town."

"'Tis unfortunate that Theo's party for David and Lynn is the same night as yours. But"—the marquess's blue eyes twinkled—"given that they met in the middle of a snowstorm, perfect timing is a bit much to expect."

"I suppose it is." Although he smiled at Bellingham's quip, Michael's tone was more glum than jovial.

Dunnley gave him a searching look, but instead of questioning him, offered aid. "How many gentlemen do you need? Even though we can't join your party, we can suggest men who might be able to attend."

"At least two."

"Both young and eligible? Or one young and one . . . not so young?" Bellingham's tone was dry.

"At least one eligible bachelor. The other will be escorting a married lady whose husband is unable to attend." For some inexplicable reason, Michael was reluctant to divulge the ladies' identities, even to these two trusted friends.

His discretion garnered him another of Dunnley's scrutinizing glances. Michael had no doubt that Theo would quiz him further when they were alone. For now, Dunnley contented himself with making several helpful suggestions. "Blackburn would be a good choice. Howe, too. Or Sherworth. The latter two regularly attend the Opera. And Blackburn often escorts his mother there."

All three men were eligible and personable, but Michael feared Lady Diana would deem Howe, a mere baron, a poor choice. Especially when her twin was escorted by a duke. "Blackburn is an excellent suggestion. I don't know Howe or Sherworth as well. They may not be very sympathetic to my plight."

"I can drop a word in Sherworth's ear," the marquess offered.

"Thank you, sir. I would appreciate it."

"I will do the same for Howe," Dunnley volunteered.

"Thank you, Theo. For that, and for your suggestions."

After a few minutes of more general conversation, Bellingham pulled out his watch, then rose to his feet. "I will see the two of you in Lords a bit later. Right now, I must toddle over to Brooks's and meet Liverpool. At this hour, I may find Sherworth there, too."

To Michael's surprise, Theo also stood. "I promised to call on my godmother this afternoon, so I will save my questions about your Opera party until the first debate."

Michael only smiled. If the weather cooperated, he would be on his way to Kesteven House then.

At twenty minutes before the hour of five, Michael cast a final, appraising look at the sky, then nodded to Fairfax House's young head groom, who barked an order to his minions, sending two scrambling to lead the matched chestnuts from their boxes, while a third pulled the curricle out of the carriage house and ran a polishing cloth over the glossy black enamel panels. The horses were backed into the traces, and the head groom himself harnessed the pair, quickly but carefully, to the curricle. Michael stowed an extra carriage rug under the seat, tapped his hat more firmly onto his head when a gust of wind threatened to snatch it, then climbed aboard and picked up the reins. Giving the horses their office, he saluted the stable staff with his whip and drove out of the mews.

"Warm enough, Tom?" he called to his tiger, perched behind him on the small seat.

"I'll do, Yer Grace" was the wizened ex-jockey's reply.

Michael fully expected that Lady Deborah would elect to postpone their drive, but he intended to give her—or her mother—the choice. Delighted surprise wreathed her countenance when he was announced, and she rose quickly to her feet. "I will be ready in a few moments, Your Grace."

"Look outside first, my lady. Although it isn't raining, it

looks as if it might at any moment." He tucked Lady Deborah's hand in the crook of his arm and escorted her to the window.

As she assessed the weather, a slight frown creased her brow. "It does appear that we are in for more rain, but those dark clouds have covered the sky all afternoon."

"Indeed they have," Lady Kesteven said from the next window, "but with surprisingly little result."

Lady Deborah turned to him, an impish smile twitching the corners of her mouth. "I am game if you are."

"Absolutely, my lady." He offered her a deep bow. "I am yours to command."

Behind him, her twin snorted. Lady Deborah, however, beamed at him, her sunny smile exhorting his heart to perform even more spectacular acrobatics. "I will get my bonnet and spencer."

"I suggest a wide-brimmed bonnet. And perhaps a cloak instead of—or in addition to—a spencer. I have carriage rugs, of course, but . . ." He shrugged, not quite certain what he was trying to say.

Still smiling, she nodded. "Those are excellent suggestions. I will return in a minute."

Lady Kesteven waved him to a seat and, after escorting her back to hers, he took the chair beside her. "If it starts raining, we will turn back immediately. My tiger has three grown daughters, so he is a vigilant chaperone."

"Your *tiger* has children?" Lady Diana's voice was laced with mockery. "Tigers are supposed to be young boys."

"Much as it goes against the grain to dispute a lady, the most important requirement for a tiger is not youth but size. They must be small enough to sit comfortably on the rear seat. Many tigers are young boys, but mine is not. He is a former jockey."

"You must be the only gentleman in the *ton* whose tiger isn't a young boy."

"Not at all. Elston's former batman, Higgins, often serves as his tiger, and is also an ex-jockey. Sundbury's tiger is, too."

"Did they ever race against your man?" Lady Kesteven asked.

"Higgins and Smedley—my tiger—raced many times. To hear them tell it, they were archrivals. Sundbury's man is a bit older, but he raced against Higgins and Smedley a few times at the start of their careers. He swears he beat them every time, but they claim—and the racing books prove—he did not."

The marchioness laughed. "How intriguing!"

Lady Deborah returned, looking pretty as a picture in a velvet spencer slightly darker than her gown, gloves of the same pale pink hue, and a wide-brimmed chipstraw bonnet with matching ribands. A cloak of amethyst merino was draped over her arm, and in her other hand, she carried a furled umbrella.

Crossing to her, he shook out the cloak and draped it over her shoulders. "My intrepid lady," he murmured for her ears alone. Then, in a normal voice as he offered his arm, "Ready?"

Smiling shyly, she nodded. "Ready."

He sketched a bow to the marchioness, then whisked his prize down the stairs and out to his curricle.

As they bowled along Brook Street, Deborah admired Fairfax's competent handling of his horses. The pair seemed a bit skittish, the off leader shying a bit when the wind gusted, which it seemed to be doing with increasing frequency, but he kept them up to their bits seemingly without effort. In truth, she admired everything about the duke, from the perfect fit of his dark blue morning coat and buff pantaloons to the understated elegance of his nubby silk waistcoat, neatly tied cravat, and gleaming Hessians. And she could not help but wonder what he thought of her.

She did not want to distract him, but neither did she want him to think she was a ninny with no conversation. "I was not sure you would return," she ventured after they crossed New Bond Street.

"What?" His eyes slewed to hers. "Did you think I

would sit tamely in White's or the House when there was a chance, however slight, that you would drive with me?"

With me or with one of the Woodhurst twins? She shrugged off the thought. "I didn't know."

"After my disappointment yesterday, nothing short of a downpour would have kept me away this afternoon."

Oh my, that does sound promising—if it is my company specifically that he sought. "Were you disappointed yesterday?" she asked, greatly daring, then blushed at the boldness of her question.

"Exceedingly disappointed."

Such honesty deserved an equally candid response. "So was I."

He smiled and darted another glance at her. "Given the weather, I did not know if you would agree to come today, nor if your mother would permit it, but I am delighted that you did."

"What would you have done if Mama had forbidden the drive?"

"There isn't much I could have done, save invite you to drive with me tomorrow, or Monday. Although if I'd felt bold, I might have asked you to play the pianoforte for me."

"Are you fond of music?" She was curious, not only what he would answer, but how.

"Yes, I am. I am an indifferent performer, but—"

"Oh!" A gust of wind threatened to snatch Deborah's bonnet, and she clapped a hand to the crown. Fairfax, not having a free hand, lost his curly-brimmed beaver, which sailed across the cobblestones and went skittering down Duke Street.

Somewhat to her surprise, he laughed, then slowed his horses and inquired, "Do you wish to turn back?"

"No! Not unless you think it isn't safe," she amended. She was enjoying this welcome respite from the tension that had permeated the house for the past few days. And from her sister's sniping.

He studied the swaying tree branches in Grosvenor Square's central garden, then his horses. "I don't think we are in any danger."

"Then, may we please continue?"

"Of course." His smile, though rare, was charming.

"And would you please continue what you were saying before the wind stole your hat?"

She had never seen a man blush, but Fairfax did. "I am afraid I don't remember what I was saying."

"I asked if you were a music lover, and you said yes, then you started to say something about being an indifferent performer."

"I do like music, particularly chamber music and the music of Bach, but I don't play well enough to do the music justice."

Deborah would have bet her entire quarterly allowance that Fairfax played very well, but just did not like to perform for an audience. "Which Bach—the London Bach or his father?"

"His father. Johann Sebastian."

"Really? He is my very favorite composer."

His eyes widened in surprise, and he darted another glance at her. "Is he, indeed? I commend your taste, Lady Deborah. So few people know of his work."

"Did you attend Mrs. Broughton's musicale last year, Your Grace?"

"I thought we agreed that you would call me Fairfax? And no, I don't believe I attended the musicale. Why do you ask?"

"Lord Bellingham and Beth—Lady Weymouth—are both exceedingly fond of Bach, and they played two of his works at the musicale."

"I am sorry to have missed it. Which pieces did they play?"

She waited until he had negotiated the turn through the Grosvenor Gate before answering. "The concerto for two violins. I am not altogether certain, but I believe its title is Double Concerto in d minor. Later, Beth played 'Jesu, Joy of Man's Desiring'."

"I am very sorry to have missed that!"

"It was marvelous. When Beth finished, there were more than a few people blinking back tears."

"I have heard a number of people praise Lady Weymouth's talent, but I have never had the privilege of hearing her play. Perhaps this Season I shall."

"Most likely not, Fairfax."

"Why do you think it unlikely? Since Weymouth himself plays, I cannot imagine him barring his wife from performing at a musicale. And my standing with Lord Liverpool is good enough that he won't complain if I sneak out of the House one evening to attend a musicale."

Now it was Deborah's turn to blush. "Beth will not be attending many social events this year. She is . . . in a delicate condition."

"I didn't know. I imagine she and Weymouth are delighted."

"Indeed they are." They smiled at one another in perfect accord.

An idea flashed into Deborah's mind. A rather outrageous one. As she considered it, she glanced around. "I have never seen Hyde Park so empty at this hour!"

"We have the place virtually to ourselves." He sounded almost pleased. "I daresay few members of the *ton* wished to risk a wetting this afternoon."

"I suppose not. Most come as much—or more—to see and be seen than to enjoy the fresh air and their companion." Belatedly realizing that sounded a bit forward, she blushed.

The duke did not seem to notice and gave her another of his rare smiles. "I hope you are enjoying my company as much as I am enjoying yours, Lady Deborah."

"I am." *Drat my fair skin and its tendency to color!* "I hope you won't take offense if I say that I am also enjoying being out of the house."

"Have you not—" He broke off, his expression chagrined.

"Have I not what?"

He huffed out a rather strangled laugh, clearly embarrassed. "I started to ask if you had not had an outing for days, but realized I knew the answer, since I saw you on Bond Street Tuesday morning."

"That was our last outing, and things have been . . ." She

fought the urge to clap a hand over her mouth. *What is wrong with me today?*

Turning to her, he arched a brow and prompted, "Things have been . . . ?"

She hesitated, biting her lip, not at all certain she wanted to confide in him. Or even if she could confide in a man. When his expression turned grave, she realized that allowing his imagination to run rampant might be worse than answering, no matter how difficult it seemed. Hoping he would understand—and, perhaps, sympathize—she took a deep breath for courage. "Things have been a bit uncomfortable at home. Between Diana and me mostly, but also a bit between Diana and Mama."

"I am sorry to hear it." He slowed the horses almost to a stop and covered her clenched hands with one of his own. "Is there anything I can do to help?"

"I don't think so, but it is kind of you to ask."

"Be assured that I shall respect your confidence, my lady."

"I know that, Fairfax—I would not have said anything had I not been certain of that—but I thank you for your promise."

He set the horses back to a walk, then said, rather tentatively, "I would have thought that, being twins, you and Diana were closer than most siblings. Or"—he darted a glance at her—"is that just an old wives' tale?"

"We have always been close, until recently. But not for the past few months, although I am not sure why." Not for anything would she tell a man that her sister was determined to wed a wealthy peer of high rank whether she loved him or not.

"You are very different. Not in appearance, obviously, but your personalities and interests are quite different. Or so it seems to me."

"Indeed they are, but I don't think many people realize it. Furthermore—"

The skies opened, and rain fell in torrents. Fairfax turned the curricle and raced back to Hanover Square. Deborah could not help but wonder if the storm was a curse or a blessing. While it had cut short their conversation and her opportunity to learn more about the duke, it had also saved her from confiding things she might later come to regret. And from acting on her rather outrageous idea until she'd had time to ponder it at length.

Chapter Eight

Tuesday, 12 April 1814

The ten days after his drive in Hyde Park with Lady Deborah were the longest—and most frustrating— days of Michael's life. He'd traveled up Town on Satur- day—much to Meecham's shock, and despite his appalled protests that His Grace should be confined to the ducal bed with his devoted valet cosseting him—to assure himself that she'd taken no ill from their wetting and to deliver a large bouquet of flowers, only to be told that the Woodhurst ladies were not receiving. He'd returned to The Oaks, and to his bed, but he'd been far more worried about Deborah's health than his own. Monday had been the same—and he'd retreated to his own bed feeling slightly put out. Tuesday, Thursday, and Friday, they were out when he called. Or, more precisely, they were "not at home"—either out or not willing to receive him. Yesterday was Easter Monday, so he hadn't called. Nor had he called today—but only because he was certain he would see Lady Deborah tonight, at the open- ing ball of the Season.

So here he stood, dressed in his finest evening attire, frus- trated and determined to hunt her down. But first he had to find her. And given the throng of people straining the seams of Lady Oglethorpe's ballroom, finding Lady Deborah would not be as easy a task as he'd imagined.

Especially since, in the quarter hour he had been here, it was appallingly apparent that quite a number of ladies, young and old, were on the hunt for *him.*

He'd been accosted before he'd even greeted his hostess.
It seemed that every woman he knew had a daughter, sister,
goddaughter, granddaughter, or niece whom she envisioned
as his duchess. The men weren't quite as bad, but at least a
dozen had introduced him to their daughters or sisters or
nieces. He'd previously met most of the young ladies, but
the matchmakers dismissed that as irrelevant. Their only
concern was bringing the girls to his notice—although
some of them could not, by any stretch of the imagination,
be considered "girls," since they were nearly as old as he.

He might as well be wearing a demmed sign! DUKE SEEK-
ING A BRIDE. Or PRIZE CATCH HUNTING FOR A WIFE.

It was enough to try the patience of a saint. And Michael
was feeling more savage than saintly. Not only was he annoyed by the blatant matchmaking—or, to state the case
frankly, title grubbing—he had not yet found the lady he
sought.

He had dreamt of her *every* night. Pleasant dreams, to be
sure, but they had become rather shocking. Not only because of their increasingly sensual content, but also because
of the feelings they evoked in him. He wanted to care for
Lady Deborah, protect her, cherish her—and ravish her.

Never before had he dreamt about a woman of his acquaintance. But for the past ten days, he'd dreamt of her.
Only her.

After Baron Allingham had stopped him to introduce his
sister, a woman Michael had known for nearly a decade and
who had several more years in her dish than he, he had
latched on to the Earl of Blackburn like a drowning man
grabs a rope. Dunnley had joined them a short time later,
and now that his taller friends were shielding him from the
sight of most of the people in the room, the three of them
were enjoying a nice, safe chat about politics while Michael
was trying to catch his breath. And tamp down his irritation.
And recover his aplomb.

He was also scanning the ballroom for Lady Deborah or
her mother. But it was difficult to do that unobtrusively
while engaged in conversation. And he did not want anyone,

not even Dunnley, to know that he was looking for someone. A female someone.

"Gentlemen, I see three young ladies who appear to need partners for the next set," Dunnley said suddenly, smiling an apology for interrupting the earl.

"Which young ladies?" Michael asked, feeling thoroughly out of sorts. "I would rather not have my toes trod upon this early in the evening."

Blackburn scanned the groups of ladies nearby and smiled. "Little danger of that with these three, I think." As they strolled toward the trio, he asked, "Which lady do you wish to partner, Dunnley?"

"Have to dance with all of them," Michael mumbled, craning his neck in an attempt to see. "Lest you want their mamas making comments about rag-manners and ungentlemanly behavior."

"I have no objection to dancing with all three of them," Blackburn said, somewhat to Michael's surprise, since the earl was absent from more social events than he attended. "They are friends of Karla's—er, Lady Elston's—so I feel certain all three are very nice young ladies."

A cluster of young men in front of them scattered to find their partners, allowing Michael to see the trio: Lady Christina Fairchild, Lady Sarah Mallory, and one of the Woodhurst twins. "You are assuming that is Lady Deborah." It was a logical assumption, since Lady Diana seemed to dislike the ladies of "The Six." Or, perhaps, disliked her exclusion from the group.

Reaching the trio, all three men bowed. After greetings were exchanged, Dunnley asked, "Might we have the honor of partnering you three lovely ladies in the next dance?"

All three glanced to the left. Michael and his companions did, too, saw the girls' mothers, and bowed to them. The older women nodded permission, then Lady Sarah Mallory said, "We would be honored, Your Grace. My lords."

"Perhaps we should use precedence to determine which gentleman is a lady's first partner." Dunnley's suggestion was a good one, although Michael would have preferred to dance first with Lady Deborah.

"That should serve very well." Bowing to the inevitable—and wondering if Dunnley had a reason for wanting Lady Sarah as his first partner—Michael offered his arm to Lady Tina and led her to the dance floor.

When the musicians struck up a waltz, he wanted to howl in frustration. Blackburn wouldn't have cared whether he waltzed with Lady Deborah or Lady Tina, but Michael most certainly did. Deborah was the partner he wanted for this most intimate of dances. She was the one he wanted to talk to, but so far he had not had the opportunity to exchange more than a smile with her.

By the middle of the waltz, Michael had to admit that he might have fared far worse. Tina Fairchild might still be a bit of a hoyden, and her chatter would tire an elephant's ears, but there wasn't a drop of malice in her, and her vivacity had a charm of its own. In addition, she was such a tiny little thing that a man of only average height felt tall beside her.

Having Lady Tina as his partner for this dance was not such a terrible fate. Being forced to waltz with Lady Diana Woodhurst—he steeled his muscles against a shudder—would be a cruel punishment.

Deborah smiled and accepted the Earl of Blackburn's arm. He was an attractive man, slightly above average height, with his mother's gray-rimmed hazel eyes and the same off-center silver streak in his mahogany hair, although his was neither as wide or as deep as Lady Blackburn's. Deborah did not know the earl well, but he was a highly respected member of government, an undersecretary in the Foreign Office.

When the musicians played the opening measures of a waltz, she stifled a sigh of regret. She would much rather have Fairfax as her partner since she had not yet been able to exchange more than a smile with him and had much for which to thank him. But Lord Blackburn proved to be a very skilled dancer and a surprisingly good conversationalist for a man who reputedly preferred political meetings to social events.

Of course, it may have helped that she asked several

questions about the progress of the war, then solicited his opinion on how much longer it would take to defeat Napoleon. But halfway through the set, Blackburn surprised her. With a merry twinkle in those remarkable eyes, he said, "Despite what you may have heard, Lady Deborah, I am able to converse about other subjects."

She blushed, even though she knew he was teasing, and he smiled. "I had no idea young ladies were so knowledgeable about political affairs."

The compliment, though indirect, pleased her far more than the fawning flattery she often heard. "I don't know that all young ladies are. I daresay it depends on their fathers' interest and knowledge, and whether or not such matters are regularly discussed during dinner, as they are in our home."

"You give yourself too little credit. The fact that a lady often hears politics discussed doesn't guarantee her interest. In fact, there are members of Lords who don't understand the ramifications of recent events as well as you do."

There is nothing indirect about that! "Thank you, Lord Blackburn. That is quite the nicest compliment I have ever received." It was also one that would please her father as much as it did her. The antics and sartorial excesses of her brother, Henry, and some of his foppish friends often caused the marquess to animadvert on the foolishness of young men "these days"—as if he had several hundred years in his dish, instead of only fifty-nine—but her father held a very high opinion of Blackburn.

"Tell me, will I have the pleasure of hearing you perform this Season?" he asked.

"Yes, at the Duchess of Greenwich's musicale next month, although I have not yet decided what to play."

"If you are seeking suggestions, I recommend Handel, Bach, Mozart, Haydn, or Scarlatti. Perhaps Beethoven, if you will be playing the pianoforte."

"If you could choose only two composers, which two would you choose? The Greenwiches have a harpsichord and a pianoforte, so I can play either. Or both, I suppose."

"I am particularly fond of Bach, Handel, and Mozart. I

like Beethoven's music, too, but not everyone does, so that may not be the best choice."

"I like them all, too, which is why it is so difficult to decide. Perhaps Bach and Mozart. Or Bach and Handel," she mused. "What is your favorite work by those three composers? Your favorite for the harpsichord or pianoforte?"

"Hmmm . . . It is difficult to choose." He swept her into a turn. "The *Italian Concerto*."

"I hadn't considered the *Italian Concerto*, but that is an excellent suggestion. Thank you."

When he offered no other suggestions, she prompted, "What are your favorite works by Handel and Mozart? Favorites for the pianoforte," she amended, smiling.

"For Mozart . . . one of the sonatas, but I couldn't tell you which one unless I heard it. They are all called sonata in G or D or F or P, making it difficult for someone who isn't a musician to remember the appropriate letter."

"There is no key of P, my lord," she teased. "But I agree that it was shockingly remiss of Mozart—and the other composers—to title their works by form and key. You would think that men of such creative genius could come up with more memorable titles."

"No key of P, you say?" The earl raised a brow in mock astonishment.

Grinning, Deborah shook her head. "No. Only A through G."

The waltz soared to an end, and Deborah dropped into a curtsy. Blackburn bowed, then placed her hand on his arm to escort her back to her mother. As they strolled around the room, she realized that he had not completed his answer to her question. "You didn't tell me which of Handel's works is your favorite."

After several moments' thought, he offered her a rueful smile. "I cannot immediately recall any pieces he wrote for the harpsichord. I know the *Water Music* and his oratorios—*Messiah* is my favorite—but . . ." He shrugged.

"Your suggestion of the *Italian Concerto* and a Mozart sonata were very helpful," she said sincerely. "Thank you, my lord, for helping me decide."

"It was my pleasure, Lady Deborah."

When they reached the marchioness, the earl bowed over Deborah's hand again, thanked her for dancing with him, and requested a set later in the evening. Surprised but not at all displeased, she agreed, and they decided on the first country dance after supper.

Diana and her partner, Sir Edward Smithson, joined them a few minutes later. Deborah did not like the baronet. His manner was shockingly forward, his gaze too leering. Just the thought of dancing with him made her feel shivery inside, and she could not imagine why her sister had agreed to waltz with him. Doing her best to ignore him, Deborah looked around for her friends—and wished she could change places with one of them. Sarah and Tina stood nearby, talking to the Duchess of Greenwich, Fairfax, and Lord Dunnley.

Ever the gentleman, Lord Blackburn asked Diana if she would dance the next set with him. Deborah hoped that Sir Edward would not follow the earl's example, but to her dismay, he did. As much as she wanted to refuse—and she did, very much—she could not. Not unless she wanted to sit out all the rest of the sets this evening. Since she'd just promised to dance with the earl after supper, she had no choice but to grant Sir Edward's request. And to pray the next set would be a country dance.

As he talked to Lady Tina and her mother, Michael allowed his gaze to drift in search of Lady Deborah. She was so lovely, and the blue sash on her white gown matched the color of her eyes. Her smile faded a bit when she, her mother, and Blackburn were joined by Lady Diana and Sir Edward Smithson, and Michael commended her good sense. Smithson was a libertine and a thoroughgoing reprobate. At Eton, his bullying ways had earned him the nickname "Nasty Ned," and the epithet still fit—possibly even better than it had twenty years ago.

Lady Sarah and Dunnley approached, and Michael smiled and stepped back a pace, so they could join the conversation. Known amongst the bachelors of the *ton* as "The

Welsh Beauty," Lady Sarah was tall and slender, with eyes the vivid blue of a summer sky, a sweet smile, and hair the blue-black of a raven's wing. Like her friend, Lady Sarah wore a cream-colored gown, but her sash was blue instead of pink. Where Lady Tina could only be described as vivacious, Lady Sarah was serene. When he'd first met her last Season, he'd found her reserve a bit daunting—and sometimes still did—but he'd come to realize that she was very shy.

The musicians played the opening bars of the next set, and Michael asked Lady Sarah to dance. She accepted with a smile, then tilted her head as if to better hear the music. "Do you think Lady Oglethorpe will choose the Sir Roger de Coverley for the final set, too, or another dance?"

"Her choices are often unconventional. The first set was a Scottish reel, so perhaps she will end with an allemande or the waltz promenade. Although many hostesses deem the minuet old-fashioned, she usually has at least two, but never as the first set."

"I like the minuet, too. And the Sir Roger de Coverley is lively and fun, but it doesn't allow much conversation with one's partner."

She was right on both counts, so at the end of the set, he escorted her to the refreshment room.

"Are you enjoying the ball, Your Grace?"

"Indeed I am. I enjoy dancing, although I cannot claim any expertise at it." Michael knew the steps and rarely trod on his partners' toes, but he did not have Dunnley's dash.

She glanced at him, her eyes wide with astonishment. "You are a very good dancer," she averred. "Any lady would be pleased to have you as a partner."

"You are very kind to say so, Lady Sarah."

"It is not mere politeness, Your Grace," she protested. "It is quite true."

"Thank you, my lady." He handed her a glass of lemonade, then motioned toward a nearby table. "Would you like to sit down for a minute?"

She acquiesced with a nod and a smile. Once they were seated, the words of her staunch avowal seemed to echo in his mind. "Do you ever wonder why gentlemen ask you to dance?"

Although he'd feared that the question would sound foolish, she gave it serious thought. "No, I don't believe I ever have."

"You have never wondered if a man asked you to dance because you are an acclaimed Beauty," he persisted, "or because of the size of your dowry?"

"No, I haven't." After a moment's hesitation, she ventured a question of her own. "Why do you ask? Do you consider such factors before you ask a lady to dance?"

"No, of course not!"

Despite the vehemence of his reply, she smiled, then lifted a brow, inviting him to answer her first question. Glancing away, he confessed, "I often wonder if I am accepted because I am a wealthy duke or because a lady likes me, plain Michael Winslow."

"Oh, Fairfax!" Placing a hand on his arm as if to comfort him, she said pensively, "I suppose every high-ranking peer must contend with a certain amount of toadying. There probably are ladies who enjoy being seen with you as much as they enjoy your company, but others—many others— delight in your company without ever giving a thought to your rank."

"You obviously fall into the latter category."

"Yes, I do. You are an admirable man, Michael Winslow, duke or not."

"Thank you, Lady Sarah." Taking her hand, he raised it to his lips and brushed a kiss across her gloved knuckles as a tribute to her candor. Then he stood and assisted her to rise. "I'd best escort you back to your mother before the next set begins."

When they reached Lady Tregaron, Michael bowed and thanked Lady Sarah for dancing with him, then bespoke a set after supper. Easing them into conversation with the Woodhurst twins, Lady Tina, Dunnley, Blackburn, and Nasty Ned, Michael debated which twin he should dance with first—pleasure then duty, or duty before pleasure— but Dunnley made the decision for him by requesting the next set with Lady Diana, the following one with her sister. Wishing he'd been a bit quicker, Michael smiled at Lady Deborah and asked her to honor him with the next dance, then with punctilious courtesy requested the subsequent set with her twin. As the other gentlemen followed their lead, the group shifted and reformed, but Michael did not lose his coveted place between Lady Sarah and Lady Deborah.

He almost groaned when he heard the dance's opening chords. Not only was it not the minuet or allemande he'd been hoping for, it was a country dance whose patterns permitted only the briefest snatches of conversation with one's partner. Offering his arm to lead Lady Deborah to the dance floor, he made so bold as to tell her, "Since it was too soon for another waltz, I was hoping for a minuet."

She glanced at him and smiled, dimples flashing. "So was I."

"If you have not yet promised the supper dance, I hope you will grant it to me, so that we will have a chance to talk a bit."

"I would be honored to have supper with you, Fairfax." Any marriage-minded miss would have said the same, but Lady Deborah's delighted smile was a far cry from the smug satisfaction or preening that usually accompanied the polite acceptance.

From the bits of conversation they exchanged during the dance, he learnt that she, too, had taken a chill after their rain-aborted drive in the park. She thanked him for his flowers and for calling, and also apologized for not being able to receive him—at first, because she was sick, then because they had not been at home when he called.

At the end of the set, he tucked her hand in the crook of his arm and escorted her to the refreshment room, hoping for an opportunity to ask her some of the questions he'd asked Lady Sarah. Lady Deborah's opening query was different than her friend's, but it paved the way equally well.

"Lady Oglethorpe's ball is a splendid start to the Season, isn't it?"

"I quite agree. I enjoy dancing, although I haven't the grace and skill some men do."

Like her friend, Lady Deborah's eyes widened in astonishment. "You are a very good dancer, Fairfax!"

"It is very kind of you to say so—"

"I am not just being polite," she asserted, her interruption
lending weight to her claim. "You are one of my very favorite partners. And any woman here would be delighted to
have you as her partner."

"Thank you, my lady. You are one of my favorites, too."
Surveying the beverages offered, he asked, "Lemonade,
wine, or punch?"

"Lemonade, please."

Handing her a glass, Michael took one for himself, then
gestured at the tables scattered around the room. "Would
you like to sit down for a minute?"

"Yes, I would."

More pleased than he could say to know that he was one
of her very favorite partners—and a bit jealous of the other
favorites, whoever they might be—he seated her, then took
the chair beside hers. After a drink of the cool, refreshing
lemonade, he continued his questions. "Do you ever wonder
why gentlemen ask you to dance?"

"Yes! Most of the time."

"Why? Do you think they ask because you are an acclaimed Beauty? Or because they know the size of your
dowry?"

"No. Well, I suppose some may ask for one of those reasons, but I think most ask because they want to be seen with
one of 'the beautiful Woodhurst twins' on their arm." She
laughed, but there was no amusement in it. "Some men
don't even bother to ask which twin I am before leading me
to the dance floor. Then they wonder why I dismiss their
flattery as Spanish coin."

Understanding her distaste of being viewed as a thing instead of a person all too well, Michael touched her hand
fleetingly to show his sympathy. And wished he dared hold
her hand. "Be assured, Lady Deborah, that I have never
asked you to dance—or to drive in the park—without
knowing who you are. Nor will I ever do so."

"Thank you, Fairfax, but you and Dunnley and a few others are the only men with whom I don't feel that way."

"I am glad to be amongst their number."

Her expression rather quizzical, she commented, "This is a strange conversation."

"Not the usual ballroom fare, that's true," he agreed. "But men, especially peers, often wonder if a lady accepts them as her partner because of their title and wealth, or because she likes them, or because she would take any partner rather than sit out a set."

"Really?" Once again, her beautiful blue eyes widened in surprise. "Do you?"

"Wonder if a lady wants me as her partner because I am a wealthy duke, or because she likes me, plain Michael Winslow?" He nodded. "Yes. Quite often."

"Well, I like you, Michael Winslow, and the fact that you have a title has nothing to do with it. And you are *not* plain," she said fiercely. "I can't deny that there are ladies who seem more interested in men's titles than in the men themselves—some girls make no secret of it—but I am *not* one of them."

"I have never thought that you were, Lady Deborah."

"I am glad." She smiled again, warming his heart. "I—"

"Forgive me for interrupting you, but I'd best escort you back now, before the next set begins." He stood, taking her hand to assist her in rising, then brought it to his lips and brushed a kiss across her gloved knuckles. "Thank you for your candor, my lady." He liked the sound of that—liked it very much—and hoped that she would agree to be his lady.

"I thank you for yours, as well. And for not laughing at my . . . foolishness."

"There is nothing foolish about wanting to be admired for yourself."

"Thank you, Fairfax. You truly are a very nice man, as well as an admirable one."

He halted, then lifted her hand from its resting place on his crooked arm and raised it to his lips again. "And you, my lady, are a very nice, and very admirable, young woman."

When they reached their friends—unfortunately, the

group still included Lady Diana and Sir Edward Smithson—Michael bowed over Lady Deborah's hand and thanked her for dancing with him. Easing them into the group, with Lady Deborah next to Dunnley and himself next to Lady Tina, who had been deserted by her last partner, the rag-mannered baronet, Michael paid little attention to what was said. Instead, he studied the two figures on the opposite side of the circle—Lady Sarah and Nasty Ned. Smithson was standing behind her, ogling her bosom and whispering in her ear. Her rigid posture bore mute testimony to the fact that his words distressed her.

Debating the best way to rescue her without calling attention to her plight, Michael almost groaned when the musicians struck up the next tune. The minuet he had hoped to dance with Lady Deborah he would now be forced to dance with her sister.

Dunnley offered his arm to Lady Deborah, and Michael turned to look for her twin. As he did, Smithson moved in front of Lady Sarah and offered his hand to lead her to the dance floor. When she stepped forward, she appeared to stumble, ripping her gown. She stammered out an apology, then fled from the room. Wishing he could follow, Michael mentally saluted her. He would have bet his entire fortune that her "stumble" was by design, not an accident. Adopting his haughtiest, most unapproachable mien, he girded himself for a thoroughly unenjoyable half hour.

Diana snickered when Sarah Mallory tripped on her hem and had to leave the ballroom to have her gown repaired. But when Smithson swore viciously and stalked off without another word, Diana stared after him, wondering what had happened to the charming, slightly wicked man who had waltzed with her. Diana had not been pleased when she'd been forced to accept him as her partner—an oversight for which she would take her admirers to task later—but she'd enjoyed the dance. And his flattering, slightly naughty compliments. Between those and the fact that he'd held her too close for most of the set, she'd felt beautiful and desirable. And she'd enjoyed the heady sensations. Quite a lot, in fact.

Enough to grant him another dance—the supper dance, which she hoped would be a waltz.

When the Duke of Fairfax bowed and offered his arm to lead her to the dance floor, Diana wanted to crow at her success. Although she'd been annoyed that Tina Fairchild had snagged him as her partner for the waltz—*what a waste!*—Diana knew he would never consider marrying such a hoyden, even if she was a duke's daughter. Sarah Mallory and Deborah had country dances with him, with little opportunity for conversation. She, Diana, had snared a minuet—and she intended to use every minute of it to work her wiles on the duke.

Snapping open her fan and waving it languidly, she smiled at Fairfax. "Are you enjoying the ball, Your Grace?"

"For the most part."

What kind of answer is that? Choosing to ignore both the brevity and the curtness of his reply, she tried a different tack, determined to draw him out. "Lady Oglethorpe has outdone herself with the decorations, don't you think?"

"I suppose so." He glanced around, then shrugged. "If you like flowers."

"*Everyone* likes flowers."

"Do they?" His tone was supercilious, and one brow arched mockingly. "Like this?" He gestured at the banks of flowers, which were beginning to wilt from the heat of the hundreds of candles in the chandeliers, as well as the exertions of hundreds of bodies.

"Perhaps not quite like this." Diana hated feeling in the wrong, and decided he would have to ask the next question.

They joined the line of dancers, their position cause for her to break the short silence. "Shouldn't we be at the front? You are the highest-ranking peer present." Her coy reminder provoked a scowl.

"Perhaps so, but I am quite content here."

He might be, but she was not; she wanted to flaunt the prize she'd caught. Fuming, she waited for his conversational gambit.

And waited. And waited.

Despite the reproving glances she shot at him, the duke

said nothing, his gaze directed resolutely forward as if memorizing the weave of the coat of the gentleman in front of them. Since she could not convince Fairfax of her worthiness to be his duchess by remaining silent, Diana stifled a sigh and began chatting about the other guests. "Lady Padbury has grown quite stout, hasn't she?" She paused to allow the duke to comment, but he made no reply. "It is unfortunate that Lydia Lane bears such a close resemblance to her mother. A gentleman need only look at Lady Padbury to see what Miss Lane will look like in twenty or thirty years." Another pause, another silence. "Look at Selwyn's cravat! I would be amazed if he can turn his head an inch."

Comment, pause, silence. Comment, pause, silence. The pattern remained unchanged down the length of the ballroom and through the turn at its end.

"Miss Merrick should never wear yellow. It makes her look sallow."

When they started back up the other side, the duke finally spoke. "Lady Diana, is it possible for you to say something nice about someone?"

She laughed gaily, although she was not at all certain he was teasing. "Of course I can."

"Since you spent the first half of the dance making derogatory remarks, perhaps you will restrict yourself to compliments for the rest of it?"

No gentleman had ever made such a request, but Diana dared not ignore the note of command in it. "Um . . . Lady Lorring's gown is pretty. I wonder what that color is called?"

"That is a compliment on the gown, not of Lady Lorring."

She huffed out a breath, wondering if he intended to criticize everything she said. "Well, she looks very nice in it."

"Yes, she does."

Surprised that he deigned to comment, but pleased that he had, she looked around for someone to compliment—someone she hadn't already disparaged. "The Duchess of St. Ives is looking quite well."

"For such an old lady, do you mean?" A hint of mockery laced his voice.

That was precisely what she'd meant, but she was not about to admit it. "Ah, no. I heard that she was ill over the winter."

"Did you? How strange that my grandmother, who is one of Her Grace's closest friends, failed to mention it to me."

Diana shrugged. Having invented the illness out of whole cloth, there was little else she could do, save search for another person to compliment. "Lady Sefton looks very nice tonight, doesn't she? That shade of blue suits her well."

"She does, indeed, look lovely. But then, she always does."

Infuriating man! Spotting her sister just ahead, smiling at Viscount Dunnley, Diana redoubled her efforts. Fairfax was the biggest catch on the Marriage Mart, and she was determined to wring an offer from him before the end of the Season. It was the only sure way to best her twin and to show her family and the *ton* that Deborah the Perfect had imperfections.

Deborah's conversation with Lord Dunnley had progressed from the decorations, to what makes a great hostess, but had floundered shortly after he'd asked her to call him Dunnley. But not because of the decreased formality.

"Tell me, please," he asked, smiling, "is there a secret to telling you and your sister apart?"

"I am the wrong person to ask. Beth or Elston might be able to answer your question. As far as I know, they are the only people outside the family who can tell us apart."

"Really? None of your court of admirers can do so?"

"If so, they haven't let on that they can." She shrugged, then added, "I do not know how Beth tells us apart, but Elston does it—at least, he did initially—by the pitch of our voices. Shortly after we met, he was able to identify us, and when I asked him how he knew who I was, he said that my voice was slightly higher pitched than Diana's."

He frowned. "The difference must be very slight."

"A quarter step, he said."

"Being a violist, he is able to detect such subtle nuances, but I fear my ear is not as acute."

"I doubt many people can detect such slight differences."

"We spoke of your admirers earlier. I know there are some men in your court who are not in your sister's, and vice versa, but—" He broke off as if reluctant to finish the question.

She, however, had no such qualms. "But you wonder if the men in our courts can tell us apart?"

He smiled ruefully. "Yes, I do—ungentlemanly as such a thought is."

"It is a perfectly logical question. One that troubles me a great deal. It is my opinion that they cannot. They court us merely because we are popular, and because other members of their set do. The fact that we are twins accounts for most of our popularity—"

"No, Lady Deborah, it does not."

"Yes, Dunnley, it does. 'The beautiful Woodhurst twins,'" she quoted with a grimace of distaste, "are the rage because we are twins."

"For some callow fellows that may be true," he conceded, "but not for most."

"I did not mean to imply that all men are so shallow. Certainly you are not, or you would not have asked how to distinguish between us."

"You dislike it, don't you?" It was obviously something he had not heretofore considered. "You want to be admired and courted for yourself, not because you are a twin."

"Yes, I do. And it is often quite difficult to determine if a man is interested in me, or if he merely wants to be seen with one of the Woodhurst twins on his arm."

"I daresay that presents quite a conundrum." As they circled each other, he seemed to ponder her dilemma. "I wish I could solve your problem, but I cannot. However, it may comfort you to know that all the eligible peers on the Marriage Mart find themselves in the same quandary—wondering if they are admired for themselves or for their titles and wealth."

"Really? I had no idea gentlemen worried about such things." She hadn't until Fairfax mentioned it earlier.

"That is undoubtedly because you are too smart, and too sensible, to marry a man merely because he has a title and a fortune. I imagine you are hoping to make a love match. Or, at the very least, to marry a man you like and respect."

"Of course I am. Preferably a love match." *With a man who can tell me apart from my sister. If such an unmarried gentleman exists.* "Is that not what you—and every other gentleman—hopes for?"

"I cannot speak for any other man, but I certainly hope that, when the time comes for me to choose a bride, I will find a lady who loves and respects me."

It was quite heartening to know that two men she liked and admired wanted to marry for love. Unfortunately, neither one of them could tell her and Diana apart.

Chapter Nine

"*H*e did *what?*"

Certain she'd misheard, Diana stared at James Martin as he repeated the message he'd been asked to convey. "Sir Edward left an hour or more ago. He asked me to take you in to supper."

The cad! She, an acclaimed Beauty and one of the celebrated Woodhurst twins, had been abandoned like a mongrel puppy left on the side of the road. Stood up for supper, as well as the dance she'd been looking forward to, by a mere baronet!

And he had not even had the decency to tell her in person. Or to take his leave of her.

To think she'd thought him charming. *Charming, ha!* He was despicable. A mannerless muckworm. An ill-bred, uncouth bounder. A churl.

She would pay Sir Edward back in kind, she vowed. But right now, she needed to find another partner. Condescending to have supper with a baronet was one thing. A mere mister was something else entirely.

The sight of Fairfax approaching prompted her to gather the reins of her fleeting composure. Supper with him was just the thing to restore her spirits. And to further her plans. Nodding a dismissal to Mr. Martin, she donned a coquettish smile and sallied forth to snare the duke.

Oh yes, he is a far better choice than the loutish baronet or vapid, lackluster Mr. Martin.

"Your Grace, have you come to take me to supper?"

He looked at her as if she'd lost her wits. Or perhaps it was her manners he thought lost. "No, Lady Diana. I am promised to your sister for supper."

Not my sister! Absolutely not. After the insult she'd been dealt, the thought of him supping with Deb was insupportable. Diana forced a laugh. "How foolish you are! You can't even recognize your own supper partner. I daresay I ought to be offended, but since we are identical twins, I will forgive you."

"There is no reason for you to forgive me. You are not my supper partner."

He sounded quite certain, but she was committed now. "You are mistaken, Your Grace. *I* am Deborah."

Pulling a quizzing glass from his pocket, he surveyed her from head to toe. He seldom wielded the glass, which added knee-weakening power to the gesture. "I am not mistaken. I am promised to Deborah, and you are not she."

Pretending puzzlement, she tilted her head to one side. "I can't imagine why you think so—"

"Several reasons. First of all, I noticed earlier that Deborah's sash was almost the same shade as Sarah Mallory's, and you are wearing a yellow one—"

"You must have confused us—"

He continued as if she hadn't interrupted. "Furthermore, you condemn yourself with every argument."

"Fairfax, Diana—" Her mother glanced from one of them to the other. "Is aught amiss?"

Diana almost stamped her foot in vexation. Another minute or so and she would have convinced him. She stepped back a pace, hoping to slip away, but her mother grasped her arm. Firmly.

The duke bowed to her mother. "Lady Diana has been trying to convince me that she is her sister, to whom I am promised for supper."

Shock was the first expression to cross the marchioness's face, then mortification. Anger quickly followed.

Hoping to defuse her mother's ire and restore her standing with the duke, Diana rolled her eyes. "It was a joke, Your Grace."

"I think not." Her mother was so angry, she was almost stuttering.

"It was, Mama," Diana insisted. "Deborah and I thought it would be fun to play a little trick on the duke."

"That is not true," her sister gasped, suddenly appearing beside them. She was accompanied by Dunnley, her partner for the last set.

Diana rained mental curses on her sister's head, determined to play out the hand she had dealt herself. "Don't lie, Deb." She sighed, hoping to sound aggrieved. "It was all your idea."

"I knew nothing of this!" her sister protested, her expression stricken. "I would never have agreed to such a deception."

"Don't lie, Deb." This time Diana made the accusation in tones of righteous indignation. "You have agreed many times."

"When we were children! And only a few times—the last when we were eight or nine."

Diana gritted her teeth. Despite her best efforts she could not seem to wriggle out of this. "It *was* a joke."

Neither her mother nor her sister believed her. Not for a moment. Diana couldn't tell if the duke did or not; his face was like a mask—one carved from stone.

"I am sorry," she added, before her mother demanded the apology. And Diana was sorry, but not for her attempted deception; she was sorry only that she'd been caught.

"I beg your pardon, Fairfax. I though my children had outgrown such childish stunts." The marchioness sank into a curtsy, but the duke caught her hand, arresting the motion.

"If there is any blame to be laid, my lady, none of it falls to you."

When her mother stepped away, Diana followed. It was either that or be dragged like a recalcitrant child. Only then did she realize that the confrontation had drawn a crowd. Among the dozen or so people watching and listening in rapt fascination were Lady Moreton and her son, Rupert, both notorious gossips. The other faces were a blur, too indistinctly seen to

identify in the brief glimpse she was permitted as her mother
led her away.

Blind to everything save the pain of her sister's betrayal,
Deborah ducked her head and directed her steps toward the
nearest door, which stood open to the evening air—and to the
garden. The dark night beckoned, promising a safe refuge
from the *ton*'s prying eyes, if not from the pain stabbing her
heart. Just as she reached the central fountain, her tears spilled
over, halting her progress. A moment later, she was folded
into an embrace, her face pressed against a snowy white cravat. A very stiff, elaborately tied cravat.

"Henry?" she gasped before the sobs racking her chest
robbed her of breath.

"Right here, puss." Her brother rubbed her back, softly
humming the lullaby their nurse had sung when she rocked
them to sleep.

Long, endless minutes later, when her sobs had dwindled
to an occasional hiccuping breath, her tears from a torrent to
a drizzle, Deborah felt utterly drained. She was no closer
to understanding her sister's actions, but was too exhausted to
make the effort tonight.

"Henry, will you take me home, please?"

"Here. Mop your face." He handed her a handkerchief.
"Of course I will take you home. Why else would I be standing here letting you dampen my cravat?"

She'd done more than dampen it—it was thoroughly
drenched, the once pristine folds now limp and soggy. But she
appreciated his attempt to cheer her, even though it had not
succeeded.

"How did you come to be out here, anyway?" She had not
seen him before she left the ballroom, but she'd seen little
save her sister's deceitful face—and the duke's expression-
less one.

"Howe and I came on the scene near the end of it. I sent
him to the card room for Papa, then I followed you."

"P-Papa knows what happened?"

"Probably not all of it. Like I said, Howe and I only saw

the end. I told him to tell Papa to take Mama and Di home, then send the carriage back for us."

Touched by his concern—when they were children, he'd usually sided with Diana—she essayed a watery smile. "You are a good brother, Henry. Thank you."

"It is easy to be a good brother when one has a sister as sweet as you."

It was probably the nicest compliment he'd ever given her, and tears pooled again in her eyes. She blinked them back, but not before her brother saw them. "Hey! No more waterworks, please."

Deborah closed her eyes and rested her head against his shoulder. "I am sorry." The tears were not just because of his compliment, though; the pain of her sister's deceit still gnawed at her. "Wh-why do you think Diana did it?"

"Did what? Pretended to be you, or lied?"

"Either. Both."

"Who knows? Maybe she pretended to be you because she was jealous."

"Of me?" she asked, incredulous. "How could she be?"

He shrugged. "I don't know. Maybe she didn't have a partner for the supper dance and thought to steal yours."

"But she did have a partner! I don't know who it was, only that she had one."

"Then I don't know. Ask her why."

She huffed out a breath. "I doubt that she would tell me."

"Perhaps not."

"Why do you think she lied?"

"Same reason as always—she knew Mama was angry and hoped to shift the blame."

After several beats of silence, Deborah asked the most important question. "Do you think Fairfax believed her?"

Henry's answer did not come as quickly as before. "I don't know that, either. His expression didn't reveal anything—at least, not that I could see—and I don't know him well enough to speculate. But I do know that he is a very intelligent man, and a fair one. I would guess—and this is only a guess—that if he had believed Di was you, there would not have a been a scene. The fact that she lied about being you might make him question everything else she said."

Tears welled again. Deborah could only hope her brother was right.

Standing in the shadows beneath a beech tree, Michael's heart ached with each tear Deborah shed. He wanted to be the one holding her, the one comforting her. He wanted to wipe her tears, and to try to assuage the pain of her sister's betrayal. But he had not reacted quickly enough. Dukes do not dash out of ballrooms in a lady's wake, as her brother had, so Michael's arms were empty.

Once again, the man was paying the price for the duke's folly.

When would he learn? How many times would he suffer because of the demmed ducal dignity? It was deeply in-grained—perhaps so deeply that he would never be able to shed it—but it was the worst, the most insidious kind of false pride. His ducal demeanor had paved his way many a time, gotten him through any number of unpleasant situations, but it could not brighten his day like Deborah's smile. Nor would it warm his heart and bring joy to his life the way being near her did.

Tomorrow he would do better. Tomorrow he would call on Deborah and offer his apologies for that ghastly scene. He would tell her the answers to some of her questions, and help her find the others. And, perhaps, tomorrow she would give him another chance. If he was very fortunate, tomorrow night he would be able to hold her in his arms and waltz with her.

Michael could only hope that she would not condemn him for his inadvertent role in her sister's betrayal. Because he now knew, with absolutely surety, that Deborah Woodhurst was the perfect wife for him. The thought of another man hav-ing the right to hold and comfort her pierced him to the core.

Tomorrow would be better, Michael vowed. He and Deb-orah had made a good start tonight, revealing some of their hopes and fears. And tomorrow he would show her more of the man beneath the ducal façade.

If he remembered how.

Chapter Ten

*R*ising at his usual hour, Michael dressed without his valet's assistance, then made his way downstairs and slipped outside without being spotted by his overly solicitous servants. A ride around the estate was the perfect way to put the events of the previous evening into perspective. By the time he returned to the house an hour later, he had a plan. Two of them, actually. One mapped out his afternoon and evening; the other was less precise—more strategy than tactics—and would be implemented only if Lady Diana attempted another deception. Much of the first plan depended on Lady Deborah, specifically on whether or not she would forgive him for his unwitting role in her twin's betrayal, and allow him to continue his courtship. The second scheme required the cooperation of his second cousin, Sir Frederick Walsingham. Mentally composing a letter to his cousin, Michael headed for the breakfast room—and halted in his tracks just across the threshold.

His better day had just taken a turn for the worse, and it was only eight o'clock.

"Good morning, Fairfax." The dowager sat in his place at the round table in the bay window overlooking the gardens, looking quite pleased with herself. "That coat is a disgrace. And those boots . . ." She fanned herself as though she feared she would swoon.

"Good morning, Grandmère." He kissed her cheek. "My coat and boots are comfortable—perfect for a solitary

morning ride. Neither the grooms nor my horse were offended. Nor has Sanders ever complained about my attire."
He nodded a greeting to the butler.

"I should hope the servants do not complain!"

"Had I known that you intended to join me for breakfast—"

"I don't need your permission, boy!"

"—I would have bathed and changed clothes before
coming to the table." Ignoring her argumentative interruption, Michael took the chair across from her.

As Sanders arranged napkin, china, and silverware, he
whispered, "I am sorry, Your Grace. I stepped out to check
on things in the kitchen, and when I returned, Her Grace was
firmly ensconced in your place."

Michael nodded to reassure the butler. The dowager
never paid attention to the servants, so they could whisper to
him with impunity, but he did not have the same freedom.

Her attitude toward those beneath her sometimes seemed
callous, but she was a product of the *ancien régime,* despite
having lived in England for more than half a century. And
despite the fact that every member of her family had lost
their heads. One of Michael's self-appointed tasks was to
ensure that she kept hers. Whether she used it or not was beyond his control.

Before she could take him to task for some failure, real or
imagined, he asked, "Have you decided yet whether or not
to attend the Opera on Saturday?"

"Not yet. I was thinking I might ask some of my friends
to join us in our box."

"You may ask a few, but I have invited five, so there are
already seven, including the two of us. Eight, if you will
have an escort."

"You will, of course, escort me." It was an imperious
command. One he could not leave unchallenged.

"No, Grandmère, not this time." Anticipating her objection, he added, "I cannot hope to find a bride if I am constantly squiring you around Town. But I will gladly invite
another gentleman to escort you."

Mollified, she nodded. "One of your older, less frivolous friends, please."

Frivolous friends, indeed! He reached for his coffee, determined that this shared breakfast would not end in an argument, as the last one had. *Who else can I invite?* If his cousin agreed to come up to Town and arrived betimes, Freddie could escort her. He was not a favorite of the dowager's, but he was not frivolous.

Her next question was inevitable, but still intrusive. "Who have you invited to the Opera?"

"I have agreed to escort Lady Kesteven and her daughters. Apparently Kesteven has another engagement." Michael wondered if Lord Henry was planning to attend. If so, he could escort the dowager. "Blackburn and Sherworth have also been pressed into duty."

"The twins would be a good choice as your duchess."

"One of them, perhaps. I do not intend to set up a harem."

His attempt at humor was met with a scowl. "Don't be impertinent. Those two are like peas in a pod."

"In appearance, yes. But their characters are quite different."

She waved a hand dismissively. "Just pick one and be done with it."

"I have just begun considering the young ladies on your list. Since there are quite a number of them, I am nowhere near ready to 'be done with it.'" He hoped the reference to her list—and its size—would buy him some time. "And lest you have forgotten, allow me to remind you that I alone will choose my bride."

"So you have told me. Several times. But I still say that I, having held the position, am better able to judge the ladies' suitability."

"Undoubtedly you did that before including them on your list." He forked another bite of ham and scrambled eggs into his mouth, to fortify himself for the rest of her arguments.

"I want to pay calls this afternoon."

"What time do you wish to leave? I will order the coachman to have the carriage ready for you."

"For *us*. You will accompany me."

The order, imperious as ever, made him sigh. With little thought for the consequences, he voiced a long-held wish. "Grandmère, it would be nice if, every once in a while, you would *ask* me to do something, instead of issuing commands. I have seldom ever refused you—and only when I had a previous commitment—so your high-handed demands gain you naught but my irritation."

Surprised, she blinked. Several times. "It is just my way, Fairfax."

"I know, Grandmère, but it is not a very pleasant way. I am nine-and-twenty, not nine."

The dowager said nothing, but she did nod. Content to have made his point without sparking an argument, he addressed her demand. "I have several engagements of my own today. You can either travel up to Town with me this morning, or with your companion later." Michael found it difficult to remember the companion's name—probably because they rarely stayed for more than a week or two. "I should be finished about three o'clock, and could join you then."

"Ermintrude and I will travel up by carriage after nuncheon. I would like you to pay a few calls with me, so meet us at three o'clock at Cathcart House."

Lady Cathcart was Michael's least favorite of his grandmother's friends, but having allowed her to pick the meeting place, he had little choice but to agree. "Yes. I may not be there on the stroke of three, but I shouldn't be too much later than that."

Recalling his plans for the evening, he inquired, "Will you attend Almack's or—"

"Faugh! Old women have no use for Almack's. Nor Almack's for them."

Michael released the breath he hadn't realized he was holding. Almack's—or any social event—was easier if he did not have to dance attendance on his grandmother in between dances with his partners. "I intend to attend tonight's assembly, so I will eat dinner at one of my clubs."

"Dance with the girls on the list tonight. Please." The politeness was obviously an afterthought, but at least she had remembered it.

"I promise to dance with several of them." *Lady Deborah, Lady Sarah, and Lady Tina.* He could not remember the names of any other young ladies on his grandmother's list, but since only the first two were on *his* list, the memory lapse was of little concern. Except . . . "Grandmère, I will not accompany you this afternoon if you intend to call on any of the ladies on your list."

The dowager bristled. "Why not?"

"Because I refuse to raise expectations I may not be able to fulfill."

"Paying one call does not commit you to offer for a girl."

"If you and I call together, the visit might be misconstrued. And it could raise expectations in a young lady's— or her mother's—mind."

"That is—"

"Sensible," Michael inserted smoothly.

"—ridiculous."

"Those are my terms." He would not be swayed, no matter what his grandmother said. Or did. "You may call on whomever you like, but I will sit in the carriage if you stop at the home of any young lady on your list."

Before any darts—verbal or otherwise—could be thrown, Michael rose. As he left the room, he reminded himself to memorize the names on the demmed list before he departed. If his grandmother was planning to bamboozle him—and he fully expected that she would try—she would soon realize her mistake.

A better day, ha! Well, perhaps it was . . . on Mars.

This is a better day? Glancing from the scowl on her father's face to the frown creasing her mother's brow, Deborah could see little change from the previous night. On the other hand, she was not being subjected to her sister's sulks and screeches this morning, nor forced to watch Henry's fidgeting, and was grateful to be spared both.

Deborah did not mind Henry's twitches and squirming so much; she knew he felt badly for her, and had found last

night's confrontations—and there had been two at home in
addition to the one at the ball—as discomfiting as she had.
But her sister's antics and tantrums were extremely annoying. If anyone had the right to sulk or scream, Deborah believed it was she. She had been betrayed. She had been
humiliated in front of half the *ton*—and Fairfax.

Diana was reaping what she had sown—and disliking
the crop. Deborah felt caught in a whirlwind, without the
least notion where she would land—but hoping that she
would not find herself in the suds, alongside her sister.

Last night was behind them, but there was still the future
to be faced. And a very uncertain one it seemed at the moment.

She would have to face Diana again; there was no way to
avoid that. Deborah hoped that particular encounter would
be a long time coming. Never would be a sufficient interval.
Next year was nearly as suitable. Unfortunately, she knew it
would occur much sooner. Probably sometime today. Her
parents had decreed that Diana could not leave the house
until she told the truth and apologized—to Deborah, to
them, and to Fairfax. An apology to Lord and Lady
Oglethorpe might also be required; her parents were of two
minds about that, and were still considering the matter.

Deborah doubted that Diana would tell the truth—at
least, not all of it—but she was certain to offer the necessary
apologies, albeit insincerely, before this evening. Today was
Wednesday; tonight was Almack's. Diana would not miss
the assembly, no matter what she had to do—or say—in
order to attend.

It was only nine o'clock in the morning. There were still
many hours in which the day could improve. Or get worse.

Deborah was hard pressed not to groan at the prospect.

Studying her image in a hand mirror, Diana decided that
her face bore no visible sign of the largely sleepless night
she'd spent—a blessing for which she was extremely grateful. It was bad enough that she felt worn to a thread; it would
be much worse if everyone else realized it. Especially since

she would spend a large part of the day pretending contrition and spouting apologies.

Everything had gone wrong last night. And it was all Sir Edward's fault!

If he hadn't deserted her, she would not have tried to snare the Duke of Fairfax as her supper partner. And if she hadn't attempted that, her family would not be furiously angry with her.

She could not understand why they were so upset. So she had told a lie or two. Where was the harm in that? She'd told lies before, and surely would again.

But how was she to know that the duke would see through her deception? She could not have known that he was aware Lord Dunnley had danced the previous set with her sister. Nor that the duke had passed them in their stroll around the ballroom. What were the chances of that in a room of such size?

A knock on the door heralded the entrance of one of the younger chambermaids, carrying a breakfast tray. "Good morning, my lady."

There was nothing good about this morning as far as Diana was concerned. If there were, she would not be cowering in her bedchamber, afraid to face her family. She nodded, acknowledging the greeting. "Where is Ogden?"

"Mrs. Ogden had errands to do, so she asked me to bring up your tray and help you dress. She and Mrs. Pettibone are teaching me about being a lady's maid, you know."

Diana hadn't known, but the information might prove useful. Ogden had made no secret of her opinion about Diana's deception—and character—last night, and would probably have more to say on the subject today. If this girl was skilled, she might prove useful. "What is your name?"

"Ginny." The girl set the tray across Diana's lap, then bobbed a curtsy. She was pretty enough, for a servant, but not too pretty. Her brown hair was attractively arranged beneath her mobcap, and her uniform and apron were neat and clean.

Diana motioned to the dressing room. "While I eat, you can lay out my gown and things."

"What do you want to wear, my lady?"

"Did Ogden not tell you which gown I would wear?"

The maid shook her head. "No, my lady. She just said to bring up your tray and help you dress."

Was Ogden's omission deliberate, or had no oversight occurred? "Is my sister up? Or, rather, has she gone down for breakfast?"

"I don't know, my lady."

Rapidly losing patience, Diana snapped, "You need to find out. And if Deborah is up and dressed, I need to know what gown she is wearing." Snidely, she added, "Surely you have noticed that we are identical twins. We always dress alike."

"But—"

"Don't argue." She pointed to the door. "And don't return until you know the answers to both questions." *Lud! Who would have thought that those old women forever complaining about how difficult it was to find good servants were right?*

The problem last night, Diana thought lying back against the pillows and sipping her chocolate, was that she and Deborah had not been dressed identically. The duke had mentioned their different colored sashes as one of the reasons he'd known she was not Deborah. That, and the fact that Deb had been Dunnley's partner for the previous set. Perhaps it was not so surprising that Fairfax had known the latter—Dunnley was his best friend—but Diana was, frankly, astonished that he'd noticed the difference in their attire. She would not have thought that such a minor detail would have made the least impression on him. Although always elegantly attired, he was not a dandy. Nor would she have thought him the kind of man who paid much attention to clothing—his or anyone else's.

But apparently he did. At least to what she and her sister wore. And that, coupled with her sister's sudden, unreasonable desire to dress even more different, posed a problem. Not an insurmountable one, but an annoying one. It would require a bit of advance planning if ever she wished to impersonate her sister again. And if the duke continued to ask

Deb to be his supper partner, Diana was quite certain that she would again attempt the deception.

She had made a few mistakes last night, there was no denying that. But given that she'd launched the impersonation on an impulse, she had not fared too badly. And she'd obtained information that would prove invaluable in furthering her scheme to snare the duke.

Even if it had, temporarily, put her in her family's black books.

Neither Fairfax nor Dunnley could tell her and Deb apart; Diana was certain of that. She had asked Lord Dunnley outright last night, and he had lamented that he could not. The duke could not, either. She had asked him several times in the past, when he seemed to know which twin she was, and he had always had a logical explanation—invariably referring to some bit of conversation that had allowed him to guess her identity.

Under other circumstances, she probably would not have worried if Lord Dunnley could tell her and Deborah apart. But Diana knew that the viscount and the Duke of Fairfax were friends. The best of friends. She could not take the chance that the viscount could distinguish her from her twin—and possibly foil her plans.

Although she intended to capture a far loftier title than his viscountcy, Lord Dunnley intrigued her. He was handsome, wealthy, charming, and a leader of the *ton*. He was also reputed to be quite the rake, and she thought he might do nicely as a lover. After she'd given her husband an heir to the dukedom, of course. It was really quite unfortunate that Fairfax, not Dunnley, was the duke. Fairfax was wealthy, but no one would call him handsome. Nor was anyone likely to claim that he was charming, rakish, or a leader of Society. A force to be reckoned with in Parliament, perhaps, but not in the *beau monde*.

Ah, well. She would do better next time. And today was bound to be a better day. Once she pretended contrition and made all the stupid apologies her parents demanded, she could plan how to snare the duke's interest tonight.

After twenty-one years of having her sister's achievements held up as an example, Diana was looking forward to a lifetime of flaunting her superior choice of husband. Failure . . .

Just the thought of that humiliation made her shudder. But she would not fail, Diana vowed. She would do whatever was necessary to succeed.

Nothing could be worse than last night's fiasco.

Deborah was beginning to wonder whether her sister was going to sulk in her bedchamber all day, or emerge and make the required apologies so that life could return to some semblance of normalcy. Their relationship would never be the same, and Deborah mourned the loss. She did not know if she would ever trust her sister again—indeed, right now, mere civility seemed almost impossible—but if Diana was truly repentant, perhaps they could, in time, find a comfortable footing.

Diana entered the drawing room a few minutes before two o'clock—just in time to entertain callers, Deborah thought cynically. Her sister was apparently not aware that their mother had given Driscoll orders that they were not at home to anyone. Diana halted just over the threshold, seemingly taken aback to find her father and brother present, too. Their parents sat side by side on a sofa and looked, as Henry had said, as stern as judges at the Old Bailey. He and Deborah sat in nearby chairs—Henry in the wing chair their mother usually chose, Deborah in the seat Fairfax had occupied both times he'd called.

Deborah could not help but wonder if her sister's choice of a simple white muslin gown with a pink sash was unconscious or contrived. Di looked liked innocence personified, and no doubt hoped to sway opinion in her favor.

Advancing toward them, Diana flicked a rather uncertain gaze from their parents to Deborah, then at Henry, before looking back at their parents. "I am sorry for what happened last night."

"Is that the best apology you can contrive?" Their father's outraged bellow was as atypical as a thunderclap on a sunny day.

As Diana sought words to appease him, Mama sputtered, "'What happened?' You impersonated your sister—or tried to—lied to the Duke of Fairfax, attempted to place the blame on your sister, and dishonored the family name at the opening ball of the Season, in front of almost every member of the *ton,* and you want to dismiss it as 'what happened last night'? Oh no, young lady." The marchioness shook her head. "That is a woefully inadequate apology."

Diana seemed to pale a bit with each charge. "It was a *joke,* Mama," she insisted, as she had last night. "Yes, I pretended to be Deb, and I had to lie to the duke to do it, but—"

Deborah shot to her feet. "And was it a *joke* when you lied to Fairfax and told him that I agreed to the deception? I don't see anything funny in that."

Her sister glanced at her as if surprised—either by the question or her incensed tone—but a shrug was Diana's only response. The nonchalant gesture infuriated Deborah all the more.

"Is your failure to answer your sister because there is no acceptable reason for your behavior?" Papa's tone was edged with steel.

Diana huffed out a breath. "I wanted the duke to notice me."

Henry snickered. "He noticed you, all right."

"He danced the minuet with you!" The indignant rejoinder came from their mother. "How could you possibly think he didn't notice you?"

"You'd been talking to Fairfax for several minutes when you lied about me," Deborah reminded her sister, "so you cannot claim you did it to gain his notice."

Her sister's reluctance to answer was apparent, but with all four of them waiting with varying degrees of patience for her reply, she had to say something. The silence grew until finally, tired of Diana's evasions, Deborah stated her opinion. "You hoped to make yourself look better by making me look bad, didn't you?"

"Oh, for heaven's sake, Deb! What difference does it

make now? It is over and done with. Water under the bridge." Diana waved her hand dismissively.

Disgust, anger, and pain surged through Deborah, in equally bitter proportions. Fearing she might lose her composure or say something she would regret later, she left the room.

Today was definitely *not* a better day.

A better day? Perhaps. The afternoon could have been worse.

Michael sank onto a chair in a corner at White's and raised a snifter of brandy in a celebratory toast. He had survived the round of calls with his grandmother—and with his bachelorhood intact. If that wasn't worthy of a toast or three, nothing short of the defeat of Napoleon was.

"Well met, Fairfax!"

Recognizing Dunnley's voice, Michael mustered a smile. "If you are looking for intelligent conversation, you won't get it from me. I just spent two hours paying calls with my grandmother."

Theo settled into the chair beside his. "Since when do you dislike making morning calls? Or is the fact that you did so with your grandmother the reason for your complaint?"

"I don't mind making them, generally—at least, I haven't until this year. But Grandmère has decided that it is time for me to marry and set up my nursery, so she is constantly singing the praises of some chit or other. Even that wouldn't be so bad were each one not more featherheaded than the last." Michael groaned, remembering the worst of the widgeons. "I swear, Dunnley, I heard enough talk about bonnets and ribands and plumes and other such falderal today to open a millinery shop!"

Totally unsympathetic to his plight, Theo laughed. "You should do it. You'd be the biggest prize on the Marriage Mart—a duke with a millinery shop." A moment later, he shook his head. "What am I saying? You already are the Catch of the Season."

"Yes," Michael said glumly, "and that's at least half the problem."

"Problem? What problem?"

"How am I supposed to know if a young lady is interested in me, or if she merely wants to snare my title and fortune?"

"Well—" Dunnley broke off as a waiter approached with a bottle. Apparently, Theo, too, was in need of a restorative. "I can't deny that many marriages are made for gain, and have been for hundreds of years, but I can think of a number of young ladies who are not likely to choose a husband because of his rank and fortune. Any number of people like you, Michael—and the fact that you are a duke has nothing to do with it."

"You sound like Sarah Mallory."

"Do I?"

Michael nodded. "She said much the same thing to me last night."

"She is an intelligent young woman. She doesn't say a lot—I think she is a bit shy—but when she does speak, her conversation is worth listening to."

"I agree, although I'd say she is more than just a bit shy. Why, she makes me seem almost gregarious, and God knows I am not." Michael raised one finger. "She is one who won't choose a husband by his rank and the size of his purse. Who are the other young ladies you mentioned?"

"Deborah Woodhurst." After a moment's hesitation, Theo added, "But I am not certain the same can be said of her twin."

"I don't think so, either." When Theo did not immediately add to the list, Michael prompted, "Who else? Besides Harriett Broughton and Tina Fairchild. They are the only others I can think of."

"I don't know Miss Broughton well enough to say."

"Take my word for it. She is as shy as I am, so no matter how high a man's title or how deep his pockets, she won't marry him unless she genuinely likes him."

Instead of listing more names—or, perhaps, out of names to list—Theo changed the subject. "Speaking of the Woodhurst twins, what was that business with Lady Diana trying to claim her sister's dance with you last night?"

Michael groaned again; he'd been asked variations of the question several times this afternoon. "I haven't got the slightest idea. But then, Lady Diana ain't the most rational female in the *ton*. Maybe she was just jealous that her sister had a partner when she herself did not, so she tried to steal Deborah's partner—me."

"That is possible, I suppose, but it seems unlikely. I don't think either of the twins have sat out a dance since they got the nod to waltz last year. Besides, I had the impression that young Martin was Lady Diana's partner. If not, why was he standing there?"

"Martin minor, d'you mean?" He used the young man's nickname at school. "He was there, wasn't he?" Last night, he had noticed Martin standing near Lady Diana, but had not wondered why he was there.

Theo nodded, then asked, "Can you really tell the twins apart, Fairfax, or were you bluffing last night?"

"I can't bluff worth a damn, as you well know. I think I have lost every game of brag I ever played. Of course I can tell the twins apart. Not from across the room, though. I have to be within a few feet of them to know which is which."

"Can you tell them apart if only one is present? Or do they have to be side by side so you can compare them?"

"They don't have to be together. I don't think Lady Deborah was there at the beginning of last night's contretemps." A moment later, Michael corrected himself. "I *know* she was not there at first."

"No, she wasn't," Theo agreed. "She was my partner for the set of country dances that had just ended, and we stopped to speak with several people as we strolled around the room. When we walked up, Lady Kesteven was sputtering in outrage at her younger daughter's audacious lies and shocking want of conduct."

"How did Lady Deborah react when she realized her twin was trying to steal her partner?"

"She was . . . stunned. She hid her distress well, but I believe she felt betrayed—either by Diana's lies or by Diana herself."

"And rightly so. What did Lady Deborah say when she realized what was happening?"

"Did you not hear her call her sister's bluff?"

"Yes, I heard that, but I wondered . . ." Michael huffed out a breath. "I wondered if Lady Deborah commented on her sister's behavior."

"Not in my hearing. But I imagine she—and Lady Kesteven, too—had a great deal to say about it later, after they left the ball."

"I don't understand why Lady Diana did it—I don't think she likes me above half—but I don't want to talk about her anymore."

Nodding in understanding, Theo again turned the subject. "How do you tell Lady Deborah and Lady Diana apart?"

Michael shrugged. "I don't know how I know which twin is which. I just do." Not even to his best friend was he willing to admit that being near Deborah caused his heart to perform amazing acrobatic feats.

"Would you be able to tell them apart if you were in a dark room and couldn't see them clearly?"

"You've got more questions than a grumpy headmaster this afternoon, don't you? I don't know if I could or not."

"Are there any young ladies you would know in a dark room—or a dark garden?"

A very grumpy headmaster. Wondering which young lady—or ladies—had prompted his friend's questions, Michael gamely attempted to answer. "In this hypothetical dark room or garden, how close am I standing to these young ladies?"

"Two or three feet. An arm's length away.

"Hmmm . . . The Woodhurst twins, probably. Maybe Miss Castleton—Lady Weymouth. Possibly Miss Broughton and Lady Sarah Mallory."

"Why those four—er, those five? And how would you know them?"

"I don't know that I would, Theo." The only young lady Michael had ever seen in a dark garden was Deborah, but to his regret, last night could not be considered an encounter. "I have a different feeling around Lady Diana than when I am with her sister. Lady Weymouth because . . . I don't know why. Or how. I just think maybe I could recognize her and the others in a dark room."

Despite the answers he'd given, Michael was absolutely certain that he—or, rather, his heart—would know Deborah anywhere, regardless of the conditions. Sunlight, moonlight, or no light at all; it wouldn't matter. The other names were pure obfuscation.

Since Dunnley seemed to be out of questions, Michael asked one. "Am I right in thinking that you asked how I tell the Woodhurst twins apart because you cannot?"

"I cannot. Lady Deborah told me last night that only two people outside the family can. Three, now that your name has been added to the list."

Shock rendered Michael speechless for a moment, then he blurted, "Please keep it to yourself! Lady Diana may try another deception, and my ability to tell the twins apart is the only weapon I have." *Only I and two other people out-side the Woodhurst family can distinguish between the twins? Incredible!*

"I will keep your secret, old trout. Lady Diana might do for the wife of my worst enemy, but not for my best friend."

Chapter Eleven

$\mathcal{D}$eborah shifted uneasily, uncomfortably aware of the silence and the tensions pulsing through the town coach. The absence of the lighthearted chatter with which they usually whiled away the drive to a social event was bad enough, but her uncertainty about their reception this evening was even worse. She felt too emotionally battered to attempt conversation, and there was nothing she could do about the *ton*'s fickleness, save deal with it when the time came. Which it would, all too soon.

Diana's behavior last night, or the confrontation in the drawing room this afternoon, had affected the entire family, although in different ways and to varying degrees. Her indifference and nonchalant attempts to make light of the situation had shocked everyone—Deborah most of all. Even more alarming, battle lines had been drawn, with the family split into two camps. Deborah, the marquess, and Henry were in one; Diana and the marchioness in the other, although only in regard to public appearances. Thus, Deborah had been coerced "for the good of the family" into accompanying their mother and Diana when they called on Lady Oglethorpe, but had resented every minute of it, and of the other half dozen calls they'd made, feeling like she was being punished, too. She'd resented it even more when they returned home and learnt that Fairfax had called a few minutes after their departure.

Diana had not yet apologized to the duke, but Mama, who, at breakfast, had been adamant about all four apologies, had argued that Diana should be allowed to attend Almack's tonight, and to make her apology there. Deborah had accepted her sister's insincere apology with a terse nod, but had not yet forgiven or forgotten. Perhaps someday she would be able to do both, but right now, the pain of betrayal was still too raw.

Tonight, battered emotions or not, she must face the *ton*—and Fairfax. If the *beau monde* chose to believe the lies Diana had told last night, Deborah's reputation would be tarnished as badly as her sister's. If the duke believed them, her heart—and her hopes—would be shattered. Taking a deep breath for courage, she glanced down at her white ball gown with its amaranth sash, smoothed her gloves from wrist to elbow, and prepared to face the Polite World.

A better day, ha. Only in fairy tales.

This had been the strangest—and most frustrating—day of Michael's life. And it was getting stranger by the minute.

He'd expected that normalcy would prevail the moment he stepped foot within the precincts of Almack's. Instead, he was being interrogated by Lady Cowper, Mrs. Drummond-Burrell, and Lady Jersey about the Oglethorpe ball. Did the patronesses of these hallowed halls want his opinion of the decorations or the quality of the entertainment? Indeed, they did not; they wanted a word for word accounting of last night's "contretemps."

"Do tell me all about it, Fairfax," Lady Cowper cajoled. "Did Diana Woodhurst pretend to be her sister?"

"I heard she did it because she wanted to dance the supper dance with you." An inveterate gossip, Sally Jersey *heard* more than most. "Isn't that right, Fairfax?"

If these arbiters of right and wrong were all but begging to hear every detail, then every matron and dowager present tonight would, too. Not to mention the quidnuncs, wits, and tabbies—of both sexes.

"Diana was jealous," Mrs. Drummond-Burrell opined. "She didn't have a partner, so she tried to steal her sister's."

"And lied, repeatedly, to do it." Lady Jersey again. "Lady Smithson heard almost all of it."

Malice and mendacity, the stuff of *on dits* and scuttlebutt. Everyone—from Paragons of Propriety to Rag-mannered Rapscallions, from Pattern-cards of Pomposity to Verisimilitudinous Vixens—loved a hint of scandal. Provided no taint of it clung to them or their family, of course.

Michael was not inclined to oblige their curiosity. Diana Woodhurst had set her course, and could sink or swim on her own, battling the tide of gossip and innuendo. But Deborah did not deserve to suffer the same fate. Nor would she, if he had anything to say about it.

And he did. There was quite a lot he wanted to say on the subject. But what he had to say was for her ears alone.

"Fairfax!" Lady Jersey poked him in the ribs with her fan.

To Michael's relief—Sally Jersey was *very* persistent— the Marquess of Kesteven crested the stairs, with his wife on one arm and one of the twins on the other. Lord Henry escorted the second twin. Giving his interrogators a semblance of a smile, Michael stepped away, so the Woodhursts could greet the patronesses.

But he did not go far, just a few paces to the side. He wanted to be close enough to discover which twin wore the blue sash, and who the pinkish-purple. And to ask Deborah to dance with him. Perhaps she would grant him two sets, to make up for missing the supper dance last night. If he was very fortunate, and if she did not hold him to blame for last night's debacle, one of them would be a waltz.

Watching the Woodhurst family bow or curtsy and greet the patronesses, he reminded himself not to address the twins by name until they identified themselves. The last thing Michael wanted was for Diana to realize that he could tell them apart. No, not quite. The very last thing he wanted was to end up married to her instead of her sweet sister. To avoid that ghastly fate, he was determined to keep Diana— and, regrettably, Deborah, too—unaware that he could distinguish them. It was a powerful weapon in his battle to avoid Diana's snares while attempting to win her sister's heart.

Kesteven, his wife, and the blue-sashed twin approached.

"Fairfax, Diana has something she wishes to say to you," the marquess said. "Would you grant us a few minutes of your time?"

Michael looked at the girl and asked, "Lady Diana?"

"Yes, Your Grace." She dipped a curtsy.

"A blue sash this evening, I see." He looked over at her sister. "And a purplish one for Lady Deborah."

"Amaranth, Fairfax," Lady Kesteven chided with a smile. "That color is called amaranth."

"Is it indeed, my lady?" He feigned an expression of astonishment. "It looks like pinkish-purple to me, but if you say it is amaranth, I shan't argue. That is easier to say, if less descriptive."

He greeted Deborah and Henry, then suggested, "Why don't we move to the far side of the room? There are several unoccupied chairs, so you ladies can be comfortable yet have an excellent view of the entire room." *It is also out of earshot of the gossip-hungry patronesses.* He offered his arm to the marchioness. She wasn't the lady he wanted to escort, but given a choice between Lady Kesteven and her younger daughter, he would choose the marchioness every time.

Once the ladies were seated, Diana showed no inclination to speak her piece. After both her parents sent her "what are you waiting for?" looks, Michael mentally girded his loins and his defenses, then stepped into the breach. "You wanted to speak with me, Lady Diana?"

"Yes, Your Grace." She did not meet his gaze—not even after her mother prodded her to her feet.

Head bent, eyes fixedly downcast, Diana launched into an apology. "I am sorry for my behavior last night. It was wrong of me to lie to you, and ill-mannered of me to cause a scene at Lady Oglethorpe's ball."

It sounded like a rehearsed speech—delivered by rote, without a hint of inflection in her voice. "I know what you did, and why it was wrong," he reminded her, his voice as flat as hers. "I want to know why you did it."

Her gaze darted to his for an instant, her expression a mixture of surprise and annoyance. Apparently, Michael thought wryly, his role was to politely and formally accept her apology. He would do that eventually, though it went against the grain to accept an apology from someone who was neither repentant nor remorseful. Because it did, and because she seemed to be sorry only that she'd been caught, he wanted to know the reasons for her deception. Perhaps once he knew why she'd done it, he would be able to judge whether she was likely to attempt the ruse again.

"Lady Diana?" he prodded, letting a measure of chill hauteur seep into his voice.

"I am reluctant to say, Your Grace." It was a blatant attempt to stall, although it was undoubtedly true. Her reluctance was as apparent as if she were wearing a sign. A very large sign.

Michael frowned to show his displeasure. Realizing that she could not see his expression with her head down, he used the same frosty tone to compel an explanation. "That is obvious. But given that you embarrassed me in front of half the *ton* last night, I believe you owe me a full account."

The demand brought her eyes up again, if only for a moment, and she skewered him with a glare. If looks could kill, he would be measuring his length on the assembly room floor. "No doubt you will think me quite foolish, Your Grace, but Mr. Martin had just informed me that my partner for the supper dance had left the ball an hour earlier and asked him to partner me instead."

"Go on," he prodded when it seemed she would stop there.

"I don't know Mr. Martin very well, so I was reluctant to agree. Then I saw you and thought I'd ask you to take me in to supper instead."

The frank admission caused Lady Kesteven to choke on a breath. The marquess glowered and crossed his arms over his chest. As unaware of her parents' reactions as she'd been of his, Diana continued, "When I asked if you'd come to take me to supper and you said you were promised to my sister, I . . . I thought it would be a great lark to convince you I was Deb."

Michael had believed her explanation until the last statement, which did not ring true. To test his theory, he asked,

"So all the lies you told me were to convince me you were Lady Deborah?"

"Yes, Your Grace, they were." For the first time, she looked him in the eye.

Assuming a perplexed frown, he moved in for the kill. "But if your decision to impersonate your sister was conceived on impulse, when you learnt she was my supper partner, how could Lady Deborah have been party to the deception?"

Her cheeks flaming—in embarrassment or anger at being caught in another lie—Diana resumed her perusal of the floor. "She wasn't. Deb knew nothing about it."

"Why did you lie about your sister's involvement?"

The answer to this question was much longer in coming. So long, in fact, that he began to think she would not reply. Her father removed that option by demanding "Why, Diana?" in a tone that brooked no denial.

She studied the toe of her slipper while tracing patterns on the floor. It was the first time she'd given the slightest indication of unease. Michael wondered whether it presaged the truth or another lie. The silence stretched, as if she, too, were trying to decide.

While she debated, Michael glanced at Deborah, noting, with some surprise, that she and the other members of the family were awaiting her sister's response. Although he had posed the question for Deborah's benefit—it was one she'd asked her brother last night—Michael had done so mostly so that Deborah would be publicly vindicated; he thought the family would have already discussed the matter. That did not appear to be the case, and Michael wondered why they had not. Perhaps they'd tried, and Diana's replies had been as evasive—or as mendacious—as the responses with which she'd attempted to fob him off.

Deborah was avoiding his eye now, almost as if she were embarrassed. Indeed, she had met his gaze only fleetingly when she'd greeted him. Soon, he would do his best to convince Deborah that he still held her in the highest regard. For now, aware of nearby ears straining to hear Diana's reply to his question, he would settle for righting the wrong she had committed when she betrayed her twin. To that end, he demanded, in his coldest, most haughty voice, "Tell the truth and be done with it. You lied enough for a lifetime last night, Lady Diana."

Flashing him a look of pure loathing, Diana retorted, "I lied because I knew Mama was furious. I thought she wouldn't be as angry if she believed Deb were party to the scheme."

Michael believed the first statement, but not the last. "But Lady Deborah wasn't aware of your attempted deception, was she?"

"No, she wasn't. I already told you that." Her tone was peevish.

Hoping to needle her into telling the truth, he speculated, "I think, knowing your mother was angry, you sacrificed your sister in the hope of saving yourself. Perhaps you also hoped to look better in my eyes. Is that an accurate assessment of your reasons for betraying your sister?"

"Perhaps," she hedged.

Sick of Diana's duplicity, her lies and evasions, he threw a final verbal gauntlet. "I think those were precisely your reasons. You sacrificed your sister's good name in the hope of saving your own. You hoped that by tarnishing her sterling reputation, the lack of shine of your own would not be as apparent."

"Yes!" she retorted, provoked beyond caution. "That is exactly what I hoped."

Michael heard Deborah's startled gasp, saw the pain that flashed across her features as she turned away, wrapping her arms around her waist as if she'd sustained a blow. The marquess and marchioness gaped at Diana as if they'd never seen her before, while Henry wore an expression of deep disgust.

"Now that you have finally told the truth, I accept your apology." Michael gave Diana a curt nod in lieu of a bow, then he turned his back and walked away, slighting her as surely as she'd slighted her sister. When he reached Deborah, he favored her with a smile and a deep obeisance.

"Would you honor me with your company for a stroll around the room, my lady?"

"Indeed I would, Your Grace." Deborah's smile was a bit strained, but she rose with alacrity and took his arm.

Deborah could only marvel at Fairfax's ability to cut through her sister's lies and evasions. Seemingly without effort, he had obtained answers to the questions that had been tormenting her ever since her sister's betrayal. Even though he'd wrung the truth from Diana, and had done so in as public a forum as her betrayal, Deborah was still surprised when, after coldly accepting her sister's apology, he approached her with a smile and asked her to promenade around the ballroom with him. Surprised, but very pleased.

Her smile a bit wobbly, she accepted his invitation, and his arm, wondering if he truly wanted her company, or if he was still in his role of knight errant, on a quest to redeem her reputation in the eyes of the *beau monde*. She waited until they were out of her family's earshot—and, for the moment, anyone else's—before asking, "How did you know?"

"How did I know what?"

"That Diana was lying."

"Two things gave her away. She never looked me in the eye until the end, and her apology and her initial explanation sounded like rote recitations."

"Did you know—before she admitted it, I mean—that I was unaware of her deception?" Deborah was not certain she wanted to hear his answer, but she felt compelled to ask the question.

"Of course. I knew that last night."

"You did?" Surprise rendered her voice almost a squeak. "But how?"

He nodded in response to two gentlemen's greetings, but did not stop to talk. "Her arguments were quite plausible, which is one reason I wanted her to vindicate you in as public a setting as she'd defamed you. As for how I knew, I am a fairly good judge of character, and I did not believe that you would show such disrespect to me. Or to any partner, for that matter."

"I wouldn't," she assured him.

"But I must confess, I asked your sister some of those questions not only for my benefit, but also for yours. I followed you out of the ballroom last night, and overheard part of your conversation with your brother."

"Oh dear." Deborah's heart sank.

He covered her hand with his. "Don't be alarmed. I would never tell anyone what I saw, and nothing you did or said affected my regard for you. To be quite frank, I was jealous of your brother."

Not sure what to make of that last statement, she chose to ignore it, at least for now. "Thank you for reassuring me. I shall be equally frank and tell you that my opinion of you is higher than ever. Not only did you see through Diana's deception last night, you saw through her lies and evasions tonight. And you got her to tell the truth. None of us were able to do that."

"Perhaps because you didn't make her angry."

His wry assessment startled a laugh from her, but when she thought about it, she realized he was right. "No, we didn't. We were angry, but she was cool and composed. And very much in control—of herself and of the situation," she added, with a moue of dismay. "How did you know that making her angry would result in a confession?"

"I didn't. I goaded her because her evasions angered me. I was as surprised as you were that they provoked her into telling the truth."

Lord Blackburn greeted them, and Fairfax stopped to talk to the earl and his mother. Blackburn requested a dance, and Deborah suggested the first country dance, hoping that Fairfax would ask her to partner him for the opening set. Or to save a dance or two for him.

As soon as they resumed their promenade, he did. "I hope that you will grant me a set. Preferably two."

"Of course I will. Which sets would you like?"

"If the choice were mine, I would pick two waltzes."

Startlement—and delighted surprise—made her stammer over her reply. "T-two waltzes might be misconstrued as a . . . partiality for my company." *Surely, he must realize that?*

"Are you so certain it would be a misconception?" His voice dropped almost to a whisper. "Deborah, I do enjoy your company—very much. But if you think two waltzes is unwise, then will you grant me a waltz and the first minuet?"

"Yes, of course I will." The response was automatic—and abstracted. Her mind was almost entirely engaged trying to puzzle out his cryptic question. *Is he saying that he is partial to my company? Or does he mean that two waltzes might not be considered showing preference for a lady's company?*

She glanced at him, hoping that his expression would provide a clue, but found instead a look of patient expectancy. Playing his last comment back in her mind, she realized that he was waiting for her to tell him which sets she would dance with him. "The first minuet might be the opening set. Or did you mean the first minuet after the opening set?"

"I would be pleased to dance the first minuet with you, whether it is the opening set or not."

"The first minuet it is, then." Wanting to space out their dances, more for her pleasure than because the tabbies might gossip, she suggested, "Shall we say the third waltz? Or have you already promised it?"

"The third waltz is fine. The only dances I have bespoken are these two with you, and one with Lady Sarah."

Sarah, who was her best friend, had not been here when the Woodhursts arrived, so he must have requested the dance last night, at the Oglethorpe ball. Foolish as it was, Deborah was jealous . . . until she realized that her abrupt departure from the ballroom, and the ball, had made it impossible for him to bespeak a dance with her in advance. That thought, for some inexplicable reason, reminded her of the flowers Fairfax had brought her when he called this afternoon. Flowers for which she had not yet thanked him.

"Oh, Fairfax, you must think me the most rag-mannered of females! I was so awed by your ability to pull the truth from Diana that I forgot to thank you for your bouquet. The flowers are lovely! Especially the orchid. I have never received a bouquet with such a dazzling array of beautiful blooms. Were they grown in the succession house on your estate?" Then, before she forgot again, "I am sorry we were not at home when you called."

"I am glad the bouquet found favor with you. And yes, the flowers were grown at The Oaks. Gibbs—my head gardener—will be delighted when I convey your compliments." He smiled, and his blue-green eyes seemed to twinkle. "I will call again. What days are you At Home? Or do you and your mother not care for such a regimented schedule?"

"We are At Home on Tuesdays and Fridays."

He nodded, and Deborah wondered if he was committing that fact to memory. She wanted to ask him why he did not live in Mayfair or St. James's—she had been curious for weeks, since he mentioned it during his first call—but she feared that he might think she was prying. Before she could decide, they reached her family, and she lost her chance, at least for the nonce. Bowing over her hand, he thanked her for her company and conversation. Softly, he added, "I eagerly await the first minuet." Then, after bowing to her mother and a quiet word with Henry, Fairfax took himself off to greet the Mallorys and the Fairchilds, who had arrived during their promenade around the room.

Gazing after him, Deborah pondered what it was about him that drew the eye. He was neither tall nor short, fat nor thin. He wore a black velvet coat and white satin knee breeches, like many of the other men in the room, but it was he who captured her attention. And he who had captured her heart.

How might she capture his?

Contemplating the ways a young lady could bring herself to a gentleman's attention without risking her reputation, she realized there were very few of them. Quite a niggardly number, in fact, when one considered the many ways in which a gentleman could garner a lady's notice. But if she

wanted to win Fairfax's regard—and she did, very much—
she had to do *something*.

What, exactly, that something would be, she did not
know, only that it would not be bold or deceitful. Her sister
might resort to such shabby tricks, but Deborah would not.
If she could not win his heart fairly, then she did not deserve
him.

Michael strolled around the room, talking politics or
sports with the gentlemen, the latest *on dits* or the entertainments in store this Season with the ladies. And castigating
himself for a fool. He'd had a matchless opportunity to
make Deborah aware of his interest, but at the last second,
he'd shied away from such a soul-baring statement.

Would it have been so difficult to say, "Two waltzes
could not be misconstrued as a partiality for your company
because I am partial to it"? Or, "I am decidedly partial to
your company, so two waltzes could not be misconstrued"?
It must have been, since all he'd done was tell her that he enjoyed her company. He'd managed to tack on "very much"
at the end, but it was not very much at all compared to what
he could have said if he hadn't turned craven.

Never before had he shirked from responsibility, or not
done whatever was necessary to achieve a goal. That he had
failed now, on a matter of such personal importance, bothered him a great deal. But Almack's was not the place to
consider the matter—a fact that was borne in on him by the
man who came up behind him, leant over his shoulder, and
whispered, "Brown studies are not permitted within these
hallowed halls, old trout. The patronesses have rules, you
know."

The patronesses had dozens of rules, and changed them
at their whim. But that was another subject better not considered here. Turning, he met Dunnley's gray eyes, which
twinkled with merriment at having caught him out. "I am
surprised that you can still recognize a study of any color,"
Michael reposted. "I doubt you have had a serious thought
since we came down from Oxford." It was a gross exagger-
ation, and quite inaccurate, but such raillery had formed part

of their friendship since their days at Eton, when they'd teased each other about their scholarly habits—or the apparent lack thereof.

Theo was the only person with whom Michael could be himself, the only person who knew him well enough that teasing was natural. And Theo was the only person who teased him. Theo's brother, his uncles, and his late mother had done so when Michael was younger, but rarely did now.

"What is wrong?" Theo's question was accompanied by a searching look.

"Nothing." The hasty answer would not have convinced a child, even though Michael had bolstered it with a quick shake of his head. He was relieved when his friend did not press the matter, instead falling into step beside him.

Affairs of the heart were the viscount's purview—he had captured dozens of women's hearts over the years—but Michael was reluctant to air his concerns. Not only was Almack's far too public a place for such a discussion, but Theo had been full of strange—and disconcerting—questions this afternoon at White's. Michael had not even been able to drink his celebratory toast before Dunnley's arrival. Theo had probably paid calls on several ladies, too, but he didn't have a grandmother hell-bent on marrying him off to any female who would promise her a quiverful of great-grandchildren— preferably beginning within the twelvemonth. Even if Dunnley's grandmother had not passed to her heavenly reward fifteen years ago, if she were wishful of seeing him wed, she would not have resorted to shabby tricks to achieve her aim. Michael's grandmother was not so nice in her notions, for she hadn't scrupled to do just that.

Not wanting to think about grandmothers, scrupulous or otherwise, he turned to the question of his friend's questions. Michael only asked one, but he'd since thought of another. "Was there a reason for your questions this afternoon? Have you found it necessary to identify women in dark rooms, or dark gardens, recently?"

"No," Dunnley chuckled.

"You didn't tell me which ladies you could identify in that hypothetical dark room or garden."

"Tina Fairchild, Jani." Jani Brooks was Theo's mistress, and had been for several years, but he had not mentioned her of late. Lady Tina was a distant cousin of Theo's and had tagged after him since she'd been a toddler. "Perhaps Beth Weymouth and Sarah Mallory."

Michael wondered if his friend's answer was as equivocal as his own had been. Dunnley was no more interested in marrying Lady Tina than Michael was. Nor his mistress, even if Mrs. Brooks were willing to wed again, which she wasn't. Beth was Theo's eldest cousin's wife. But Sarah Mallory . . . Lady Sarah just might be the perfect wife for Theo, if the fire and emotion of her music were hints of a passionate nature.

Casting a quizzical gaze at his friend's face, Michael almost laughed aloud. Theo's bland expression revealed nothing, which said a great deal.

Well, well, well. This might prove to be a very interesting Season, indeed!

Chapter Twelve

T   *he day has certainly taken an interesting turn!* It had,
   in fact, been as full of twists and turns as a maze, but
as far as Deborah was concerned, Fairfax having singled her
out was by far the best one. And the most promising.

Steadfastly ignoring her sister—and, in turn, being ignored—she chatted with Sarah and Tina, and granted
dances to several gentlemen, including the first waltz to
Lord Dunnley. But diverting as her friends' and admirers'
conversation was, part of her mind was still puzzling over
Fairfax's cryptic remark. Glancing toward the far end of the
room, she waited impatiently for the musicians to finish tuning their instruments—a process that seemed to be taking
much longer than usual tonight. Or perhaps she was just
more eager than usual for the dancing to begin.

When the opening notes of the first set sounded, Deborah
smiled. *A minuet!*

A moment later, Fairfax bowed before her, then smiled
and offered his hand to lead her to the dance floor. "My
lady?"

Something in his inflection or his tone—or, perhaps, the
look in his eyes—made her feel as if she were the most important lady in the realm. As if she mattered more to him
than any other woman. A fanciful notion, to be sure, as foolish as it was pleasant, with no more substance than the air
she breathed, but it made her smile as she placed her hand in
his.

They took their places in the line of dancers, and Fairfax

glanced over at her and smiled again. Oh, she loved his smile! It, too, made her feel special, perhaps because his smiles were so rare. They hadn't been rare this evening, though. Indeed, far from it; he'd already bestowed several on her. They hadn't just been a polite upward curving of his lips; his blue-green eyes had seemed to smile, too. And each smile had made her heart flutter.

She wished she had a word to describe the color of his eyes. They were too blue to be called emerald, too green to be sapphire, not opaque enough to be aquamarine. She had once seen a painting of an American Indian, and the turquoises in the jewelry he wore had been closest to the color of the duke's eyes. They were, perhaps, a bit more green than she remembered the stones being—they were certainly more green than any turquoise she had ever seen—but not much.

Why she thought of his eyes in terms of gems, she could not imagine. Perhaps because the color was so unusual. Or because she valued a smile from his eyes more than a handful of diamonds and rubies. Whatever the reason, she treasured each and every smile, and she loved the color of his eyes.

"You look lovely this evening, Lady Deborah. I believe I neglected to tell you so earlier."

"Thank you, Your Grace. It is kind of you to say so." His compliment pleased her, perhaps more than it should. Deborah knew she was not looking her best this evening; the emotional turmoil of the past twenty-some hours had taken its toll. Also because she could not recall that he'd ever before complimented her appearance. Her musical performances and her dancing, yes, but not her looks. Generally, she preferred to be admired for her talent—she'd worked diligently to achieve her skill—but it was nice to know that he thought she was lovely. Very nice, indeed.

Emboldened by his praise, she dared to return a similar accolade. "You look very elegant tonight, but then, you always do."

Her words seemed to surprise him. And to please him. If the startled expression that crossed his face was an indication, he did not often receive such tributes. Or, perhaps, any compliments at all.

"Thank you, my lady."

Again, there was something different—something special—about the way he spoke the last two words. They sounded . . . almost like a caress, if such a thing was possible.

The lady behind her bumped the heel of Deborah's slipper. It was such a startling occurrence that she barely resisted the urge to look over her shoulder. The minuet's basic movements were simple enough that a child could perform them. The skill involved came from the grace with which a dancer performed the movements. The head held just so, the toe pointed. The curve of the arms. The line of the body during the bows or curtsies. Graceful flourishes of the hands. Almost anyone could dance the minuet; dancing it with style and flair was more difficult.

Deborah and her brothers and sister had been well schooled in the art of the minuet because it was their parents' favorite dance. Of all the gentlemen—younger gentlemen—of her acquaintance, Dunnley and Elston performed it best, their every movement exquisitely graceful. Fairfax danced it very well, too, but not with quite the same panache. The finest practitioners of the art, however, were Lord Bellingham and the Duke of Greenwich, with her father and the Earl of Tregaron almost as skilled.

"I am looking forward to the Opera on Saturday." And, indeed, she was. The fact that she would be in Fairfax's company for the entire evening played a significant role in her anticipation. "One of Mama's friends attended last night's performance, and she said Madame Grassini was better than ever before."

"I paid calls this afternoon with my grandmother, and a number of ladies said much the same thing, but I don't know if any of them attended the performance, or if they were repeating something they'd heard. Later, at White's, I heard Grassini's praises sung by several men who were present last night."

"You paid calls with your *grandmother?*" That was filial devotion, indeed! Deborah could think of a few men who occasionally paid calls with their mothers, but not many. And not often.

"For two hours I did, but I made several by myself first. Including my call at Kesteven House."

The second bump from behind caught Deborah with one foot in the air, and almost knocked her off balance. Fairfax saved her from a nasty tumble, then looked at her with concern. "Are you feeling unwell?"

Embarrassed—and decidedly flustered—she blurted, "The lady behind me bumped my foot again."

"Again?"

"She did it once before, but not quite as hard. And I had both feet on the ground then."

He glanced over his shoulder, directing a scorching look at the graceless clodpole. When he turned back, his lips were compressed into a tight, angry line. "Your sister."

"What?" Darting a look behind her, she met her twin's unrepentant gaze. *Why would Diana do such a thing?* It wasn't clumsiness, that was for certain. Diana knew the patterns of the minuet well, although she deemed it hopelessly old-fashioned, and danced it with careless grace. Deborah could think of two explanations for the bumping, but both seemed wildly improbable.

"Do you think your sister did it deliberately?"

"I—I don't know." It was one possibility, and if Diana were angry at her, Deborah would not have dismissed it. But Diana wasn't angry at her—or, rather, she had no reason to be—while she had every right to be angry at Diana. *She* was the one who'd been betrayed. *She'd* been dragged all over Town this afternoon, paying calls to convince the matrons of the *ton* that whatever gossip they might have heard grossly exaggerated the incident. *She'd* once again been made to feel like nothing more than half of a matching pair. Yet through it all, her sister had never admitted that she'd lied— not until the Dowager Duchess of St. Ives asked her outright if she had.

"A shilling for your thoughts, my lady."

"Shouldn't it be a penny, Your Grace?"

"I suspect yours are worth quite a bit more than a penny. You seem to be thinking quite hard."

Watching his face as she told him, Deborah did not understand why he frowned. But his only comment was, "I can't imagine anyone lying to Her Grace of St. Ives."

She thought her sister had considered it, for a moment or two. Diana was a facile prevaricator, but even she had quailed at the prospect of lying to the duchess, one of the *ton*'s most formidable beldames. Dubbed the "Tiny Tyrant" by her son, the diminutive duchess had reigned over the *beau monde* for decades. She had the power to make or break anyone's reputation—with the possible exception of members of the royal family, although most of them had destroyed their own.

"I know many young ladies find the prospect of calling on her daunting, but I have always liked her," Deborah admitted. "After her staunch partisanship today, I quite adore her."

"I have known her since I was a small boy, and I like her, too. I am glad to know she stood your champion today. I shall have to do something special to thank her."

She looked askance at him. He caught her gaze and asked, "What is it, my lady? Is aught amiss?"

"You make it sound as if no one ever takes my side. And as if I need a champion."

"Everyone needs a champion from time to time. And it does seem to me that your sister has things her way more often than you do."

Another bump, this one not as hard. Fairfax either felt it or recognized it for what it was because he turned to glare at Diana. Rapidly coming to the conclusion that her second explanation was correct, Deborah waited until the next turn, when there was no chance of being overheard, to tell him her suspicion. "I think Diana is dancing so close to eavesdrop on our conversation."

He considered the idea, glanced over his shoulder, then agreed. "You may be right, although I can't imagine why she would want to listen."

Then he smiled—a rather mischievous grin—and asked in a near whisper, "How do you suggest we foil her?"

"Foil her?"

"We could say nothing for the rest of the dance, or save any meaningful conversation until later, during the third waltz, or we could save it until tomorrow afternoon, if you would like to drive in the park with me?"

"I would enjoy driving in the park with you tomorrow." *An understatement if ever there was one!* "I think it will look a bit strange, to Diana and to others, if we remain silent for the rest of the minuet—it might seem we have quarreled— but it would probably be best if we limit ourselves to subjects in which Diana has no interest."

"Such as . . . ?"

"Music."

Her suggestion seemed to surprise him, but he accepted it readily enough. "Is there a particular aspect of music you wish to discuss?"

Deborah took a deeper than usual breath, wondering if she was brave enough to make the request she'd been considering since their rain-aborted drive in the park. "Do you remember last time we drove in the park?"

"Of course I do." His smile, as well as his tone, made it seem as if he remembered every moment of the time he had spent with her. "We both were drenched when it suddenly began to rain."

Her sister bumped into her again, straining to hear their low-voiced conversation. Deborah glared at her, but the duke's glower was fierce enough to cow the most stout-hearted warrior.

"Just before the skies opened, we were discussing the music of Bach. Johann Sebastian Bach, not the London Bach."

He nodded. "I remember. I also remember that you seemed to like his music as much as I do."

"I was wondering if you would like to perform one of his concerti for two harpsichords with me at the Duchess of Greenwich's musicale next month. Or, perhaps, the pieces for two harpsichords from *The Art of the Fugue*."

He was distinctly taken aback by her request, but he did not immediately refuse. "I have never performed in public, Lady Deborah."

"Why not?" She was truly curious. She had been playing for her parents' dinner guests since she was ten or eleven years old, and for other people's guests since she'd let down her hems, put up her hair, and gone into company.

"My grandmother thinks music is an ungentlemanly pastime."

"Is she acquainted with Lord Bellingham? Or Lord Marlowe?" They were the only peer musicians she knew who were above sixty.

"She knows Bellingham. I am not certain if she knows Marlowe."

"Does she consider Lord Bellingham a gentleman?" Deborah could not imagine anyone thinking the marquess was not.

"Of course she does. How could anyone believe otherwise?"

She smiled. "I was just thinking the same thing. He will be performing at the duchess's musicale."

Fairfax flushed a bit, but she could see no reason for embarrassment. When a possible explanation occurred to her, it seemed so ludicrous that she blurted, "Surely your grandmother cannot think musical performances are acceptable for a marquess, but not for a duke?"

"No!" He took a deep breath, as if rattled. Or, perhaps, bracing himself to explain. "I didn't mean she thinks performing music for the *ton*'s entertainment is beneath a duke's dignity. That is, she may—she has some antiquated notions of proper ducal behavior—but that isn't the reason she objects." Another deep breath. "She thinks music is a rather unmanly pursuit. That I should spend my time hunting and shooting, or racing my curricle, or . . ."

"Do you like hunting, shooting, and curricle racing?"

"Well, I don't *dis*like them, but I generally prefer more intellectual pursuits."

"Do you think it is beneath your dignity to perform at a *ton* event?"

"No."

Hoping she would not offend him, she said gently, "I understand your desire to please your grandmother. But you shouldn't have to do things contrary to your own inclinations in order to please her. After all, Fairfax, you are the duke. And you are an intelligent man—wise enough to know what you should and shouldn't do. Why hunt or shoot if you would rather play the harpsichord?"

He stared at her, unblinking. Fearing she had overstepped—greatly—she stammered, "I—I beg your pardon—"

"No, Deborah." He covered her hand with his. "You said nothing for which you need apologize. You only voiced opinions I have held for years."

Relieved, she smiled. Having come this far, she ventured another step, hoping to persuade him. "Then, if you don't think it is beneath your dignity to perform at a musicale, why shouldn't you?"

Surprisingly, he chuckled. "Game as a pebble, aren't you?"

"I don't know what that means, so I can't answer."

"In this case, my dear, it means that you weren't shy about asking for what you wanted." Then, serious again, he requested, "May I think about it for a day or two?"

"Of course."

"Thank you. I promise you an answer by Friday. Will you be attending the Enderby ball tomorrow night? And . . . um, I cannot remember what engagements, if any, I have Friday evening."

"I cannot recall where we are promised, either. If you haven't decided by tomorrow evening, you can give me your answer on Saturday."

He nodded, accepting her solution. "Are there two harpsichords at Greenwich House?"

"I believe so, but I am not altogether certain. I didn't want to inquire until I'd asked you to play, because I knew Tina would pester me with questions."

"Ask the duchess," he suggested dryly.

"I will." Then, because she wanted the decision to be his

alone, not influenced by other factors, she proposed an alternative. "If Greenwich House has only one harpsichord, one of Bach's sons—Wilhelm, I think—wrote a duet for two performers on one harpsichord."

"That might be better, unless there are two harpsichords at Kesteven House. Fairfax House has only one, although I could have the harpsichord from The Oaks—my estate near Kew—brought up to Town."

The minuet was rapidly drawing to an end, much to Deborah's regret. "I will talk to the duchess while you decide if you want to perform with me. Then—"

"Deborah, it is not a question of performing *with you,* but of performing at all. Regardless of what I decide about the Greenwich musicale, I would like to play the harpsichord duet with you."

"You would?" She smiled, delighted and very pleased.

"Indeed I would. In fact, if you have copies of both parts . . . Are the parts written separately, or are they on the same score?"

Frowning in concentration, she tried to summon a mental picture of the music. "I cannot recall. I haven't played it for several years."

"If you have the music here in Town, perhaps you will show it to me tomorrow. Then I will set my secretary the task of finding the score for me."

"I am almost certain it is here. I brought it last year, hoping to meet someone who would play it with me." The final notes of the minuet sounded, and she dropped into a curtsy.

Fairfax bowed, then led her from the dance floor. "May I make a request of you?"

"Of course you may. It is only fair, since I made one of you."

"Since your sister thwarted our plans to have supper together last night, might I be your supper partner at the Enderby ball? Or at one of the balls next week, if you are already promised to another gentleman tomorrow?"

She smiled again, more pleased than she could say. "I would be honored to have supper with you tomorrow night, Fairfax. Or at any ball," she added daringly, hoping he would understand the message underlying her words. "I enjoy your company and conversation."

"Thank you, Lady Deborah." Stopping, he bowed over her hand. "That is one of the nicest compliments I have ever received."

Flustered by the unexpected salute—his lips had brushed her gloved knuckles—and by his obvious pleasure, she was not certain what to say. "I d-didn't . . . It wasn't intended as a compliment, Your Grace. It is a fact—a simple statement of the truth."

"That is an even better compliment." He tucked her hand back into the crook of his arm, resting his hand over hers, and resumed walking. "I enjoy your company and conversation, too, my lady."

A shiver raced up her spine—part pleasure at his words, part a thrill at the caressing inflection he gave the honorific. "Thank you," she said. Then, more softly, "I am glad."

A few steps later, she darted a glance at him—and found him looking at her. "I think you need more—or better—friends."

"A duke has many acquaintances, but very few real friends."

Recognizing the truth of his words, she felt a pang of . . . something. "You have one more friend than you perhaps realized."

Their arrival at her mother's side prevented her from saying more. Prevented him from saying more, too. Smiling, he bowed over her hand again. "Thank you for the dance and your company, Lady Deborah."

"Thank you, Your Grace."

Watching him as he walked away, she could still feel the imprint of his lips against her glove.

Suddenly weak-kneed, she plopped down on a chair. *I have fallen head over heels in love with Fairfax, yet I don't know if he can tell Diana and me apart or not.*

Chapter Thirteen

She likes me! Michael felt the urge to dance a jig. But a duke who danced a jig at Almack's when not a single note of music was to be heard would suffer an even more ignoble fate than a duke who danced a jig down Bond Street at midday, so Michael restrained himself. But it was more difficult than it ought to have been.

Relinquishing Deborah's hand, Michael turned and walked away, his pace steady but measured, hoping that no one would greet him and that the next set would not be one he had promised. Deborah's "simple statement of fact" had delighted him. Her soft-voiced "You have one more friend than you perhaps realized" had demmed near unmanned him. Either would have had a powerful—and profound—impact. Hearing them together, one after the other, had almost brought him to his knees, and he needed a few moments of solitude to regain control of his rioting emotions.

Unfortunately, Almack's was not a place designed for solitary contemplation. Head down, hands clasped behind his back, he left the ballroom, nodding at the patronesses as he passed, and crossed the anteroom to the large apartment on the far side. Reaching the window, he gripped the sill with both hands, and stared blindly into the night.

He found it difficult to believe that he had so far forgotten himself as to kiss Deborah's hand in public. Not only that, he had chosen one of the most public settings imaginable—one in which the salute was certain to have been ob-

served. He didn't regret having done it—kissing a lady's
hand was one of the few ways a gentleman could show his
regard for her—but he did regret the location, and the fact
that he might have caused her embarrassment.

He had fallen tip over tail in love with Deborah. He was
not certain when his admiration and respect had deepened to
love, but they had. Unquestionably, they had.

His fingers relaxed, tension released like a spring uncoil-
ing. Propping a shoulder against the window frame, he pondered the wonder and the mystery of love. It was, he
thought, a force of nature, like waves crashing on a shore, or
the sun rising in the east. No doubt there were scientific explanations for love, too, but he preferred to enjoy magnifi-
cent natural phenomena without considering the rules and
laws governing their existence.

Perhaps love was why the urge to protect her that he'd
felt since the moment he'd met her had become, in the past
two days, an ineffable *need* to protect her. Last night, in
Lady Oglethorpe's garden, the fact that he did not have the
right to protect and comfort Deborah had pained him—a
throbbing ache in his chest. Tonight, the pain had not been
physical, but mental anguish that she'd had to hear her sister's cruel words.

No, it had been longer than two days. He'd felt the need
to protect her since his first call at Kesteven House, almost
a fortnight ago. He'd been angry that the marchioness had
not done more to stop Diana's sniping. And he'd done his
best to end it, without overstepping the bounds that con-
strained a gentleman's behavior.

Faintly, he heard the opening notes of the next set. In-
clining his head toward the door, he concentrated on the
music and, with relief, recognized the tune of a popular
country dance. Of the dozen or so dances yet to occur this
evening, he had bespoken only the first three waltzes—with
Sarah Mallory, Tina Fairchild, and Deborah, respectively—
so he returned to his ruminations.

Last night, Lady Kesteven had intervened promptly—
probably the moment she suspected that his conversation
with Diana was edging toward argument. He could not fault

the marchioness in that regard, but he could—and did—fault her and the marquess for not punishing Diana for what she had done last night.

The fact that she was here this evening seemed to indicate that her parents had chosen to overlook her lies and shocking behavior. To Lord and Lady Kesteven's credit, they had been as appalled as he to hear Diana's reasons for betraying her sister. But why the devil had they not demanded an explanation last night? Or earlier today? Then punished her for her transgressions.

If she were his daughter, Michael would lock her in the nearest dungeon until she had learnt courtesy and decorum and the wages of sin. How would she learn that actions have consequences if she never had to face them?

Diana sowed a lot of discord and hurt, but seldom had to reap what she'd sown. But that was about to change. He would do everything in his power to ensure that it did, particularly if Deborah was the person being hurt.

He laughed wryly at his bold assertion. He'd never attempted to wield power outside of Parliament or Westminster, but he did not doubt that he could. If Dunnley was right—and he invariably was about such things—then Fairfax, both dukedom and man, had almost as much clout in the social arena as in the political realm.

It was time and past for Deborah to have a champion. And what better man to fight on her behalf than he, who loved her?

It was also time—long past time—for Diana to receive her comeuppance. He was just the man for that task, too, particularly if she continued to torment her sweet sister. He did not know if Diana had intended to trip Deborah during the minuet or merely to eavesdrop. Nor did he care. But now that he knew Diana would not scruple at deception or dishonesty, he would be on his guard. He suspected—strongly suspected—that her ultimate goal was his title and fortune, but she was doomed to failure. No matter what she did.

Michael had a trick or two to play in this game. And he had an ace up his sleeve.

One that he could, in all honor, play.

And would play if Diana continued her scheming.
With a little help from his cousin.

Fuming, Diana watched the Duke of Fairfax lead her sister to the dance floor for a second set, this one a waltz. How dare he ignore her! She had apologized, and he'd accepted her apology. That should have marked the end of his displeasure, yet he'd ignored her all evening.

Because of him, she'd sat out three sets this evening. A number that would soon increase if no one solicited her hand for this waltz. Or if the patronesses did not present her with a partner. None of them had made the slightest attempt to do so this evening, although they'd provided partners for other girls. No doubt the blame for that could be laid at the duke's door, too; he had been talking with three of them when she and her family had arrived.

Sir Edward Smithson bowed before her. "Will you honor me with this dance, my lady?"

"I ought to refuse since you abandoned me last night, but I will grant your request." Despite all the problems that arose in its wake, his desertion paled in comparison with the humiliation of sitting out another set.

"Ah, Lady Diana. I would have begged your pardon immediately, but I was not entirely certain of your identity. Please forgive me. Did Martin not explain that I was called away last night?"

"No. He said only that you'd left the ball earlier." It was difficult to stay angry at a man when he was holding her so closely, even though his explanation was highly improbable.

"I am sorry. I shall take him to task for his lapse."

"Perhaps you should take yourself to task for not telling me yourself."

It was a bold statement for a young lady to make. An expression of annoyance crossed Sir Edward's face, then he dropped his gaze, giving every appearance of contrition. "You are quite right, Lady Diana. I did not behave as a gentleman ought, and I cannot, in honor, berate Martin for his failure to do something I myself failed to do."

Diana had pretended remorse often enough to recognize

the ploy. But she could hardly cut up stiff about his insincere apology when all the ones she'd made today had been equally false.

After a minute or so, he drew her closer. "You seem a bit down-pin this evening. Is something wrong?"

Has he not heard what happened, or is he testing me? Unable to decide, she deemed it best not deviate too much from the story she'd told last night—and countless times today. "I attempted to play a joke on my sister and Fairfax at Lady Oglethorpe's ball, but it did not work out as I'd planned. Now, they—and my parents—are angry at me."

"Fairfax has never appreciated a good joke, but I am sorry to hear that your family is upset." His hand slid up her back, trailed by a pleasant tingle. "Were your sister's friends involved?"

"No, but they are angry at me, too." Not that she cared for their opinions, but including them might garner her a bit more sympathy.

"I daresay that if you and I put our heads together, we could come up with a scheme for you to get back at them. If, that is, you wish to turn the tables on them." He shrugged. "It seems only fair."

There was nothing she wanted more, but it would not do to appear too eager. "That might be amusing. What do you have in mind?"

"Nothing yet, but I will think on it. If you grant me a waltz tomorrow night at the Enderby ball, we can talk more then."

Discussing their plans under the noses of the high sticklers was vastly appealing. It added a fillip of danger—and of pleasure. "Very well, Sir Edward. Shall we say the second waltz?"

He nodded, smiling. "The second waltz."

Suddenly, his smile seemed . . . almost predatory. She knew then, with utter certainty, that his offer had not been born of altruism, but because he, too, sought revenge. Against whom she did not know—yet—but she was quite sure it wasn't her sister. Fairfax seemed an equally unlikely choice, as did Sarah Mallory and Tina Fairchild, but even so,

Diana was convinced that Sir Edward intended to settle an old score.

Well, well, well! The Season is becoming more interesting by the day. She had no objection to helping the baronet mete out vengeance in return for his assistance in achieving her goal. Not that she intended to tell him her real objective.

As he whirled Deborah into a turn, Michael realized, with some astonishment, that he could remember none of the sets he'd danced this evening, nor the ladies with whom he'd danced them, save for the opening minuet and the waltzes. The minuet—or, perhaps, Deborah's conversation and questions—had led to the revelation that he loved her. The waltzes had proven enlightening, too, if only because of the different feelings they had evoked. Waltzing with Lady Sarah Mallory had been pleasant and enjoyable; the second waltz, with Lady Tina Fairchild, had been enjoyable and amusing. This one, with Deborah, was wondrous—like dancing high in the heavens among the stars. But it was also torturous because, with the patronesses, tabbies, and quidnuncs watching, he could not hold her as closely as he wished.

He smiled, happy just to be in the company of the woman he loved. "Are you enjoying yourself this evening, my lady?" He had discovered during their first dance that he derived great pleasure from calling her "his lady." Probably more than was wise, given that she was unaware of his feelings.

"Yes, I am. More than I thought I would."

The qualifier surprised him. Concerned him, too. "Did you not expect to enjoy yourself this evening?"

"I . . ." Her gaze dropped to the vicinity of the top button of his waistcoat. "I was a bit worried about how we would be received."

"Because of your sister's deceit last night?"

She nodded, clearly distressed, but he was not certain why she was upset.

"Surely you did not expect *your* reception to be different?"

Her teeth biting her lower lip, she nodded, then softly confessed, "I did. Or, rather, I was worried that it would be. Last night quite a number of people heard Diana say that I was party to her deception."

"And the same number heard your denials."

"B-but it was just my word against hers." She met his gaze, her beautiful blue eyes clouded with worry. "How could they know which of us was telling the truth?"

"Any number of reasons, my dear. Your sister was at the center of the controversy. It was she who apologized. And she who was pulled away by your mother, for all the world like a contumacious child."

Drawing her closer, he quietly added a final argument. "Unless the *ton* decided over the winter to eschew gossip— an unlikely possibility at best—then at least a dozen ears were straining to hear your sister's apology to me and our subsequent conversation. Her final explanation was loud enough to be overheard by people nearby, even if the rest of what she said was not. And her last statement vindicated you absolutely and indisputably."

She winced, and hoping to comfort her, he reduced the distance between them by another inch. "In addition to all that, I have danced with you twice this evening, and ignored her. If nothing else, that will make it clear to the *beau monde* that you were her victim as surely as I was."

"Only to people who can tell us apart. And there are only two people here tonight who can—my mother and Henry."

Much as he wanted to tell her that he also had that ability, this was not the time for such a revelation—last night was proof of that!—nor was Almack's the place for it. "I suspect there are others of whom you are unaware."

Deborah's gaze scanned the room. When her eyes again met his, a wrinkle between her brows indicated her puzzlement. "Neither Beth nor Elston is here tonight."

"I meant, I suspect there are other people who can tell you and your sister apart. People whom you don't realize can distinguish between you."

"Who?" Then, a moment later, "*You? Can you tell us apart?*"

He almost told her then. Almost. But the risks were still too great: They were still at Almack's, and he still dared not take the chance of her sister finding out. Instead, he answered Deborah's questions with a smile—one she could interpret any way she wished.

Before his eyes, Deborah drooped like a flower deprived of water and sunlight. Her smile faded, then disappeared; her head dipped toward the floor; her shoulders sagged. After a moment, she rallied, but not without an effort.

Michael knew that he'd disappointed her, and damned himself for it. Had she seemed aware of her sister's designs on him, he might well have told her then and there, and resigned himself to dealing with the consequences. Unfortunately—or perhaps not—Deborah was blissfully oblivious of her sister's intent. But, regrettably, also unmindful of his plight. Thus, if he were to confess his ability to tell them apart, not only would he increase the odds of Deborah's sister learning his secret, but he also would run the risk that Deborah's love for her sister would blind her to her twin's predilection for perfidy. If that proved to be the case, it would be he, not Diana, who plummeted in Deborah's esteem—a consequence that would sound the death knell to his hopes and dreams.

Of course, Deborah would be more likely to believe him if she knew him better. That was his goal for the nonce. He could not expect her to reciprocate his feelings, once he apprised her of them, until she knew more about him. About the man beneath the ducal façade.

How can I best—and most easily—do that? Most easily for me and for Deborah? Music had been the subject of the conversation that led to her revelations, and could, perhaps, serve the same purpose for him.

"Deborah, have you had an opportunity to ask the duchess if there are two harpsichords at Greenwich House? Or has she been engaged in conversation whenever you attempted to do so? She and your mother and Lady Tregaron seem to be having a long—and rather lively—discussion this evening."

She laughed, the sound as delicate and rippling as an

arpeggio. "Indeed they are. Mama and Lady Tregaron suddenly realized earlier this evening that they are hosting balls one night after the other, and they have been comparing notes ever since."

"How can that be? Both invitations were sent a month or more ago."

"I know." A little giggle escaped, thwarting her attempt to resume her usual dignified decorum. "I don't understand it, either. Sarah and I have known all along that her parents' ball is the day before ours, but somehow it escaped Mama's and Lady Tregaron's notice until this evening."

She shook her head, still amazed at her mother's obliviousness. "I believe Her Grace is commiserating and offering advice. And probably thanking heaven that she chose to have a musicale this year. But I was able to ask her earlier. She *thinks* there is another harpsichord in the schoolroom wing, but she isn't certain. She said that she would check tomorrow." Bemusement pleated her brow, her beautiful blue eyes beseeching him to explain the incomprehensible. Then, in a fierce whisper, she blurted, "How could anyone not know how many harpsichords they have?"

Before he'd formulated an answer, she said, in a measured tone as if speaking her thoughts aloud, "I know that Greenwich House is quite large, but even so . . . I daresay I could list the musical instruments at every one of my father's estates, even those we rarely visit. And you knew there was only one harpsichord at Fairfax House, even though, by all accounts, you never live there."

"I spent two Seasons at Fairfax House—the most recent, three years ago. And, like you, I know what instruments can be found at each of my estates, even the most far-flung ones. But Her Grace's interest in music may not be as strong as ours. Or maybe it was when she was younger, but has waned over the years."

"Perhaps you are right. She did say there was an old clavichord, and asked if that would serve. I . . . I said I wasn't sure." She glanced away, her cheeks flushed a delicate rose. "I have heard both instruments played, of course, but not together. I wouldn't think they would blend very well."

"I have never heard them played together, either, but I suspect the clavichord would overpower the harpsichord."

Nodding in agreement, Deborah smiled. Given his desire to continue basking in the glow of her regard, Michael knew he would agree to perform the duet with her if the music was not beyond his abilities. "If I am going to have the harpsichord at The Oaks brought up to Town, there is no reason it couldn't be moved from Fairfax House to Greenwich House for the musicale. Actually—"

"But if you do that, you won't be able to practice!"

He leant in to confide something else. Something no one knew. "For the past several weeks, I have been debating whether I should move to Fairfax House for the Season. If I decide to perform with you at the duchess's musicale, I will definitely move to Town." With a rueful smile, he confessed, "I will need the time I usually spend traveling each day for extra practice."

"May I ask you a question, Your Grace?"

He wanted to shake her for such unnecessary formality, chide her for her hesitation, kiss her to reassure her. Instead, he drew her another inch closer. "Fairfax, please. And of course you may ask me a question. As many as you like, whenever you wish."

"Ever since you first mentioned your estate near Kew, I have wondered why you prefer to live there instead of in Town."

It was a chance to tell her something about his life. About himself. Almack's was not the place he would have chosen for his first attempt at soul baring—given a choice, it was the last place he would have picked—but this was the best opportunity he was likely to have tonight. Michael was determined to make the most of it.

If he remembered how.

His gaze riveted to hers, he sent a prayer winging heavenward and dug deep within himself. "I am, at heart, a country gentleman. I prefer the relaxed pace and simpler pursuits of country life to the frantic whirl of activity in Town, but my position requires that I spend the spring, and most of the winter, here. My estate at Kew is a small park, like most residences along the Thames, but living there, I feel as if I am in the country. I wake up to the sound of bird calls, can walk or ride around the grounds every morning, see vegetables and herbs growing in the kitchen garden. The house dates from the reign of Elizabeth—small but snug, and quite lovely. Compared to St. James's Square, The Oaks is pastoral. Serene."

"It sounds lovely." It was the merest breath of sound, as if she'd spoken her thoughts aloud.

Encouraged by her rapt attention, Michael nodded. "It is. There are disadvantages to living so far from Westminster, but, overall, I prefer it."

She smiled. "I can understand why you would. There are days when I wish I could escape to the country."

"Perhaps in a week or two, when the weather is a bit warmer, I can get up a riding party to Richmond, and show you The Oaks."

"I could do that—find a date that suits most of our friends and make the arrangements. If . . . if you would like me to, that is."

The idea of the two of them working together was appealing. Vastly appealing. "I would like that. Thank you. I only ask that you choose a Wednesday—"

"Because Lords won't be in session." She nodded. "More gentlemen will accept the invitation if the excursion is on Wednesday, I think, because they won't have to worry that they might miss an important debate."

"Exactly so, my lady." He smiled, approval mingled with delight. "Then, if you are sure you don't mind making the arrangements, I will leave everything in your capable hands."

"Perhaps tomorrow, during our drive in the park, we can discuss what you have in mind and whom you wish to invite."

"An excellent idea. Also, if possible, we should decide what duet to play. I know the duchess's musicale is next month, but I don't remember the date."

"May the twelfth."

"That is less than a month away!" Michael's stomach knotted at the thought.

"Four weeks from tomorrow."

"That isn't a great deal of time. I think it would be best not to attempt a concerto. We can probably find five or seven willing string players—however many are required—but two of the best are likely to return to their estate ere then, and less skilled musicians will need more time to learn their parts."

"I hadn't considered that." From her pensive tone, he guessed that she was thinking of the same men he was—Weymouth, a cellist, and Elston, a violist—since their wives were members of "The Six." "The fewer people involved, the easier it will be to schedule rehearsals."

"Yes. We need to speak to your mother about practicing together. If she has no objection, I will have the harpsichord moved to Kesteven House. You can't come to Fairfax House without ruining your reputation unless your father or brother, as well as your mother or a chaperone, accompanies you. And if your family is there, I would spend more time acting as host than rehearsing."

"You speak as if you have already decided."

It wasn't quite a question, but since the waltz was almost at an end, Michael chose to treat it as one. To reveal a bit more of himself—and his feelings—to her. "I told you I would like to play with you, Deborah. If the music isn't beyond my abilities, I will perform a duet with you at the duchess's musicale."

"Just like that?"

"Yes."

A frown momentarily creased her brow. "Why?"

"Because you asked me to."

Chapter Fourteen

Thursday, 14 April 1814

Because you asked me to. The words had bounced through Deborah's brain all night, ricocheting from one side of her skull to another, until it seemed their echo would never fade. The phrase—and the enigmatic smile Fairfax had given her when she'd asked if he could tell her and her sister apart—competed for her attention until dawn, when she had finally fallen asleep, exhausted. And dreamt of him.

When she awoke, the morning was half gone, but her thoughts were still a tangled jumble. Propping herself against the pillows, she rang for Ogden, hoping the middle-aged maid would bring a tray of tea and toast, not just a cup of chocolate. The dresser, wise to the ways of the twins, did just that. After a searching look at her favorite's face, she plumped up the pillows and bade her charge to ring when she was ready to dress.

As she sipped tea and nibbled on a piece of toast, Deborah pondered whether any man, other than her father and brothers, had ever done something just because she'd asked. Last Season, her admirers had brought glasses of lemonade or punch when she'd requested one, or walked in Hyde Park instead of driving, but that was not at all the same thing as Fairfax agreeing to perform a duet with her at a musicale. She sensed that he was a very private man, perhaps even a bit shy—at least outside of Parliament and Westminster, where, according to her father, the duke was a gifted speaker and a force to be reckoned with. Sensed, too, that tonight

Fairfax had shown her a side of himself that few people had ever seen.

Slipping out of bed, she danced around the room, feeling almost giddy with delight. Almost better than the thought that Fairfax admired her was knowing that his admiration was hers alone, not something shared with her twin. Deborah did not begrudge her sister a man's love and esteem; she just did not want to share it.

With Fairfax, Deborah knew that she had nothing to fear. His reaction to Diana's apology last night had made it quite clear that he found her behavior contemptible. Nor had he been pleased with Diana's repeated attempts to eavesdrop during the minuet.

But, an inner voice cautioned, *just because he did not allow Diana to see that rare side of himself last night, does not mean that he will never allow her to see it.*

The wise little voice was right, of course. But even so, Deborah thought that her sister might find it difficult to regain the duke's favor.

If, in fact, he could tell the two of them apart.

Why did he not answer when I asked him if he could? It was merely a variation of the question that had plagued her all night, but Deborah was no more certain of the answer in sunlight than she'd been under the moon's glow.

Reaching for the bellpull, she rang for Ogden, then wandered into the dressing room to decide what to wear this afternoon. Not only did she have the drive in the park with Fairfax to look forward to, but also showing him the duet scores. Perhaps he would even play for her. Or with her.

Deborah spun another turn, hugging her happiness to herself.

Diana slid an arm from beneath the quilt and groped for the bellpull, wondering why no one had brought her chocolate. After last night's debacle, she needed a new tactic to win the duke's attention away from her sister. Something that would rivet his attention on her. Something . . .

Jumping out of bed, she ran to the dressing room and plucked the primrose silk ball gown from its peg. If she had a suitable shawl to wear with it, and if she could convince her sister that they should wear the gowns to the opera on Saturday, Diana could achieve two goals at once. She could wear the unfortunate gown and ensure that the duke's attention never wavered.

After she altered the neckline, that is.

After his morning ride and breakfast, Michael surprised Sanders, two footmen, and a maid by going to the music room instead of his study. He spent a few minutes searching for *The Art of the Fugue*, considerably longer studying the three movements for two harpsichords, each of which had two sections. The two *contrapunctus* movements both had a *rectus* and an *inversus;* the fugue movement also had two contrasting sections. In all three movements, the two harpsichord parts appeared to be about equally difficult—somewhat to his regret; he'd been halfheartedly hoping that one would be easier. Slowly playing through all three movements, wincing every time he struck a wrong note, then repeating the exercise—and the wincing—for the second harpsichord part was enough to convince him that neither part was beyond his ability. A challenge, perhaps, but nothing he could not master with practice.

Hours and hours of practice.

Michael was willing to spend the necessary time if doing so would increase his opportunities to see—and court—Deborah. But to have the extra time, he would have to move to Fairfax House.

Removing his spectacles—and not at all certain how he felt about Deborah seeing him wearing them—he picked up the score and went in search of his secretary.

And found him, as expected, in his small office adjacent to Michael's study.

"Good morning, Your Grace." Ian Drummond rose to greet his employer.

"Good morning, Mr. Drummond." Michael sat in the chair in front of Drummond's desk, set the score aside, donned his spectacles again, and began reading and signing the pile of letters awaiting his attention. When he finished,

Drummond had his notebook open and a pencil poised to take notes.

A quiet Scot in his late thirties whose quick wit masked a brilliant mind, Ian Drummond had been Michael's secretary since he'd reached his majority and formally taken up the reins and responsibilities of the dukedom. Drummond had once been a talented, extremely successful barrister, but left the law after learning that a client for whom he'd just won an acquittal was guilty of the heinous crime. Michael's solicitor had advised against hiring the former barrister, but Michael had taken a chance on the Scotsman and had never regretted his decision.

"What else do you have for me this morning, Ian?"

"Invitations, sir. Later this afternoon, I should have all the information you requested for your next speech in Lords." Initially, Drummond had been unwaveringly formal, but after two or three years, Michael had limited his secretary to only one "Your Grace" a day, and had himself relaxed enough to occasionally call the Scotsman by his first name.

The stack of invitations was soon sorted into accept and reject piles, the latter much larger than the former; reports from the bailiffs of two of the dukedom's estates summarized and detailed instructions issued regarding the questions and problems raised. When an arched eyebrow produced nothing more, Michael picked up *The Art of the Fugue*. "I need another copy of this score."

"Another copy of the score," Drummond muttered, his flummoxed expression one that Michael had never seen before. "Do you recall where you obtained this one, Your Grace?"

"No," Michael said cheerfully, enjoying—probably more than he should—having stumped his redoubtable secretary. "You might try Longman's or Napier's."

"Longman's or Napier's," the former barrister echoed, in much the same tone he'd have said "Timbuktu."

"In Cheapside and Lincoln's Inn Fields, Ian, not the outer reaches of Mongolia. Longman has a second shop on . . . I don't remember where. And you can try Birchall's on New Bond Street."

While the secretary's pencil was still skimming across the page, Michael made his second request. "Where will I find the best harpsichords in London?"

"Down the hall to your left, sir. And at Fairfax House and the Hanover Square assembly room."

Hiding a smile at the other man's dry tone, Michael did his best to match it. "Quite possibly. But if I wanted to buy another one, in which shops will I find the best instruments?"

"One in each of your homes isn't enough?"

"Possibly not."

"Should this possibly necessary harpsichord be Italian, Flemish, English, French, or German, sir? Two manuals or one? Two or three strings per note? Gilded, painted, inlaid, veneered, or plain? And how soon would you want it, if you were to decide you need another one?"

Michael blinked at the spate of questions, knowing that his secretary was an appreciative listener, but not a performer. "Probably English, since I will want it immediately. Two manuals, three strings. The finish is not important, as long as the instrument is attractive."

The Scotsman darted a glance at him, then returned to his task. Finally, after completing his notes and another glance, he ventured, "Your Grace, may I ask why you need—might need—a second harpsichord?"

"You may ask, Drummond, if you cease the 'your graceing.' You are already well over your quota for the day."

Abashed, the secretary rubbed his nose. "Sorry, sir. It was unintentional."

Michael nodded, accepting the apology, leaned back in his seat, and removed his spectacles. "I have been asked to play a duet for two harpsichords at the Duchess of Greenwich's musicale."

Auburn brows soaring, the older man goggled. "And you agreed?"

"I agreed to consider it. Having done so, I will agree to perform."

"Her Grace will love that," Drummond muttered.

Deliberately misunderstanding, Michael agreed. "Her Grace of Greenwich will, no doubt, be pleased, although she has never heard me play." He met the other man's "you know I meant our duchess" look with a bland smile. Which faltered at the next question.

"If the Duchess of Greenwich didn't ask you to play, who did?"

"Another lady."

"Must be a special lady." The soft-voiced retort sounded almost hopeful. Drummond was as anxious as the dowager to see the duke married and the succession secured.

"Yes." Michael's tone, while pleasant, did not encourage further questions. He had no intention of confiding Deborah's name to his secretary, even though he trusted the man, and his discretion, implicitly.

"One more thing, Drummond." Michael had deliberately saved this item on his mental agenda for last. "We will be moving to Fairfax House within the next few days."

"We will?" The Scotsman lifted his hands to cover his ears, then removed them and frowned. "My hearing must be failing. I heard no surprised exclamations earlier, nor do I hear the bustle that usually accompanies our removal from one residence to another."

"You are the first to know. We will move as soon as you and Sanders make the necessary arrangements."

"Perhaps you will wait until tomorrow afternoon to inform Her Grace." There was a faint but hopeful hint of query to the words.

"I hadn't planned on it. Is there some reason I should wait until then?"

"It is my half day off," the secretary reminded him. "And I would prefer not to be present when you inform Her Grace."

Michael hid a smile, well aware that his grandmother's reaction was likely to be explosive. "I plan to tell my grandmother this morning. She may choose to remain at The Oaks if she wishes." He devoutly hoped that she would. His life would be much less trying—and his courtship of Deborah easier, not to mention much less likely to come to the dowager's notice—if she did.

"In fact"—he pulled out his watch and rose to his feet—"I intend to tell Sanders now, then my grandmother."

Drummond nodded, his expression glum. "I will consult with Sanders and begin making arrangements, sir."

Deborah was practicing the second harpsichord part of the twelfth movement of *The Art of the Fugue* when Fairfax was announced. After greeting her mother and sister, he spent several minutes in quiet conversation with the marchioness, looking up only once, when Deborah's fingers faltered as her concern—and her fear that something was wrong—mounted. His smile reassured her that all was well, and although she wondered what they were discussing, the intricate fingering of the section she was playing soon demanded all her attention.

When she finished the movement, she glanced over her shoulder—and was started to find him and her mother standing behind her. After he greeted Deborah, her mother explained, "Diana and I are going to pay calls this afternoon, so while you and Fairfax practice your duet, Ogden will serve as your chaperone. We should be back in time for tea, but if we aren't, don't get so lost in the music that you forget your duties as a hostess."

She kissed Deborah's cheek, then crossed to the bellpull.

"Mama, I believe you are mistaken." Diana rose to her feet on the words and was now looking daggers at Fairfax and Deborah.

"How so, dear?" The marchioness rang for Ogden, then turned to the three of them.

"The last time His Grace took Deborah for a drive in the park, he promised he would take me next."

Deborah's cheeks flamed in mortification, not only at her sister's audacity in reminding Fairfax of his promise, but also for expecting him to keep it after her deception and lies Tuesday night. Wanting to sink, and uncertain whether she should do or say anything, Deborah darted at glance at Fairfax.

"I said I would take you for a drive *another time,* Lady Diana, not the next time." Fairfax's tone was only slightly frosty, but it, coupled with his rigid bearing, condemned Diana's behavior. "You are otherwise engaged this afternoon, so we will defer our drive."

"I can make calls anytime—"

"You are paying calls with me this afternoon, Diana." Despite the marchioness's implacable tone, Diana opened her mouth to protest. Any words she might have uttered were overridden by their mother's next command. "Go up and get your bonnet and spencer. *Now.*"

Too embarrassed even to peek at Fairfax, Deborah watched her sister flounce out of the room. No doubt everyone present knew that, in addition to paying calls, Diana would also be receiving a frightful scold. Probably before the carriage turned out of Hanover Square.

Turning to the cabinet in which she kept her music, Deborah made a pretense of searching for the duet. Behind her, she heard, as if from a distance, her mother apologizing to Fairfax for both Diana's behavior and her own departure. In that same vague way, Deborah was aware of Ogden's entrance, her mother's instructions to the maid, and her mother wishing her a pleasant afternoon. Even more vaguely, Deborah heard Fairfax issue a sharp order. But not until he slipped his arm around her waist and guided her to the nearest chair, then pressed her head toward her knees, was Deborah truly aware of anything except her acute discomfiture.

"I am not going to swoon." She propped her elbows on her legs and covered her face with her hands.

"You are very pale." Fairfax's concern was apparent in his voice, as well as in the protective arm he'd wrapped around her shoulders.

With every moment that passed, her embarrassment increased, but the hazy, faraway sensation began to recede.

The longer she waited, the harder it would be to face him. Deborah sat upright, folding her hands in her lap and staring down at them. "I beg your pardon, Fairfax. I am not usually so . . . missish." Clenching her hands more tightly together, she dragged in a breath. "I also want to apologize for my sister—"

"No." He covered her hands with his, his touch warm but fleeting. "Your sister is quite capable of apologizing, should she wish to do so."

"'Tis jealous Lady Diana is," Ogden opined. "Make no mistake about it."

"J-jealous?" Perplexed, Deborah looked over at the maid. "Jealous of what?"

"Of you, my lady. She has been for a long time."

"No, Ogden." Deborah shook her head to emphasize the words. "You are mistaken."

"Nay, lass, I am not." The maid's eyes were kind, but her tone was resolute.

"But Diana has no reason to be jealous of me!"

"Mebbe, mebbe not." Ogden shrugged. "But iffen she has set her cap for His Grace, and he's a-courting you—"

"He isn't courting me—"

"I am." Fairfax's warm hand again covered hers.

"—then your sister may feel she has reason to be jealous," the maid finished, ignoring both interruptions.

Distracted both by his words and the feeling of being almost in his embrace, Deborah glanced at him in surprise. "You are?"

He bent his head closer to hers, catching her gaze. "I am. Unless you object . . . ?" He arched a brow, inviting her to state her preference.

"I don't object." Her voice sounded as breathless as if she'd just run a footrace—and matched the pounding of her heart.

His smile dawned like the most glorious sunrise, first curving his lips, then brightening his eyes. "I am very glad to hear it, my lady."

A thrill coursed down her spine at his emphasis on the last two words. They again seemed both a verbal caress and an endearment—almost a claiming.

"Ahem!"

At the maid's admonishment, Deborah straightened, a blush staining her cheeks when she realized that she'd leant closer to Fairfax. Still smiling, he brushed the back of one finger against the flag of color, then trailed it down her cheek to trace the line of her jaw.

"Lady Deborah, I thought you and His Grace were going to practice duets on the harpsichord." Ogden's reminder brought Deborah abruptly back to the present.

"Yes, we are." She rose to her feet, aided by Fairfax's hand under her elbow. His touch was, as always, gentle yet firm and supportive, but not nearly as pleasant as having his arm around her. Improper as such a thought was—and it was improper enough to heat her cheeks again—it did not feel *wrong*. But even so, she ducked her face to avoid his gaze.

"Don't be embarrassed, darling girl."

The fond tone of his whispered words—and the endearment—sent another frisson tingling down her spine. And all the way to her toes, which curled inside her slippers. But despite the pleasurable sensation—or, perhaps, because of it—she wondered yet again if he could tell her and Diana apart. In light of his declaration, the question loomed larger in her mind.

Focusing on the matter at hand, the task of choosing what to play at the Duchess of Greenwich's musicale, she said, "I have not yet heard from the duchess, so I still don't know if there are two harpsichords at Greenwich House or only one. Do you think we should play the duet by Wilhelm Friedemann Bach? It requires only one instrument," she reminded him.

"I am not going to answer that question until I have both seen the score and attempted to play it." His smile removed any possible sting from the words. "But if I have another harpsichord moved to Fairfax House, that same instrument could be moved to Greenwich House the day of the musicale. If the duchess is amenable, of course."

"You would be willing to do that?" Given his diffidence about performing, Deborah was surprised that he was willing to go to such lengths.

"Yes, if we decide that we want to play some of the movements from *The Art of the Fugue*. I played through them this morning, and although they are challenging, I believe I can master them in time."

She handed him the duet, then turned away to move a second chair, which a footman had carried from the dining room earlier, in front of the keyboard. An instant after her hands curled over the crest rail, Fairfax's hands came to rest on either side of hers, embracing her from behind and halting her progress. And her breath.

"I will move it." Despite his words, he made no move to release her.

Deborah darted a panicked glance at Ogden, relieved to see the maid's eyes were on the flounce she was mending. As she breathed a sigh of relief, Fairfax's cheek brushed hers. Or maybe 'twas hers that rubbed against his. She trembled, either at the pleasurable sensation or with fear of discovery. He hummed, a sound that came from deep in his chest, and said, "This is nice, isn't it?"

Nice was not the word she would have used, but Deborah nodded. Which again rubbed their cheeks together. Shivering, she quietly entreated, "Fairfax!" but the quavering word sounded more imploring than exhorting.

His chuckle was the merest wisp of sound. "I will behave if you will save a waltz for me tonight."

He stepped back, allowing her to slip past him. "I thought you wanted the supper dance? Have you changed your mind?"

"I want both, darling girl."

"You may have both—but only if you behave."

"The first waltz?"

Pleased by his choice, she nodded. "Yes, the first waltz."

Once they were seated side by side at the harpsichord, he peered at the score, then sighed. "You are about to see something few members of the *ton* have ever seen."

See or hear? Aware that he rarely, if ever, performed in company, she wondered if he'd misspoken. And was charmed when he pulled a pair of spectacles from his pocket and perched them on his nose. They made him look quite the scholar, but also boyishly endearing.

She hid a smile as he raised his voice to warn, "Mrs.

Ogden, if you are a music lover, you may wish to cover your ears."

They played through the duet twice, with Fairfax wincing whenever he struck a wrong note. She grimaced at her mistakes, too, and considering that she had played the piece many times, there were quite a number of them. Far more than there had been earlier, but it was disconcerting, in a pleasurable way, to have him sitting so close beside her, his coat sleeve brushing her arm from time to time and sending tremors rippling down her arm and into her fingers.

"This is a good choice for the duchess's musicale," Fairfax said after their second attempt. Pulling out his pocket diary, he made note of the duet's title, composer, and publisher. "Tomorrow, I will have my secretary search for the score, so I can practice at home."

"We will need to play another piece, too."

He picked up *The Art of the Fugue.* "Do you know all three of the movements for two harpsichords?"

"No, only the first two."

"In that case, I suggest we play your favorite *contrapunctus* movement and the fugue."

"Why not both *contrapunctus* movements?"

Grinning, he handed her the score. "Because if I am going to learn three new pieces for this musicale, you ought to have to learn at least one."

"That seems fair," she agreed, hiding a smile. "The twelfth and eighteenth movements, then."

"Which harpsichord part do you wish to play?"

"The second."

"Why not the first? After all, this performance was your idea."

"Because I already know the second part of the *contrapunctus.*"

"I suppose it would be ungentlemanly of me to insist that you learn the first part."

It wasn't really a question—indeed, it sounded like he was gently teasing her, although he'd never done so—so she stifled another smile and responded with a prim expression worthy of a schoolmistress and the solemnity of a judge. "Indeed it would."

"Let's try them, shall we?"

"How can we with only one harpsichord?"

"You play the right hand notes of your part, and I will play the left hand of mine."

She did not know how that would be helpful, except to set the pace, but she was enjoying their musical interlude, so she readily agreed. If nothing else, the unorthodox performance might help her to become accustomed to playing with him so close beside her.

Even if it did set their beloved Bach spinning in his grave. Or cause his ghost to haunt them forevermore.

Next, they used the same method to practice the fugue. When they finished, amidst much laughter, Deborah said, "I wish we could play these two movements at the musicale, but we would need to practice them—properly—and I don't see how we can."

"It is all arranged, my dear. I told your mother what we planned, and that I would move a second harpsichord here, if she wished, or to Fairfax House, if she could contrive a way for you to practice there with no possible threat to your reputation."

Kesteven House was neither the largest nor the smallest house on Hanover Square, and while it usually seemed commodious, it did not have a music room. "Regrettably, there isn't a room devoted to music here, like at Woodhurst Castle and some of my father's other estates." Nor did Deborah think her mother would agree to have a second harpsichord in the drawing room, even for a month.

"Lady Kesteven has granted permission for us to practice at Fairfax House a few mornings a week if your father accompanies you. Or if your brother and Ogden are present."

"Henry seldom rises before noon. Or, rather, he is seldom seen outside his chamber before noon. But my father often is at home in the morning, and I daresay he would be willing to escort me."

"If I see him this evening, either in Lords or at the Enderby ball, I will try to impress upon him the importance of his assistance." After a moment's thought, Fairfax asked, "Is your father a musician? Or a music lover?"

"He isn't a musician, but he likes to listen to me play, and he can occasionally be prevailed upon to sing."

He nodded absently, apparently already formulating a plan, and Deborah was content just to sit beside him. The next nod was decisive, and he smiled and reached for her hand, raising it to his lips. "Although I may come to regret it, I am delighted that you asked me to perform with you at the duchess's musicale."

Deborah could not decide if she was more delighted by his words or by the brush of lips against her bare hand. His words warmed her heart; the kiss sent tingles radiating up her arm and all the way down to her toes.

Chapter Fifteen

*T*he Enderby ball was not yet three hours old, but Diana had long since deemed it sadly flat. It would have been a dead bore, if not for the shocks she'd received. The first, after Lady Enderby's chill greeting, had been the astonishing news of Dunnley's and Sarah Mallory's engagement. *Sarah Mallory? How could the rakish viscount possibly think that Sarah the Ice Queen was his match?* The second blow was the sight—and not just once!—of her sister and the Duke of Fairfax talking quietly together. Nor did his attentiveness to Deborah bode well for Diana's plans.

Thus, when Sir Edward Smithson appeared just after the second waltz was announced, Diana smiled and allowed him to lead her to the dance floor, eager to hear whatever scheme he'd devised.

Since it would be rude to immediately demand to know his plan, Diana opened the conversation with the latest gossip. "What did you think of the big announcement?" She rolled her eyes to convey her opinion, hoping that he would be as frank.

"What announcement?"

"How could you have missed it? Everyone has been abuzz all evening."

He shrugged. "I have only been here for twenty or thirty minutes, and I spent most of the time in the card room. Where, I might add, the prevailing topics of conversation were the fact that Brockton is selling off his hunters and that

Cummings lost ten thousand pounds playing faro last night at Watier's."

"He did?" Gentlemen lost money at cards every day, but losses that large were unusual. She had not heard a whisper about it, either, although Mama had dragged her from one end of Mayfair to the other this afternoon, paying a dozen calls.

"So they said." Sir Edward shrugged again, his attention on something—or someone—behind her. "To what were you referring?"

His disinterest was so blatant that Diana almost did not tell him. But, remembering her very real interest in his plan to retaliate against Deborah the Perfect, her friends, and the stodgy Duke of Fairfax, she relented. "To the announcement of Dunnley's engagement to Sarah Mallory."

"What?"

Diana thought the baronet would be amused by the mismatched couple. She did not expect to shock him into immobility. Prodding him back into motion, she was momentarily shaken by his expression of black rage, until she realized his ire was not directed at her.

"Control yourself!" she hissed, pleased to discover the target of his vengeance, although she'd guessed it was Dunnley after hearing, during that interminable round of calls, that he'd cut Sir Edward last night at Almack's.

Now, if only the news of the viscount's engagement would launch a discussion of Sir Edward's plan for revenge, although she could not imagine a scheme that would achieve both his goal and hers.

"I do believe we should discuss our . . . shall we say, mutual ambition." He whirled them into a turn that took them out one of the open French doors onto a broad terrace, with stairs leading down to the garden. "But not where there is a chance we will be overheard." Striking off across the lawn at a brisk pace, he tugged her along, heedless of the damage the dew was wreaking on her dancing slippers.

Finally stopping beneath a rose arbor, he turned, gathering her into his arms to continue the dance, although the music was almost inaudible at this distance.

"Now, my lady . . ." He pulled her much closer than in the ballroom—almost against his chest—then bent his head and covered her mouth with his own.

Diana was expecting the kiss, and had been since the moment he'd led her outside. It was not her first kiss—she'd given that to the squire's son when she was fifteen—nor was it gentle and tender. Sir Edward's kisses were hard and demanding, but the feeling of warmth they engendered grew apace, spreading throughout her body like fingers of flame. She looped her arms around his neck, standing on tiptoe when his kisses became even more urgent.

His hands moved over her body like a virtuoso playing a favorite instrument, and she trembled at each new, increasingly delightful sensation. Diana knew that she ought not to permit such behavior, told herself she must be a wanton to enjoy it, but the admonitions had no effect. If this was wantonness, she reveled in it, gasping in both shock and pleasure when his fingertips brushed the tip of her breast.

His hand returned to caress her throat, but gradually moved lower, teasing the lace that edged her modestly low-cut bodice, then pausing at the center. She gasped again as he slipped his hand inside, cupping one soft mound and deftly loosening the tape at her neck until her bodice gaped. With one hand, she wanted to push him away for taking such liberties, yet with the other, she wanted to urge him on, wanted to experience more of these wondrous feelings.

The crunch of gravel on a path nearby brought Diana back to an awareness of their location. Sir Edward seemed almost as startled as she, but was quicker to recover, fastening her gown as he explained his plan. "It needs refining, but I think it will serve, don't you?"

"Y-yes." It was nothing like she expected, and she was not certain his scheme would achieve the result she desired, but if nothing else, it would set the cat amongst the pigeons. During the turmoil, she could implement a stratagem or two of her own, if necessary. "Yes," she said more confidently, "it should serve, one way or the other."

"I won't accompany you back to the ballroom. Your reputation might suffer if it were believed you were out here alone with a man. We will talk again in a few days—that will give you time to choose the best day and make the arrangements for our little jaunt."

"I? Why should I make the arrangements?"

"Because our prey would not accept an invitation from me." He kissed her again, more perfunctorily than passionately, then gave her a little shove toward the house.

All in all, Diana thought as she walked back to the ballroom, it had been an enlightening evening.

Michael turned away in disgust, wondering why Diana Woodhurst—or any young lady—would venture into a dark garden with a reprobate like Sir Edward Smithson, much less allow him to take such liberties.

The gravel shifted beneath Michael's feet, sounding as loud as a cannonade, but he was beyond caring if the lust-ridden couple heard him. In fact, he hoped they did, if only to frighten Diana into some semblance of proper behavior.

Michael had come outside for a breath of fresh air. And so that his hostess would not dragoon him into dancing the second waltz with some young lady of her acquaintance. He performed such duty dances without complaint, taking pleasure in giving pleasure to the wallflowers and less favored young ladies. But tonight, the only woman he wanted to hold in his arms was Deborah. Since he could not do that now—she was waltzing with Dunnley—he'd come outside. To reflect back on the day and, in particular, on the wonderful afternoon he'd spent with Deborah. He hadn't expected to encounter her sister out here, but he thanked God that Diana had not run into him. And he certainly had not expected to find her locked in an embrace with Nasty Ned. Or with her bodice draped around her waist.

Suddenly, achingly, Michael recalled that Deborah and Diana were twins. *Identical twins.* The same in every aspect except their character and interests.

In the feeble hope of erasing the very vivid image of Deborah now in his mind's eye, Michael leaned against a tree and tried to remember the names of all of Britain's monarchs since the expulsion of the Romans.

"The early British kings," he intoned sotto voce. "Hengest of Kent ruled from about 455 to 488. Aella of Sussex ruled from 477 to 514. Aesc, or Oeric Oisc, of Kent, from 488 to 512. Esa became king of Bernicia around 500. In 512, Octa became king of Kent. Cissa of Sussex took the throne in 514, and Cerdic of Wessex in 519. Oh, Glywysing! Glywys Cernyw of Glywysing, late in the fifth century. Then . . . was it Cunedda Wledig the Imperator? And did Cadwallon Lawhir or Gwynllyw Farfog the Bearded succeed him?

"Blasted Welshmen! I should have started with the Saxon kings."

Within the first few measures of the supper dance, Deborah became convinced that nothing could be more wonderful than waltzing with the man you loved. It wasn't just knowing that his arm encircled her, feeling his hand at her waist, the sense of intimacy even in the middle of a crowded ballroom, although that was part of what made it wonderful—and made her giddy. It was not the look in Fairfax's eyes as he smiled at her, although that was part of it, too, and contributed to her euphoria. She did not know exactly why waltzing with him felt so wonderful—and so wonderfully right—but it did.

It seemed as if they danced on a cloud high in the heavens, amidst bright stars and whirling planets, illuminated by moonbeams.

Little was said—at least, not in words—but both Deborah and Fairfax smiled throughout the dance. A wealth of conversation was taking place with their eyes—and, perhaps, in their hearts. Unfortunately, Deborah was not certain whether she was interpreting the unspoken dialogue correctly. If she was, the budding hope that her dreams might come true this Season would soon be realized. If she was not—if she was reading more into Fairfax's speaking glances than he meant, or twisting them to fit the desires of her heart—then she was likely to have her heart broken.

Near the end of the dance, her uncertainty compelled her

to break the silence. "Fairfax, I want to thank you for making today such a wonderful day."

"Me?" He seemed surprised.

"Yes. Last night and today were wonderful. You . . . you made me feel special. Important. Like—"

"You *are* special and important, Deborah."

The end of the dance prevented him from saying more. If, in fact, he had more to say. Deborah wanted to stamp her foot in vexation, for not only had the end of the set interrupted him, but she also had more she wanted to say. Or, rather, something she wanted to ask.

Fairfax tucked her hand in the crook of his arm, his hand resting over hers, then glanced at the doorway as the guests thronged toward the supper room. "Would you like to stroll on the terrace for a few minutes until the crowd disperses?" The tender look in his eyes made her feel that she was again floating on a cloud high in the heavens.

Through the open French doors leading to the terrace, she could see several other couples, although not clearly enough to identify them. Their presence, however, was enough— not that Fairfax would ever do anything to endanger her reputation. Happy just to be in his company, she smiled. "A breath of fresh air would be lovely."

Almost the moment they stepped foot on the terrace, Deborah felt better. The light breeze was chill but refreshing after the heat of the ballroom. Moonlight bathed one end of the terrace, flickering Japanese lanterns suspended from the branches of the row of trees edging the grounds limned the other. Deborah was pleased when Fairfax strolled in the direction of the softer illumination.

Despite the presence of the other couples, she felt as if the two of them were alone, with only the stars overhead and a nightingale singing to its mate to observe them.

As they reached the end of the terrace, Fairfax's hand tightened over hers, lifting it from its resting place on his arm and raising it to his lips. "Deborah, you are a very special woman. I cannot think when I have had a more enjoyable day—and it was all because of you. This afternoon and again this evening, you made me feel special. . . . Welcome and wanted."

"I should think you would feel that way every day. You are a duke."

"But the duke is special simply because he is a duke."

Deborah did not agree, but did not argue, concentrating instead on the message underlying his words. The hidden meaning eluded her, but she knew it was important. "I don't understand."

Then, between one heartbeat and the next, she did. "Do you mean that I made you feel special as a person? Not because you are a duke, but because of the man you are?"

"Yes. You made me feel that I was a special man. That Michael Winslow was special," he clarified, "not the Duke of Fairfax."

"Both are special, Michael." She would not have dared to use his given name were this not so important. "I admire and respect the Duke of Fairfax. But I admire and respect and *like* Michael Winslow, and"—she took a deep breath to bolster her courage—"and I would like to know him better."

He smiled, clearly pleased, and twined his fingers with hers. Raising their clasped hands, he brushed another kiss across her knuckles.

She dipped her head to hide her confusion. Not because of the intimacy of either gesture, but because she had not realized that he still held her hand. It felt so right in his, although she wished their gloves would melt away.

"Fairfax, did you mean what you said this afternoon?" It was the merest whisper.

He curled a finger beneath her chin, gently tilting her face up. When her gaze met his, he asked, "Did I mean what, darling girl?"

"Did you mean it when you said you were courting me?"

He stepped closer and directly in front of her, blocking her view of the people behind them. Then he kissed her, the soft, gentle caress of his lips against hers as much a declaration as the words he'd spoken this afternoon. "Yes, I meant it."

Her heart brimming with happiness, she closed her eyes and sent a prayer of thanks winging heavenward.

"Would you prefer I did not?" The uncharacteristic hesitance in his voice contrasted sharply with his firm declaration.

"No! That is, I would not prefer if you did not." Her tongue as tangled as her answer, she dragged in a breath and tried again. "Nothing would please me more than to be courted by you."

His muttered "Thank God" made her smile, and when he drew their clasped hands to his heart and rested his forehead against hers, her heart overflowed with joy.

Her hopes and dreams were half fulfilled. Tonight she would silently celebrate. Tomorrow was soon enough to worry whether the other half would ever be realized.

Chapter Sixteen

Saturday, 16 April 1814

*D*eborah could not have been more surprised when Diana, who had hardly spoken to her for the past three days, sat beside her at breakfast and asked, "What do you think we should wear to the Opera tonight?"

Taken aback, and not at all certain she could trust the olive branch her sister appeared to be offering, Deborah fumbled for a response. As if Tuesday and Wednesday evening had never happened, Diana continued, "I was thinking we could wear the gowns with the reversed colors."

"But those are evening gowns, not opera dresses! We will freeze."

"Pooh! The theater isn't that drafty. Besides, we can always wear shawls."

"Why not an opera dress?"

Her expression sheepish, Diana confessed, "You were right about the color of the primrose gown. I want to wear it as soon as possible, then have Ogden put on a new bodice in a contrasting, more flattering color."

Why is Diana willing to admit that she was wrong about the gown, but not about lying at the Oglethorpe ball? Deborah would have much preferred the latter admission, as well as a sincere apology, but she was more likely to find a Brummagen sixpence than to ever hear either.

"Please, Deb?" her sister wheedled. "I would rather wear the primrose gown when only a few gentlemen will be present to see it."

"Half the gentlemen of the *ton* will see you if you wear it tonight!"

"Yes, but from a distance. And with a shawl to distract from the unfortunate color."

Since the only disadvantage was that she might be cold, Deborah agreed. "I suppose we could. *If* I have a shawl—a warm shawl—that complements the gown." She also intended to inspect the gown itself, to be sure no "accidents" had befallen it.

"Thank you, Deb!" Diana's hug was as surprising—and seemed as sincere—as her thanks. "I have been thinking that it might be nice to invite several of our friends to ride in the country. Somewhere outside of London, where we can have a good gallop. Perhaps we could even plan a picnic?"

Deborah stared at her sister in astonishment. In the past, they had often had similar ideas at the same time, but given the discord between them the past few weeks, she had not expected it to happen again. Yet two days after she had offered to plan the excursion to Richmond that Fairfax had suggested, Diana was proposing a ride in the country and a picnic. Since she could not possibly know about Deborah's discussion with him, Deborah could not help but hope that she and her sister would soon be in accord again. "Did you have a particular destination in mind?"

"No. I just thought it might be a pleasant change from shopping and paying calls." Diana glanced from Deborah to their mother, then back. "Where do you think would be best?"

"Windsor," the marchioness suggested. "Or perhaps Richmond, though you would not need a picnic there—you could eat at the Star and Garter. It was a popular jaunt when I was your age."

"Did you have your heart set on a picnic, Di?" Deborah asked.

"No. Hmmm . . . Richmond seems the better choice, since we wouldn't have to plan a meal and arrange for the servants to transport it there."

"How many people were you thinking to invite?" their mother inquired.

"I hadn't yet considered such details, but . . . perhaps a dozen?" Again Diana looked between Deborah and their mother, either seeking their opinions or trying to gauge their reactions.

"I think there will be more than that," Deborah warned. "Even if each of us invites only three friends and an escort for each, that is a dozen people. Sixteen including us and our escorts. Not to mention Mama and an additional chaperone or two."

The strangest expression crossed Diana's face, but Deborah could not imagine why. "Were you thinking of inviting only young ladies?" she queried.

"No." Diana shook her head. "I was thinking of ladies and gentlemen, I just hadn't realized how large a group it would be."

"If we want gentlemen to attend, we should plan to go on a Wednesday. Preferably toward the end of the month, when the weather is warmer." Deborah was pleased that their plans so closely matched the excursion she and Fairfax had discussed.

"Excellent suggestions, Deb," the marchioness said.

Diana opened her mouth as if to protest, then apparently thought better of it. "After we make our lists, we will be better able to choose a date." Shortly thereafter, she rose from the table and left the morning room.

Michael was looking forward to the evening—and dreading it in equal measure. He was eager to pursue his courtship of Deborah, but considerably less enthusiastic about doing so under his grandmother's watchful eye.

It is only one night. he reminded himself. *One night out of a Season full of activities.* Since Lady Kesteven and two of his grandmother's cronies would also be present tonight, not to mention a goodly portion of the *ton,* opportunities for wooing would be almost nonexistent.

He glanced at the long case clock in the corner of the library, then, frowning, went in search of Sanders. Drummond should have arrived more than an hour ago, along with the last cavalcade of goods and servants from The

Oaks—including Meecham and Michael's newest evening attire.

The entry hall was in an uproar, the front door standing open. Several footmen labored up the stairs with trunks on their shoulders, while others carried in more trunks from outside. When the dowager stepped inside, trailed by her companion and her dresser, Michael managed, just barely, to stifle a groan.

Intercepting the trio just before they reached the staircase, he crossed his arms over his chest and directed a look of inquiry at the bane of his existence. "Grandmère? I thought you decided to stay at The Oaks?"

"I changed my mind."

"You changed your mind?" he echoed in disbelief. "You, the woman who vowed that nothing would persuade her to step foot in Fairfax House ever again?"

"Yes." Without another word of explanation, she brushed past him.

Weak-kneed at the thought of the increased scope for her meddling, Michael collapsed onto the bottom stair. This time he did not even try to hold back his moan.

Diana studied her appearance in the mirror, wondering if she had gone a bit too far when she'd altered the neckline of the primrose silk gown.

"I dunno, m'lady. It's awful low." Beside her, Ginny voiced the thought in Diana's mind.

"Nonsense! I have seen ladies wearing gowns this low at the theater."

"Have ye?" The little chambermaid turned lady's maid sounded doubtful. "Iffen you take a deep breath, you'll likely pop right out of the bodice."

"Then I won't take any deep breaths." Diana's dismissive tone curtailed further discussion. While it was true that she would have to move carefully, there was no doubt that the gown's décolletage would catch the Duke of Fairfax's eye. And the eye of every other man in his box. Deborah, in her flattering pale green gown, would be forced to converse with their mother while the gentlemen clamored for Diana's attention. She would, of course, listen to their gallantries, but most of her attention would be focused on charming the duke.

Hearing the *rap-tap* of the knocker, she donned her evening cloak. Once they reached the theater, Mama's objections would be fruitless, so Diana did not intend to unveil the altered gown until then.

I wonder if Sir Edward will be at the Opera? A frisson of excitement streaked down her spine as she considered the ways he would demonstrate his appreciation of the gown's neckline. *If only the Duke of Fairfax weren't so unattractive, and had a fraction of the baronet's dash and charm!*

Deborah smiled up at Fairfax as he seated her at the front of his box. He returned her smile, trailing a finger along her nape as he helped her remove her cloak. His hand resting on her shoulder, he looked behind her to assure that her mother and sister were receiving the same attention from their escorts. Without warning, his grip on her shoulder tightened almost to the point of pain, her mother gasped, and one of the men behind her—either Blackburn or the Earl of Sherworth—hissed a warning. Then Fairfax swore under his breath, both earls more audibly. In a voice that bore more resemblance to an animal's growl than his usual mellifluous bass, Blackburn said, "If you are trying to make a byword of your name, Lady Diana, I daresay you have succeeded. Now, where is your demmed cloak?"

Twisting in her seat to look behind her, Deborah saw her sister—more of her than she'd seen since the last time their nurse had bathed them together in the big copper tub in front of the nursery fire. She snapped her eyes shut, more to preserve her sensibilities than Diana's. But judging from the shockingly immodest décolletage of her gown, Diana no longer had any sensibilities, preservable or otherwise.

To her dismay, Deborah discovered that closing her eyes had no effect; the image was seared onto the back of her eyelids. Gripping her hands tightly in her lap to prevent herself from slapping her sister back to her senses—or senseless—Deborah listened with mounting disquiet to the

low-voiced discussion behind her. Fairfax still stood behind
her, his right hand gripping the crest rail of her chair, his fingers occasionally brushing her right shoulder, but from the
sound of it, everyone else had moved to the back of the box.

"Lady Kesteven, if you wish, I will escort Lady Diana
home," Blackburn offered.

"She cannot stay here," their mother retorted, anger pulsing beneath her tone. "But you should not escort her without
a chaperone, and if I go with you, then Deborah will be un-
chaperoned."

Sherworth volunteered to accompany Blackburn, but that
did not conform to Society's notions of propriety. It was a
breech of decorum for a young lady to ride in a closed carriage with two gentlemen unless one of them was related to
her, yet two ladies could ride in that same carriage with a
gentleman, even if none of the three were related.

Just when Deborah feared they would all have to leave,
Lord Howe entered the box with an elderly lady on his arm.
The marchioness greeted the dowager duchess and quickly
explained the problem. Fairfax then introduced Deborah and
his grandmother, and after a searching, head-to-toe scrutiny,
the dowager duchess offered to serve as Deborah's chaperone until Lady Kesteven returned. In the end, it was Howe
and Blackburn who accompanied Diana and the marchioness back to Kesteven House.

Howe's argument was simple and succinct. "I have
known Lady Diana since I was a schoolboy, and run tame in
the household for years. If necessary, I will sit on Lady
Diana in the middle of the entry hall, under Driscoll's
watchful eye, until Henry or Kesteven returns."

The baron's fervent but droll assertion drew a ghost of a
smile from the formidable dowager duchess. Once she
agreed to the change in escort, Sherworth sank into a chair,
clearly relieved to have this new, simpler duty.

As Howe bundled Diana more tightly into her cloak,
Lady Kesteven crossed to Deborah and whispered, "I am
sorry, dearling. Try not to let your sister's . . ." Words failed
her. "Don't let your sister spoil your evening. I will return as

quickly as I can." Then she and Blackburn followed Howe and Diana from the box.

A quick peek at the duchess's face was enough to make Deborah wonder if she had erred in not returning home with her mother and sister.

Her tone censorious, the dowager asked, "What kind of hoyden—"

"Grandmère, we will not discuss Lady Diana's conduct." Fairfax's tone brooked no argument.

The duchess bristled, but Sherworth distracted her with a question. "What was your favorite performance last year, Your Grace?"

The overture began before they finished their debate. With a sigh of relief, Deborah slumped, exhausted, in her chair. Fairfax leant over and whispered, "Just relax and enjoy the music, sweetheart. Don't allow a single thought of your sister to cross your mind." When he pressed a quick kiss to her cheek, Deborah knew she would survive, no matter what the evening held.

His kisses were a wondrous incentive.

Chapter Seventeen

Wednesday, 20 April 1814

*W*ednesday morning, Deborah's father escorted her to Fairfax House for her first rehearsal there. She and Fairfax had practiced the duet for two performers on one harpsichord at Kesteven House on Monday afternoon, as well as their one-handed version of the two movements from *The Art of the Fugue*, but this would be their first practice with two harpsichords.

It would also be her first encounter since Saturday night with the dowager duchess, and Deborah was far more nervous about that meeting than she was about the fugue movement she had not yet mastered.

"Chin up, my girl," her father admonished. "Neither your sister's behavior nor the duchess's grumbling need concern you."

Deborah refused to think about her sister. Doing so gave her both a headache and a heartache, the latter partly the result of Diana's repeated betrayals and partly born out of fear that Diana's increasingly scandalous conduct would give Fairfax a disgust of the entire family.

Gossip about the gown Diana wore to the Opera had been so pervasive Monday afternoon that she had attended neither Lady Moreton's rout that evening nor the dowager Countess of Sherworth's ball last night. At breakfast this morning, Diana had been trying to convince their mother to allow her to attend Almack's this evening, but Deborah had left the table before they'd reached an agreement. Or come to blows.

As her father reached for the knocker, the butler opened the door and bowed them inside. "Good morning, Lord Kesteven. My lady."

The entry hall was enormous, almost as large as the Great Hall at Woodhurst Castle. Alternating black and white Italian marble tiles gave the floor the appearance of a huge chessboard, but the rich, colorful tapestries with scenes from Greek mythology softened the effect.

"Good morning, Lady Deborah. Kesteven."

Turning toward the welcome sound of Fairfax's voice, Deborah dropped a curtsy, feeling slightly intimidated.

He arched a brow but forbore from comment, instead offering his arm to escort her through the house. "Tea and coffee in the music room, please, Sanders."

"Yes, Your Grace."

Each turn revealed walls bedecked with glorious landscapes and somber-faced portraits, some of them hundreds of years old. "If these"—she gestured the length of the hall—"are all your ancestors, they appear to be a rather dour lot," she teased.

"Yes, indeed. The dutiful but dour dukes. Well, there are a few earls amongst them, but they were not known for their joviality, either."

"Are you a throwback to one of the early dukes or earls?" She had not yet seen his portrait, nor one that bore more than a passing resemblance to him.

"I am an Original, my darling," he whispered, nuzzling her ear.

"I saw that, young man." Her father's voice was not the least bit stern, his statement more of a reminder than a reprimand.

When they entered the music room, Deborah stopped just over the threshold, her breath caught in her throat at the perfection of the room. It was of the same grandiose proportions as the rest of the house, but there were no rugs or hangings to muffle the sound, just polished oak floors and wainscoting. Two harpsichords sat side by side in the middle of the room, a pianoforte against the opposite wall, and a harp in the far corner. More than a dozen gilt chairs were lined up against the wall, and a large leather wing chair, similar to the ones in her father's study, and a side table had been placed near the door for her father's comfort. French doors stood open to the garden, and the faint trill of birdsong could be heard.

"What a wonderful room!" She squeezed Fairfax's arm in her enthusiasm. "If we lived here, Mama would be dragging me out of this room half a dozen times a day."

"Is this my seat?" The question was clearly rhetorical, since her father did not wait for a reply. "I appreciate your having a proper chair moved in here for me, Fairfax. Thank you." He opened a portfolio, rifled through the letters and papers it contained, then began reading.

Drawn as if by a lodestone, Deborah approached the harpsichords, wondering which one she would be playing. The one on the left was Flemish, and dated from early in the previous century; the one on the right was English and, at most, twenty years old.

She was not aware that Fairfax had come up behind her until he placed a hand on her shoulder. "Which instrument do you want to play, sweetheart?"

"I would be delighted to play either of them." She wanted him to make the choice. "Which one do you most often play?"

"This one." Smiling like a mischievous schoolboy, he pointed to the Flemish instrument.

"Then I shall play that one." She stepped closer to the English harpsichord.

"Not so fast, my lady." Fairfax caught her hand, halting her progress. "I suggest we play the single harpsichord duet first, on both instruments, so you can determine which keyboard's action is closest to yours. That is the instrument you will play, since I can practice on either of them at any time."

His solution was both logical and practical, so she readily agreed. As he seated her in front of the Flemish instrument, he kissed her cheek, the brush of his lips soft and tender but far too fleeting. With her father in the room, it was more than she expected, but greedily, she yearned for more.

While Fairfax moved the chair from the other harpsichord beside hers and donned his spectacles, she played scales to limber her fingers. When he repeated the same three scales, she smiled, wondering whether he'd chosen them intentionally or unconsciously.

Opening the score, she poised her hands above the keyboard, playing the opening measures without striking the keys as she waited for his signal to begin.

"Ready, my dear?"

"Ready." With Fairfax at her side, she felt able to tackle anything.

Michael was fighting an uphill battle, and losing allies and weapons at an alarming rate. His cousin, Frederick Walsingham, had agreed to come to London and assist Michael, but would not arrive until Saturday. He had also warned Michael that he would need new clothes, especially evening attire, if he was to cut a dash in Town. Or to impersonate Michael, which, in this case, amounted to the same thing. Having seen Freddie and the better portion of his wardrobe at Christmas, Michael had already put Weston to work on Freddie's sartorial imperfections.

Dunnley was in Hampshire at his principal estate, dealing with flooding problems caused by collapsed drainage ditches. Before leaving Town, he had asked Michael to keep an eye on his fiancée, Lady Sarah Mallory, who was being pestered and vaguely threatened by Sir Edward Smithson. Michael had spent the past two evenings helping Theo's brother and Sarah's brother keep her out of harm's way, but none of them knew what Nasty Ned would do.

Despite the fact that Michael had all but ignored her for the past week, Diana was still bent on snaring his coronet. And on making her sister's life miserable. The past two nights, when the gossip—or her parents—had confined Diana to her room, had been the most pleasant of the Season. Michael could only hope that she would stay there for another week or so, but he knew that wish was unlikely to be fulfilled.

Now, his hat metaphorically in hand and his heart in his throat, Michael faced another ordeal: asking for Kesteven's permission to pay his addresses to Deborah. Before leaving the Metropolis, Theo had confided that Lord Tregaron had grilled him for quite half an hour before granting permission—and his blessing. No matter how long nor how intense Kesteven's probing, Michael was determined to soldier on. Deborah was a prize worth fighting for.

Driscoll opened the door while Michael's fingers were still on the knocker. "Good afternoon, Your Grace. Was her ladyship expecting you?" The butler's frown was formidable but bemused. "None of the ladies are at home."

"Good afternoon, Driscoll. I am calling on Lord Kesteven today. I believe he is expecting me."

"His lordship, you say?" The butler seemed surprised, as well he might, since in the past, Michael had always called on the ladies of the house. "He is here, Your Grace. If you will follow me, please."

As he entered Kesteven's study, Michael felt a bit like a schoolboy called before the headmaster. *It is for Deborah. For Deborah, the woman you love, and who loves you.*

"So"—the marquess tapped a note against the edge of his desk—"you wish to pay your addresses to Deborah."

It wasn't really a query—Kesteven knew why he was calling—but Michael answered anyway. "Yes, my lord. I do."

"I have a few questions for you."

His cravat suddenly too tight, Michael clasped his hands together so he would not tug on it. "I expected that you would, sir."

"What is your annual income? Are you able to support my daughter in the style to which she is accustomed?"

"Between eighty thousand and one hundred thousand pounds, depending on the price of crops and the success of various investments." Michael was one of the wealthiest men in Britain, so Kesteven could have no complaint on that score.

"Any debts, encumbrances, or mortgages?"

"My grandmother's jointure entitles her to one-third of the income from my principal estate, Fairfax Castle. Her portion amounts to about ten thousand pounds a year."

"Anything else?"

"No, sir. Only current tradesman's bills."

Kesteven nodded; he, too, was reputed to pay bills on time.

The next question was unexpected. Not to mention ambiguous as bedamned. "Why Deborah?"

What the devil is he asking? And why? Given the choice between floundering around trying to answer a question he did not understand or asking for clarification, Michael chose the latter. And prayed his choice would not lower him in Kesteven's esteem. "Are you asking me why I want to marry one of your daughters instead of another man's daughter? Or are you asking why I want to marry Deborah instead of Diana?"

"Both, I suppose."

"I like Deborah, and I have the greatest admiration and respect for her." Michael wanted Deborah to be the first to hear that he loved her, so he merely hinted at his feelings. "Nothing would make me happier than to spend the rest of my days protecting and cherishing her."

Kesteven frowned, unappeased. "What makes you certain that it is Deborah, not Diana, you want to spend the rest of your days protecting and cherishing?"

Michael fought the urge to squirm. While the question had a relatively simple answer, it was also a potential minefield. "If you are asking if I can tell your daughters apart, the answer is yes. I can."

"Are you certain? They *are* identical twins."

"Yes, sir." He punctuated his answer with a decisive nod. "Your daughters are identical in appearance, but their characters and interests are distinctly different. So, in my opinion, are their hopes and dreams."

"How do you tell them apart? And how long have you been able to do so?"

"I have been able to tell them apart since I first met them.

As for how I do it, I don't know. Well," he added wryly, "aside from the fact that my heart performs the most amazing acrobatics whenever I am near Deborah."

"Ah." Kesteven smiled for the first time all afternoon. "You love her then?"

"Yes, sir. With all my heart."

"You have my permission to pay your addresses, but the decision will be Deborah's alone."

"I understand, sir. And thank you." Michael studied his hands, still tightly clasped in his lap, wondering if—and how—he could request a favor.

"Out with it, young man."

Michael's head jerked up at the order. "Sir?"

"There is something on your mind."

"The Spaniards could have used you, sir," he quipped, hoping to dispel the tension. "During the Inquisition."

Kesteven laughed. "Perhaps so. Now tell me what is on your mind."

"Two things, actually. I had hoped Deborah would be the first to hear that I love her, although I understand your desire to know, so I would ask that you allow me to tell her my feelings."

"Done. What else?"

"I would also ask that you not tell anyone that I can tell the twins apart." Again Michael fought the urge to squirm; the path ahead wound through fields of bogs. "As you are aware, Diana has attempted to deceive me by pretending to be her sister, and my only weapon is the fact that she doesn't know I can tell her and Deborah apart." When the marquess frowned, Michael added, "I will, of course, tell Deborah before I propose."

"Wouldn't making it known that you can tell the girls apart put an end to Diana's tricks?"

"I don't know, sir. It might also spur her to greater lengths, and I would rather not risk that."

"Indeed." Kesteven blanched at the thought. "In that case, I agree."

"Thank you, sir."

As he left the house, Michael wondered how soon he

would be able to offer for Deborah. And prayed—fervently—that she would accept him. If she did not, he would never be able to keep the promise he had made his grandmother.

He would have Deborah, and only Deborah, as his wife and duchess. No other woman would suit.

Diana was feeling increasingly desperate to fix Fairfax's attention. Her most recent attempt had been an abysmal failure, but she vowed to keep trying until she succeeded. She had set her cap for him and had resolved to snare a husband of higher rank than the man her sister chose. Stealing Fairfax out from under Deborah's nose—if, in fact, he was—would increase Diana's triumph.

Almack's was not the best place for another attempt—it was, in fact, one of the worst possible choices, since the patronesses watched like hawks for the slightest infraction—but he was here, so she would do the best she could. It was too late to start over with another man. And if she did, she would not best her sister; the only duke outside the royal family who outranked Fairfax was married. Thus, in order to achieve her goal and lord it over Deborah, she had to snare Fairfax.

Why couldn't the blasted man cooperate? They were identical twins! In the eyes of Society, a match with one of them was as good as the other.

Frowning, Diana glanced around the assembly room. Most of her admirers seemed to have deserted her, although she could not imagine why. She *had* caused a bit of a scandal, but any number of other ladies, young and old, had done the same. Including a few who were present tonight.

She shrugged off the absence of her court. Tried, too, to ignore the number of sets she sat out, although that was more difficult. How was it possible that she, one of the celebrated Woodhurst twins, was a wallflower? Had the gentlemen of the *ton* forgotten that they'd dubbed her and her sister "The English Roses" last year?

When Sir Edward Smithson requested her hand for the first waltz, she almost leapt from her seat. Not only did she enjoy dancing with him, but they would be able to discuss their plans.

"Everything is set for next Wednesday. We will ride to Richmond and eat at the Star and Garter," she reported. "Everyone we invited has accepted."

"I did not receive an invitation."

"You told me not to put your name on the guest list!"

"So I did." He pulled her a bit closer. "Who will be present?"

"Deborah and I. Fairfax and a cousin of his who will be in Town. Dunnley, Blackburn, and Howe. My brother and Sarah Mallory's brother. Sarah and Tina Fairchild."

"How many chaperones?"

"Three—"

"Why so da—so many? It will make everything more difficult."

"Because my mother, Lady Tregaron, and the Duchess of Greenwich are all determined to go. Apparently it was quite a popular excursion when they made their come-outs." She rolled her eyes at the folly of old women trying to relive their youth. "They will travel by carriage, either ahead of or behind us, so they won't be able to interfere with whatever you have planned." Despite her prompting, he had not yet confided the details of his plan.

"Divide everyone into three groups. You and I will be in the first group, in my phaeton. Your sister, Fairfax, Dunnley, and Lady Sarah *must* be in the second group. The rest don't matter—they can be in either the first or third group.

"What else?"

"That is all you need to know."

"I don't agree—"

"You can disagree all you want, Lady Diana, but I am not going to tell you the rest until Wednesday."

Infuriating man! "How can I help if I don't know what you are going to do?"

"If you want to win Fairfax from your sister, you will do exactly what I tell you Wednesday."

"Deborah has not won him!" She cringed, the overly loud words seemed to echo around her. Grabbing the reins of her fleeting temper, she informed the baronet, "And if you want *my* help on Wednesday, you will detain my sister in a lengthy conversation tonight before the third waltz."

"Another attempt at deception, Lady Diana? I would have thought you'd learnt your lesson, but I am willing to oblige you."

Deborah was surprised—and not at all pleased—when Sir Edward Smithson cornered her in the refreshment room and launched into a lengthy monologue. She did not like the baronet, did not care about his sporting exploits, and she was eager to return to the ballroom for the next set. There was certain to be another waltz soon—the third one of the evening—and she had promised it to Fairfax.

As the baronet droned on, Howe, who had been her partner for the last set, shifted impatiently from foot to foot. When the musicians began tuning their instruments, she interrupted the baronet in midspate. "Excuse me for interrupting, Sir Edward, but I need to return to the ballroom. I have a partner for the next dance."

"But I haven't finished telling you about this run. We were approaching—"

"You will have to finish the story another time. I am promised for this set."

"I am almost finished. We were . . ."

Deborah no longer bothered to listen to the boring account. Instead, she cocked her head toward the doorway, to better hear the opening bars of the next set. The moment she heard them—and it was, indeed, the waltz she'd been anticipating—she opened her mouth, determined to end the conversation no matter how rude she had to be, but Howe beat her to it. "Excuse us, Smithson. Lady Deborah and I have partners for this dance."

Tucking her arm in his, Howe led her away, giving Sir Edward no chance to argue. When they were out of earshot, the baron muttered, "What a windbag! I have never been more bored in my life."

She laughed with her brother's friend, but her laughter died when they reentered the ballroom and she spied her sister talking earnestly to Fairfax. Deborah's breath hitched; she could not get air into or out of her lungs. She and her sister were dressed identically tonight, so if Di attempted another deception, she might well succeed.

Although too far away to hear what Diana and Fairfax were saying, Deborah feared the worst. *And at Almack's, of all places! Di's attics must be to let!* Quickening her steps, she dodged this group and that, with Howe's assistance.

By the time they reached Diana and Fairfax, the duke's arms were crossed over his chest, his expression implacable as granite. "I am promised to Lady Deborah, and you are not she."

"I am!" Diana stamped her foot. "How many times do I have to tell you?"

"Perhaps," Deborah interrupted, "until you tell the truth, Diana."

"I am not Diana. You are."

"I have been Deborah since birth, and well you know it!" Deborah clenched her fists, angrier than she'd ever been in her life.

Diana turned to Howe. "Tell the duke who we are."

Fairfax shook his head. "No need, Howe. When Lady Kesteven returns, she will be happy to identify her daughters."

"But we are missing our waltz." Diana tried to take Fairfax's arm, but he stepped out of her reach.

"Give over, Diana." Fairfax offered his arm to Deborah. "I am going to waltz with your sister."

Deborah's legs were shaking so badly, she would never be able to dance. Despite Fairfax's presence at her side, she was unequal to anything at the moment except, perhaps, a bout of tears.

Chapter Eighteen

Tuesday, 26 April 1814

*D*eborah greeted Lord and Lady Abernathy, then followed her mother, brother, and sister into the ballroom. *Lud, what a crush!* The entire room, including the dance floor, was packed with people, giving a new meaning to the term "a shocking squeeze." How would she ever find her friends? More importantly, how would her partners find her?

Ahead of her, her mother and Henry moved with purpose, veering to the left as they made their way around one group of people after the other. Either they'd spotted someone they knew or a trio of chairs. At the moment, Deborah would be grateful for either one.

The skirts of her blush pink silk gown were already creased, her toes had been trod on twice. Mama and Henry forged ahead, and Deborah could do naught but follow. She did, however, hope that her mother had seen Lady Tregaron, Sarah's mother. Dunnley had been in the country for more than a week, and Sarah missed her fiancé sorely. Deborah knew her friend was worried that he would not return in time for tomorrow's jaunt to Richmond, and was determined to cheer her. But perhaps more importantly, Deborah needed Sarah's advice.

A group of gentlemen moved to one side, and Deborah saw a row of gilt spindle-back chairs lining the wall. A row that included Tina Fairchild, Sarah, Lady Tregaron, and the Duchess of Greenwich. Sarah's father and brother—the Earl of Tregaron and Viscount Llanfyllin—stood nearby, as did Dunnley's brother, Captain Middleford. Deborah was pleased to see a vacant chair beside the duchess and two more to Tina's right.

"What a horrible squeeze! How are we supposed to dance in this crush?" Grateful to be out of the worst of the crowd, she shook out her skirts—a futile effort—then sat next to Tina, whose ivory muslin gown was sadly creased.

With a sniff of disdain, Diana took the last chair, on Deborah's right.

Her ice blue silk slightly wrinkled, Sarah leant forward, smiling a welcome. "Tina and I were discussing the trip to Richmond tomorrow. We are looking forward to it."

"Are you indeed?" Diana's usual air of ennui was noticeably absent, replaced by a barely concealed excitement. From long experience, Deborah knew that boded ill for someone, and her heart sank.

"Should be fun." Henry propped himself against Diana's chair, his crimson waistcoat on display. Glaringly so, to Deborah's eyes, but she much preferred the subtle elegance of black and white evening attire, such as that worn by Lord Tregaron or Llanfyllin. Or like Fairfax and Dunnley always wore. Even Captain Middleford's uniform coat, which was red and glittered with braid and silver lace, seemed more subdued than her brother's eye-popping crimson waistcoat.

Llanfyllin agreed; Captain Middleford muttered something she couldn't quite hear. Smiling an apology, Deborah leant over Tina and whispered urgently to Sarah, "I need to talk to you later."

When the minuet was announced, Deborah glanced around the ballroom, searching for Fairfax or his cousin, Sir Frederick Walsingham. Beside her, Tina chatted without seeming to take a breath.

After a minute, Deborah gave up looking. She could see little except the backs of other guests. "Do you see Fairfax?" she asked Sarah, who was also gazing around the room.

Sarah shook her head. "No, nor Blackburn, either."

A few moments later, Tina elbowed Deborah. "Fairfax just arrived." Then, frowning, she added, "Or is that his cousin?"

Like her friends, Deborah had met the duke's cousin yesterday. And, like them, she had been surprised by the remarkable resemblance between the two men. They were exactly the same height, and shared the same features, brown hair, and blue-green eyes. Although they were second cousins, they looked as much alike as she and Diana did! The baronet's eyes were, perhaps, a bit greener than Fairfax's, but they had moved apart before she could study them closely. The only other noticeable difference was that Sir Frederick lacked Fairfax's presence, his air of command, and Walsingham's clothes had been a bit more worn than his cousin's.

"Whether it is Fairfax or Sir Frederick, his cousin is greeting Lady Abernathy now," Sarah reported.

Convinced that Fairfax was the man slightly in the lead, Deborah was surprised when the second gentleman brushed past his cousin and bowed over her hand. "I beg your pardon for my late arrival. We can still join the dance, um . . . unless you would prefer to sit it out?"

"I would much rather dance." Deborah smiled to cover her confusion. *This is Sir Frederick, isn't it?*

"Then dance we shall."

As he led her to the dance floor, she glanced over her shoulder and saw the baronet—or was it really Fairfax?—ask Tina to dance with him.

Long before the end of the minuet, Deborah was convinced that her partner was Sir Frederick. He danced well, but lacked a measure of Fairfax's grace. She waited until nearly the end of the set to question him. "What is going on?"

He arched his brows—both of them, not just the left one. "Going on? Nothing, my dear."

"I don't believe you. Why are you pretending to be Fairfax?"

"Has our close resemblance fooled you? I was certain that you, of all people, would be able to tell us apart."

"I think, sir, that you wish to fool me—or someone—and have not succeeded. At least, not with me."

"How can I convince you?"

"Shall we find a harpsichord and put it to the test?" She did not know if Sir Frederick played, but even if he did, she doubted he would kiss her when he seated her. Fairfax invariably did, to her delight. And, she supposed, his.

"I cannot say I am eager to try to fight my way out of this room—getting inside was difficult enough—but if that is what it takes . . ." Her partner again raised both brows in query.

"Perhaps after I have danced with your cousin."

Deborah's first dance with his cousin was not until later, giving her far too much time to worry about what was going on. And there was plenty to occupy her thoughts. Sarah's father, brother, and Captain Middleford rarely left Sarah's side. It seemed as if they were guarding her from something. Or someone. In between sets, Blackburn, Fairfax (or his cousin), and Sir Frederick (or his cousin) joined the protective phalanx around Sarah. Although Deborah did not want to endanger her friend, she desperately wanted to talk to her. Preferably without an audience.

After the fourth set, Sarah asked, "Will you accompany me to the ladies' retiring room?"

"Of course I will."

The gentlemen, however, were not in favor of the idea. Captain Middleford muttered something about "trouble begging to happen," and he and Llanfyllin insisted on escorting them.

Three older ladies occupied the room, but Deborah was determined to wait them out. Apparently Sarah was, too. "Sit down, Deb, and I will pin your flounce."

Deborah smiled and joined the charade. "I cannot imagine how I came to be so clumsy."

"I daresay it was your partner's fault, not yours." Pulling a packet of pins from her reticule, Sarah knelt at her feet and pretended to pin the flounce.

The moment the door closed behind the older women, Deborah blurted, "Sarah, what is going on?"

Sarah rose and pulled a chair close to Deborah's. "You said earlier that you wanted to talk to me."

"Yes, I do, but that isn't what I meant."

Sarah's smile was a feeble effort. "I know, but we can't stay here long, so tell me what is troubling you."

"Well, there are two things now. No, three."

"Let's deal with them one at a time. What was—or is— the first one?"

Deborah began with the worry that had occupied her thoughts since breakfast. "I fear—no, I am certain—that Diana is up to something. I don't know what, though. She has been acting strangely—sly and secretive—for several days, and this morning I heard her muttering about 'just desserts.' I am worried that someone will be hurt by whatever she is planning"

"You believe it is something more than insidious comments against a rival?"

"I don't know!" Deborah took a deep breath, hoping it would calm her fears. "But I think it is something worse."

"Has Diana mentioned one young lady more than others? Or one gentleman?"

"Not really. She has mentioned you—your engagement to Dunnley—a few times, but I can't recall her talking much about any other girl." These days, Deborah and her sister rarely talked at all. "The man she has talked about most is Fairfax."

"Speaking of Fairfax, does he seem . . . different tonight? Or is it just my imagination? It may well be. I have mistaken him for his cousin all evening."

"I have as well. Strange, isn't it?" Deborah tried to make light of it. "Perhaps it is a trick of the light."

The entrance of an elderly dowager ended their coze. Not because she was a high stickler, but because she was also a notorious gossip. Sarah rose, and Deborah followed more slowly, reluctant to return to the ballroom.

Before they left, Sarah stopped and, in a quiet voice that could not be overhead, said, "Deb, I doubt there is anything you can do to prevent your sister from doing whatever she plans. Unless, of course, you can find out what she intends and either put a stop to it or warn her intended victim."

"That is what I thought, but I wondered—I was hoping there was a solution I'd overlooked."

There was much still to be discussed, but Deborah knew her friend well enough to know that they would tackle the others as soon as they possibly could.

Captain Middleford and Llanfyllin stood a short distance away, talking with Howe and two military gentlemen. As they walked past, Sarah linked arms with Deborah. Llanfyllin beckoned an urgent "come here," but Sarah ignored him.

"Sarah, *what* is going on? Your father and brother . . ." Deborah did not know quite how to describe their protectiveness this evening.

"I can't tell you here"—Sarah gestured at the people clustered in the hall—"but I will explain tomorrow."

"I will hold you to that promise." Concern for her friend prompted Deborah's words. If Sarah was in danger, she wanted to know. And to help as best she could.

Outside the ballroom, they were hailed by Diana, of all people. The same Diana who had always given every indication of cordially despising all the members of "The Six," and who had not said much more than "pass the bread" to Deborah for more than a week, now insisted that she had to talk with both of them. It was puzzling, to say the least. Especially since she asked about the arrangements for tomorrow's excursion to Richmond, which she knew as well as Deborah did.

After Sarah left, Diana quickly lost interest in the subject. Hearing the opening bars of a waltz, the first one this evening, Deborah hastened toward the ballroom. She had promised the dance to Sir Frederick, which, she suspected, meant that Fairfax would be her partner.

Deborah had a number of questions for the duke, and she would not be put off by superficial resemblances and deceptions.

Warned by his cousin that Deborah was wise to their deception, Michael was, for the first time, not particularly eager to waltz with his beloved. Perhaps her determined expression ought to have put him off, but it had the opposite effect. Hiding a smile, he bowed before her, then offered his arm to lead her to the dance floor.

"You look lovely this evening, Lady Deborah."

"Thank you."

"Although I have only seen you twice, I wonder if you and your sister always dress in identical or nearly identical gowns. As best I can recall, yesterday your dresses were the same. Tonight, your gowns are the same color, but yours has little white flowers sewn on it, and your sister has dark pink flowers on hers."

"Yes, we generally do. The different trims are a compromise. She would have us dressed identically all the time, while I would prefer that we never did."

"Never?" He arched a brow as if surprised by her answer.

She ignored his question to ask one of her own. "Did you and your cousin ever dress the same when you were growing up?"

Michael felt a stab of panic, wondering if she'd asked Freddie the same question—and how he'd answered it. "We were together only for visits—Christmas and a few weeks during the summer—so it wasn't an issue."

In the same sweet tone, she asked, "Fairfax, what is going on?"

"I am Walsingham—"

"Don't lie to me, Michael Winslow!"

Mentally throwing up his hands, Michael surrendered. "I should have known that we wouldn't be able to fool you, my love." Giving her no chance to ask questions, he explained, "We are practicing the ruse tonight. Tomorrow I hope to show your sister the folly of deception. Will you keep our secret? If you will trust me until tomorrow afternoon, I promise to explain it—and more—when we are at The Oaks."

After subjecting him to an intense scrutiny, she nodded. "I will keep your secret if you give me your word that Diana will not be harmed."

"You have it. The purpose of the deception is to show her that substance is more important than surface appearance."

A glimmer of a smile brightened her eyes. "A lesson she needs to learn."

"I am hoping that she will choose to ride with the faux duke tomorrow, so I can spend the day with you."

"That would be lovely."

"I agree."

Content to be in each other's company, they danced in silence for a while. Loath though he was to break the magical spell that surrounded them whenever they were together, necessity compelled Michael to ask a question near the end of the set. "Do you think anyone else has realized that Freddie and I are masquerading as each other?"

"Sarah asked me earlier if I thought you seemed different tonight. She said she had mistaken you for your cousin all night, but she isn't sure if there is a difference, or if it is just her imagination."

Quelling the stirrings of unease, he asked, "Is she likely to mention it to anyone else?"

"Not to Diana, but possibly to Tina."

Lady Tina was a chatterbox; some might even call her a rattlepate. If she got wind of the deception, she would broadcast it to all and sundry. He winced at the vision of his carefully constructed plan collapsing like a house of cards.

"Would you like me to say something to Sarah? Or to Tina?"

"I would prefer that no one know—except you, of course—so they won't act differently around us, but . . ." Uncertain, he solicited her opinion. "What do you think would be best?"

After due consideration, she advised, "Say nothing. If either of them raises questions, I will make light of any differences they perceive."

"Are there differences between us?"

Eyes atwinkle, she smiled. "A few subtle differences, yes. Sir Frederick is not as accomplished a dancer—at least, not in the minuet. Also, when questioning something, he raises both eyebrows. You query by arching your left brow."

"Indeed?"

She laughed. "Yes, just like that."

"You, my darling girl, are a treasure. Were we not in public, I would kiss you."

"Tomorrow, perhaps?"

Her teasing delighted him. And fired his imagination. "Depend upon it, my love."

If all went well, she would get her kiss and a great deal more.

Chapter Nineteen

Wednesday, 27 April 1814

Over breakfast, the ladies of Kesteven House checked their lists. Then checked them again at the end of the meal. Satisfied that nothing had been overlooked, Deborah smiled at her mother and poured herself another cup of tea.

Diana, who had contributed little to the discussion, leant forward and propped her elbows on the table. "With such a large party, staying together will be difficult. I think we should divide into three groups. My friends and I will go in the first group. Deb, Sarah, Dunnley, and Fairfax and his cousin will be the second group. Tina, Henry, Howe, Llanfyllin, and . . . whoever is left can be the third group."

Although she wondered why her sister had not mentioned this days ago, Deborah saw some merit in the suggestion. "I daresay Tina will want to ride with Sarah and me. And Llanfyllin may prefer to ride with Sarah, too."

"He is Henry's friend!"

"Yes, but he is Sarah's brother."

Diana shrugged. "I suppose it doesn't matter which group he is in."

"Also, Blackburn might prefer to ride with Fairfax and Dunnley, instead of with Henry and his friends."

"Perhaps, but there ought to be at least one young lady in each group. And a sensible gentleman."

"Splitting into smaller groups is a good idea," their mother agreed. "Henry and his friends probably won't care if there isn't a young lady in their group. But, Diana, I don't agree that Henry isn't sensible. Nor Howe."

"Not as wise as Lord Blackburn," Diana countered.

"My dear, the earl is a decade older than your brother. Wisdom comes with age."

"Mama, you and the other ladies will have to leave well before the rest of us if you intend to be at the Star and Garter when we arrive."

"We will leave around noon. Your guests probably will not arrive on the stroke of twelve. Organizing them into groups will take time, too. You probably won't leave until quarter or half past."

Deborah was certain that her sister was plotting something. Mischief, or, heaven forbid, the "just desserts" she'd been muttering about yesterday. Deborah was equally certain that the grouping of guests played a part in the scheme, although she could find no fault with the suggested groups. Unless Di planned to elope with one of the gentlemen in the first group, which seemed unlikely. All Deborah could do was resolve to keep her eyes open for trouble.

Wearing her favorite blue velvet riding habit and carrying her gloves and crop, Deborah descended the stairs a quarter hour before their guests were expected to arrive. She had reviewed the groups of guests while dressing, and again when Ogden arranged her hair, and realized that she was not certain who, other than her sister, would be in the first group of riders. Their mother had approved the guest list, but Diana had written the invitations and kept track of the acceptances, and could have switched—or added—a name or two.

Despite the fact that Deborah could not imagine how something untoward could occur when riding with friends, worry still niggled at her mind.

It only increased when Sarah and Llanfyllin arrived.

"Sarah!" Deborah was alarmed by her friend's paleness and red-rimmed eyes. "Are you meeting Dunnley here? I thought you were going to drive in his curricle."

"I am not certain Dunnley will be here, so I decided to ride my mare."

"Did he not return to Town last night?" That was the only explanation Deborah could think of for the viscount's absence.

"He returned, but I am not certain he will come."

Deborah glanced at Llanfyllin, but he shook his head, unable to provide further explanation. Or unwilling to provide one now.

Fairfax and Sir Frederick arrived shortly before noon. Tina, accompanied by Howe, arrived a few minutes later, followed by her mother and Lady Tregaron in the countess's town chaise. The older women switched to the marchioness's more spacious coach, then, after a quick check that most of the guests were present—and an admonition not to wait too long for stragglers—the chaperones set off.

Less than a minute after their departure, Diana's friends arrived en masse. Deborah was shocked when Sir Edward Smithson halted his high-perch phaeton at the curb— he had definitely not been on the guest list!—but Diana clambered aboard, then gave the order for her friends on horseback to lead the way.

Upset by this unexpected development, Deborah joined Fairfax and his cousin, who were talking to Sarah and Llanfyllin. Pulling the duke to one side, she whispered, "I don't like this. Sir Edward wasn't invited."

"I don't like it, either, for a number of reasons, but he is here, and there isn't much we can do about it. Your sister obviously expected him. At least they will be ahead of us, so we can watch out for trouble. You might suggest to your brother that he should catch up with them and keep an eye on your sister."

Deborah leapt at the suggestion. Henry wasn't happy, but he knew his duty and was prepared to do it. After Fairfax (in the guise of his cousin) and Sir Frederick (masquerading as Fairfax) had a word with him, Henry set off at a trot.

About ten minutes past the hour, Blackburn arrived, apologizing for his tardiness. Within moments, he was deep in discussion with Fairfax and Llanfyllin, and all three men wore frowns of varying degrees.

Deborah was grateful that Fairfax had taken charge. When he suggested that the two of them, his cousin, and Sarah and her brother should leave, Deborah offered only a token protest. "What about Dunnley? He didn't send his regrets, but Sarah seems to think he might not attend."

"Since I was late arriving," Blackburn said, "I will stay and wait for Dunnley."

"I don't mind waiting a bit, either," Howe added. "Do you, Tina?"

"No. Catching up to you will give us a good excuse for a gallop." Tina grinned, always glad for just such an excuse.

"How long should we wait, Lady Deborah?" Blackburn inquired.

"What time is it now?"

Fairfax and Blackburn pulled out their watches. "Quarter past the hour."

"Wait ten or fifteen minutes," she suggested. "Mama expected us all to leave by half past."

"Ten minutes, then." The earl closed his watch with a decisive snap.

As they rode out of Hanover Square, Deborah studied her companions. Sarah was pale and listless; Llanfyllin brooding; Fairfax worried but trying to hide it. Only Sir Frederick seemed to be enjoying himself. Nothing could have been further from the jovial excursion they had all been anticipating. Deborah shivered with foreboding, fearing that worse was yet to come, but with no idea what it would be or how to prevent it from happening.

Michael did not know how to reassure Deborah. "I am sorry, sweetheart. I know this isn't the pleasant jaunt you envisioned."

His words had the opposite effect he'd intended; her frown deepened. "What is going on?"

"I don't know, exactly."

"Tell me what you do know."

For the first time in his life, Michael broke a confidence.

"Before he left for Hampshire, Dunnley told me that Sir Edward has been pestering Sarah. Behaving unpleasantly and, perhaps, making vague threats. Dunnley was very concerned because Smithson was becoming more . . . persistent and blatant, so he asked me—and his brother and Blackburn—to keep an eye on Sarah and Nasty Ned. Perhaps Llanfyllin and I are making too much of his presence here today, but . . ."

" 'Nasty Ned'?" The twinkle in her eyes bespoke amusement. "Is that Dunnley's name for Sir Edward? It seems quite fitting."

"Smithson has had the nickname since Eton. And yes, it is quite apt."

"I don't like Sir Edward, so that may affect my opinion, but I think you and Llanfyllin are right to be concerned. Even if I didn't dislike him, I trust your judgment. Neither you nor Llanfyllin are the type to fly into the boughs without reason."

"It bothers me that no one except your sister knew that Smithson was coming. And that Dunnley isn't here." Michael knew his friend was planning to attend; he'd received a note from Theo this morning.

"Do . . . You don't think Sir Edward did something to Dunnley, do you?"

"Injured him in some way, do you mean?"

She nodded and edged her mare closer to his gelding.

"No, sweetheart. Smithson is a bully. He wouldn't take on Dunnley." He covered her hand with his, hoping his touch would reassure her if his words did not.

"Why didn't Sarah and Llanfyllin leave when they saw Sir Edward?"

"I am not certain. Llanfyllin seems to think something else happened this morning—something between Sarah and Dunnley—but he doesn't know what. Apparently she left for a fitting at the dressmaker's looking forward to seeing him, and came back close to tears, convinced that he wouldn't attend. Llanfyllin expected Dunnley to be here."

Deborah glanced over at her friend, then shook her head.

"That doesn't make sense. She wouldn't have seen him at Madame Celeste's."

"Where is Madame Celeste's?"

"On Bond Street. Perhaps you remember talking to Mama and I in front of her shop before the Season began."

"Yes, I do." He remembered her sister almost bowling him over.

"Halloo!"

Glancing over his shoulder, Michael saw Blackburn, Howe, and Tina approaching. "Shall we stop and wait for them?"

She looked back, then smiled for the first time since they'd left Hanover Square. "No need for that. In a moment, Tina will have them galloping to catch up with us."

"No sign of Dunnley," Blackburn reported, "but the butler will send him along if he appears."

The earl's expression was a bit grim—Dunnley had confided in him, too—but Howe and Tina were in high spirits. Deborah perked up a bit, but sent worried glances in Sarah's direction every few minutes.

Michael knew the odds of his being betrothed by the end of the day were getting longer by the minute, but there wasn't a demmed thing he could do about it.

Diana looked at Sir Edward in disbelief. "You can't be serious!"

"Indeed I am."

"Kidnapping is against the law."

"I am not really going to kidnap Lady Sarah, just take her away for a few hours."

That sounds like kidnapping to me! "Where will you take her?"

"I am not sure. Perhaps to my hunting box."

Diana did not believe him. He would not have concocted this ridiculous plan without a specific destination in mind. "What am I supposed to say when they ask where you have taken Sarah? If you leave me behind, they are certain to interrogate me."

"Tell them I am taking her to Gretna."

"Gretna Green?"

"Of course Gretna Green," he snapped, slowing his horses. "Tell them I am taking her there."

Perhaps that had been his intent all along. Marrying Dunnley's fiancée over the anvil was a more torturous revenge than kidnapping her. A lifelong revenge, if Dunnley was truly fond of Sarah—and he'd given every appearance of it at the Enderby ball. Diana had no great liking for Sarah the Ice Queen, but at the moment, she didn't think very highly of Sir Edward, either. "What about *my* revenge?"

"Just do as I told you, then use your head."

Use my head? What kind of scheme is that? As they waited by the side of the road, Diana alternated between darting glances at her companion and at the road behind her. "Here they come!"

"Wait until they get closer. . . . Now!"

Diana began moaning.

"You are supposed to sound deathly ill, not like a mewling babe!"

She redoubled her efforts, and he jumped down from the phaeton to flag down the approaching riders. Identifying the trio in front as her sister, Fairfax or his cousin, and Blackburn, Diana clutched her stomach and closed her eyes.

Michael exchanged a look with Blackburn, then called a warning over his shoulder to the others. Llanfyllin rode closer to his sister, and Freddie moved up to guard her other side. Michael and Blackburn flanked Deborah; Howe and Tina were at the rear.

"Phaeton looks fine to me," Blackburn muttered out of the corner of his mouth. "And the horses are still in the traces."

When they were within hailing distance, Michael called, "Smithson, did you break down?"

"No. Lady Diana is ill."

Deborah spurred her horse forward. "What is wrong?"

"She is moaning like she is dying and holding her belly," Smithson said in disgust.

Sliding off her horse, Deborah ran to her sister. "Di, what is wrong?"

All Michael could hear was the word "sick" and Diana's groans.

Dismounting, he handed his reins and Deborah's to Blackburn. Tina handed hers to Howe, then scrambled off her horse to help Deborah.

Freddie, Sarah, and Llanfyllin edged closer. Shooting them a look warning them to keep their distance, Michael walked to the other side of the phaeton to offer his assistance.

"Sick . . . so sick."

"Are you going to cast up your accounts?" Tina asked.

"I don't know" was Diana's piteous reply.

Smithson cringed. "Not in the phaeton!"

Deborah glanced around. "Fairfax, can you lift her out?"

The things a man does for love! Michael and his cousin were the shortest men present—Smithson was a good five inches taller, and Blackburn three—but the twins couldn't weigh much more than eight stone. Michael did not doubt his ability to lift Diana, but she was *not* the lady he wanted in his arms.

"Lady Diana, you will please keep your accounts where they belong until your feet are on the ground," he ordered.

Fortunately for both his attire and his composure, she did. Deborah slipped an arm around her sister's waist, and Tina moved to support her on the other side.

"Take me over there." Diana waved a hand toward a cluster of bushes.

"We will, Di. Can you wrap your arms around our shoulders?"

Diana lifted one arm slightly, then moaned and clutched her stomach again.

Tina nudged Diana into motion. "You won't get there if you don't take a step."

"She seems quite ill. I wonder if there is a doctor nearby?" Blackburn came to stand beside Michael.

"There is one near Kew, and one in Putney, but I don't know of any closer."

They watched the trio's erratic progress into the field. Diana stumbled several times, bumping her companions and almost knocking over Tina, who was four or five inches shorter and a stone or two lighter.

Freddie wandered over to join them. "Not the way I expected to spend the afternoon, coz."

"Me, either, Freddie."

Ducked down behind the bushes, Diana moaned and gagged until she heard the snap of a whip and a shouted "Bloody hell!"

"My God!" Tina stared in horror, pointing a shaking finger at the road. "Deb, look!"

Diana stood, wiping her face with a handkerchief. "I am feeling better now."

Her sister barely spared her a look. "Come on! We have to help."

Tina ran toward the road with Deborah close on her heels. Diana followed slowly. She did not want to raise anyone's suspicions, so every bit of distance and time she could gain helped. She also needed a scheme of her own, but wrack her brain though she did, she could not think of a way to turn the situation to her advantage.

When she reached the road, the dust from Smithson's phaeton was settling. Llanfyllin was in pursuit, and the rest of the men were clustered around Fairfax and his cousin, one of whom was giving orders. Her sister and Tina fluttered around them, wringing their hands and exclaiming "Poor Sarah!"

A minute or two later, Fairfax—or perhaps his cousin—and Blackburn were mounted and racing after Sir Edward. Then, the moment Diana had been dreading arrived. Howe, Sir Frederick, Tina, and Deborah turned their attention to her.

Hoping she looked ill and confused, Diana asked, "What happened?"

"What happened?" Tina was furious. "I think you know exactly what happened!"

"How could I? I was behind the bushes."

"Poor Sarah!" Deborah continued to bemoan her friend's plight. "Sir Edward tricked us—"

"Was it Smithson alone?" Frederick—or Fairfax— asked. "Or were you his accomplice, Lady Diana?"

"I was sick!" Diana insisted. "You lifted me out of the carriage, didn't you?" She was not certain if he or his cousin had done it. They both wore blue coats, lighter blue waist-coats, and tan riding breeches. She had been too busy acting then to study the man carefully. Now, however, she could see his worn collar and cuffs, so she knew this man was Sir Frederick.

"I wonder." Howe said only those two words, but Diana could hear the suspicion in his voice.

"Shouldn't we follow them?" She pointed in the direction the three men had ridden.

"You ask a lot of questions for a lady who was deathly ill just minutes ago." Sir Frederick was growing increasingly suspicious. "And you don't have a mount."

"I am feeling much better. And I can ride Sarah's horse."

Tina shook her head. "No. She won't tolerate any rider except Sarah or Lady Tregaron."

"I can ride anything with four legs," Diana insisted. Riding and needlework were her only accomplishments, and she was very skilled at both.

"No one is casting aspersions on your skill as a horse-woman, Di," her sister said. "But Tina is right—"

Diana grabbed the gray's reins, ending the argument. She patted the mare's nose, then glared from Sir Frederick to Howe, waiting for one of them to throw her in the saddle.

"Are you so certain of your ability to ride the mare?" Howe asked.

"Yes. Now throw me up."

Before her skirts were settled, she was flying through the air.

Bloody hell! What else can possibly go wrong?

Kneeling next to Diana, Michael reported, "I think her arm is broken."

Deborah burst into tears. Michael rose and wrapped his arms around her. "Don't cry, sweetheart."

While she sobbed, he glanced around for Tina and Howe. They had caught Sarah's mare, and Tina was trying to calm her. Michael gestured for Howe to join him.

"Someone needs to ride for help. Do you want to go, Howe—"

"Yes!" The baron's response was immediate. "I can't deal with tears, but I can ride. Where is the nearest doctor?"

"Go to the Star and Garter. There must be a doctor in Richmond, and that is almost as close as the ones I know. Have a carriage sent back for Diana, preferably with her mother inside it. Tell Lady Tregaron what happened, but be sure to tell her that Llanfyllin, Blackburn, and Freddie are in pursuit of Smithson and Sarah. Everyone, including the pursuers, is to meet at the Star and Garter."

"I ought to have chosen the tears." Howe's mournful tone was almost comical.

"Lady Tregaron will take the news better from you than from me. She has known you for several years, hasn't she?"

"About a dozen—since Llanfyllin and I entered Harrow."

"Stay at the Star and Garter if you would, and try to keep the ladies calm. Also, see if anyone in that first group of riders knows anything about Smithson's plans."

"I will ask." After taking his leave of Tina and Deborah, Howe rode off.

Four horses, one of which no one could ride. Three women—one in pain, one in tears, and the third valiantly attempting to stave off tears and help. One man. Michael look around, shaking his head in bemusement. The romantic afternoon he had planned was in shambles. It was a shame he could not set Tina and Diana on horseback and send them off in one direction, while he threw Deborah over his saddlebow and rode off into the sunset.

Lying on the ground, her arm hurting like a sore tooth, and her goal of marrying the Duke of Fairfax further out of reach than at the start of the Season, Diana prayed for rescue and tried to think of a new plan to win the duke. But after what she had done today, the only way she would wring an offer from him was by compromising him. The sooner, the better. The scandal—and this day was sure to result in several of them—would not be as bad if she were the Duchess of Fairfax.

The welcome sound of a vehicle approaching heartened her. *Rescue!* If she could convince Fairfax to accompany her to the doctor, she could implement her new scheme.

"What the hell happened?"

Not rescue, Lord Dunnley—and he was not in a pleasant mood.

"Diana tried to ride Sarah's horse and was thrown." Deborah sounded both frightened and angry.

"Dunnley! Thank God you are here," Tina exclaimed, quite as if she thought the viscount could work miracles. "Sir Edward Smithson kidnapped Sarah."

"What happened?" Dunnley repeated his demand.

Tina yelled, "I just told you—Sir Edward kidnapped Sarah!" Then she burst into tears.

Deborah's feeble explanation consisted of "Poor Sarah!" and "He tricked us!"

Diana heard the sigh that preceded Sir Frederick's accounting of the afternoon's events. "Smithson set up a clever ambush. His phaeton was stopped at the side of the road when we rode up, and he said that Lady Diana wasn't feeling well. Deborah and Tina dismounted to ask her what was wrong, and after a minute or so, Diana, with much moaning and groaning, asked them to lead her to those bushes."

"And while everyone was watching the three of them, Smithson pulled Sarah off her horse, threw her into his rig, and took off." Disgust was rife in Dunnley's voice.

Not wanting to hear Sir Frederick describe her role in Sir Edward's scheme, Diana closed her ears to their words. Closed her eyes, too, and tried to recall everything she had ever heard about young ladies who had been compromised. In particular, what they had done to achieve that status.

Less than a minute later, Dunnley stood beside her. "Where is Smithson taking Lady Sarah?"

"To Gretna Green."

"He can't reach Gretna in a day. Where is he planning to stop tonight?"

What should I say? Sir Edward had not given her a response for this question, so she told the truth. "I don't know."

Dunnley brushed the toe of his boot against her broken arm. "I daresay you will remember if I step on your arm. Shall we try it and see?"

Her eyes flew open at the very real threat in his voice. "I don't know for certain, but possibly his hunting box."

He turned away, and she expelled a shaky breath. *Lud, she had never seen him look so dangerous, so . . . savage.* His threat seemed to have increased the throbbing in her arm, so she closed her eyes and ears again, trying to block out the pain.

She must have fallen asleep because the next thing she knew, Tina shouted, "Someone is coming!"

Pressing her ear to the ground, Diana felt the *thrump, thrump, thrump* of a horse's hooves cantering toward them. And, more faintly, she felt the *clop, clop* of a pair or team of horses at the trot.

She opened her eyes as Fairfax drew rein in front of his less elegantly garbed cousin, then dismounted. "I lost Smithson, but found a rescuer."

From the way the duke said "a rescuer," Diana did not think he meant Howe and her mother.

Sir Frederick must not have been certain because he said, "I didn't think Howe would return with Lady Kesteven this quickly."

"It isn't Lady Kesteven," the duke confirmed.

Diana closed her eyes, wondering who it was. And wondering what Mama would think when she returned with Howe and Diana was not there. But, she realized with rising excitement, if she could get Fairfax to accompany her to the doctor, and if she was alone with the duke when Mama entered, then he would have to propose.

It was perfect! She would be engaged to the Duke of Fairfax before nightfall.

*   *   *

Deborah smiled at the Dowager Duchess of St. Ives when she stepped down from her coach so that her footmen could lift Diana inside.

"Don't worry about your sister, child. My physician will attend to her, and she will be more comfortable at my house than at an inn. When your mother arrives, tell her Diana is at River Bend with me." Lowering her voice to a whisper, the duchess advised, "Forget about your sister and concentrate on that young man." She pointed her chin at Fairfax. "He looks like he has lost his best friend. Or his hope of heaven. I don't know about the first, but I am quite certain that, in his opinion, you fit the latter description to perfection."

"Do you really think so?" Deborah waited for the answer with bated breath.

"I just said so, didn't I?"

"But what should I do?" she all but wailed. Everything had gone wrong today, and she did not know how to even begin righting things.

"Do you love him, child?"

"Yes. With all my heart."

"Tell him."

With that, the duchess stepped away and looked around at the rest of the group. "You"—she pointed to Sir Frederick—"what is your name again?"

"Sir Frederick Walsingham at your service, Your Grace." He bowed with courtly grace.

"Very pretty. Now, help Lady Tina into my coach—"

"Me?" Tina started in surprise. "But—"

"I am an old woman. I will need help with Lady Diana until her mother arrives."

"But why—"

The duchess grasped Tina's arm and whispered something in her ear. Tina's eyes darted from Fairfax to Deborah, then to Sir Frederick and back to the duchess. "Yes, Your Grace."

While one of the duchess's footmen tied Tina's horse to the back of the coach, the dowager's gimlet gaze settled on Fairfax's cousin again. "You can either ride on the box with my driver or ride beside the carriage as our escort."

Sir Frederick shot a panicked look at his cousin, but bowed to the inevitable. And to the duchess again, this time more perfunctorily. "I'd be honored to serve as your escort, Your Grace."

Watching the duchess's carriage drive away with Sir Frederick riding beside it, Deborah could not help but wonder if Her Grace of St. Ives was a matchmaker or a troublemaker.

Deborah was not aware that she had voiced the question until Fairfax answered.

"A matchmaker." He grasped her shoulders as he spoke, ignoring her start of surprise and turning her to face him.

She dipped her head, averting her gaze. He squeezed her shoulders, then curled a finger under her chin and lifted her face until her eyes met his. "Deborah, if you have no interest in being matched with me, tell me now."

Wide-eyed, suddenly breathless, it was all she could do to say, "I am! Of course I am."

"Then walk with me, my lady."

Deborah nodded and wondered where they were going, but she fell into step beside him.

"Last night, I promised you an explanation. Several of them, in fact. . . ."

She did not need his explanations, but she listened, letting his voice wash over her and soothe her frazzled nerves, in the hope of hearing the answer to two simple questions: Did he love her? Could he tell her and Diana apart? She was almost certain that the answer to both questions was yes, but she wanted to know for sure.

She shivered slightly in the cooling breeze, and Fairfax slipped his arm around her waist and drew her closer, as if to share his own warmth with her.

As they strolled and he talked, his hand slid upward until it was just beneath her breast. The movement—or, perhaps, his hand itself—created a strange, mad urge to throw herself into his arms. Confused by the feeling, she peeked at him through her lashes, and he smiled, with more warmth and tenderness in his expression than she had ever seen before. Suddenly breathless, her lips parted, seeking air, and he bent his head and captured her lips in a kiss so soft, so gentle and sweet, that it seemed almost a figment of her imagination. Or her dreams.

But despite its softness, his kiss promised love and happiness, a lifetime of music and joy and dreams fulfilled.

It was a much longer kiss than the one he'd given her on the terrace during the Enderby ball. It was, in fact, a succession of lovely, wonderful kisses. And this time, his kiss did far more than curl her toes. Every nerve in her body responded, flashing to awareness. These kisses teased her senses, unleashing a passion deeper than anything she had ever read about, heard of, or imagined. She pressed closer and looped her arms around his neck. Perhaps her passion sparked his, for he held her more tightly, his kisses deeper, more urgent. His hands slid up her spine, first gently caressing, then more boldly in an enthralled—and enthralling—exploration of her curves that sent her feelings spiraling to dizzying heights.

She turned her head aside, gasping for breath or balance. Slowly, almost reluctantly—or so it seemed to her hopeful heart—he set her back on her heels. His hands on her shoulders, he stepped back a pace and gazed at her, a rueful smile quirking his lips and brightening his beautiful turquoise eyes. "Forgive me, my love. I ought not to have kissed you before you answered me."

Had he asked a question? Is that what triggered that mad wish to throw myself into his arms? She could not remember. "What did you ask me?"

He threw back his head and laughed, then dropped to one knee and clasped her hands in his. "My darling Deborah, I love you with all my heart, and I have been able to tell you and your sister apart since the day I met you. Please, my darling, will you do me the very great honor of becoming my wife, my duchess, and my love?"

"I would be honored to be your wife, Michael Winslow, and your duchess, and most especially, your love. I love you, too. More than I realized it was possible to love."

He sprang to his feet and pulled her into his arms.

Emily Woodhurst, the Marchioness of Kesteven, blinked several times, then rubbed her eyes. When she looked out the carriage window again, the sight was unchanged.

Nudging Howe awake with a well-placed elbow to the ribs, she pointed outside. "Look!"

In the middle of London to Richmond road, the Duke of Fairfax was dancing a jig, with her daughter, Deborah, in his arms.

Epilogue

*D*eborah Elizabeth Catherine Woodhurst Winslow, the Duchess of Fairfax, opened the drawer of the writing table in her study, searching for the sheet of paper on which, a year ago and many miles away, she had written her goals for 1814. Finally finding the elusive paper, she reviewed the three objectives.

She started in surprise when her husband kissed her nape, then slipped his arms around her.

"Christmas is over, my love. Do you really need to write more lists?"

"It isn't a list, Michael. Well, it is, but not the kind you mean." She explained about her family's tradition of setting goals for each year. "This is the list of my goals for 1814."

He pulled on his spectacles and picked up the paper. "I can say with certainty that you achieved the first goal."

"Yes, I succeeded beyond my wildest dreams."

"And you accomplished the second goal as well."

"Yes, I did."

"Judging from the letters we received from my cousin and your sister this morning, between us, and with Freddie's help, you achieved your third goal, too. Well done, my darling!" He punctuated his accolade with a kiss. "What do you hope to accomplish in 1815?"

"First, I shall endeavor to be the best wife and duchess in the realm."

"I have no doubt you will achieve that goal."

"Then, in July, I will give you a son or daughter. Finally—"

The list fell to the floor as the duke lifted his wife into his arms, kissed her breathless, then danced her around the room, out the door, and down the hall to their bedchamber.

The maid who found the paper the next morning could not read, but she placed the list on the duchess's writing table.

Deborah's Goals for 1814

*1. To find a man I love (preferably one who loves me)
who can tell me apart from my sister.*

The best means to achieve this may be to further my acquaintance with the following gentlemen:

>*Viscount Dunnley*
>*The Duke of Fairfax*
>*The Earl of Blackburn*
>*Viscount Llanfyllin*
>*Lord Howe*

2. To learn four new pianoforte pieces:

>*Sonata in c-sharp minor by Beethoven*
>*Sonata in E-flat Major by Mozart*
>*Sonata in F Major by Haydn*
>*Sonata in a minor by D. Scarlatti*

*3. To convince Diana that it is better to marry for love
than for money or position.*

Susannah Carleton discovered Regency romances at the ripe old age of thirty-three and promptly fell in love, since life among the *ton* in Regency England is such a diverting change from that of an engineer. She lives in northern Florida with her husband and teenage son, and when she isn't reading or writing, she enjoys solo and choral singing and needlework. Visit her Web site at www.susannahcarleton.com to learn more about Susannah and her books.